I0665188

THE OASIS TRIALS

BOOK 11 THE THAW CHRONICLES

TAMAR SLOAN

HEIDI CATHERINE

SEQUEL HOUSE

HALO

*H*alo's mother once told her that if you want to leave a mark, first you must pick up your quill. She'd been too young at the time to understand what that meant, but as she rolls the heavy metal pole along the uneven ground, she thinks she's figured it out.

If you want a dream to become a reality, then you must put in the work. Pick up your quill, your hammer, or your spade, and do what it takes to leave your mark. Or in this case, more specifically, Halo needs to pick up a pole that weighs twice as much as she does and show everyone what they can achieve with a bit of muscle and a whole lot of vision.

The pole hits a decaying tire sticking out of the ground and becomes wedged. Halo gets to her feet and heaves it over the obstacle only for her foot to disappear into a small sinkhole. Living on an island made entirely from trash has its challenges. But as she looks down at the pole that's been carefully rigged with possibly her greatest invention yet, she can't deny it also has its benefits. That's why they call this place Treasure Island, not Trash Island. *Everything* here has a purpose.

Drawing in a deep breath as she extricates her foot, she

focuses on her task. A bead of sweat rolls down her forehead and catches in her eyelashes. She blinks it away and bends to roll the pole a few feet closer to its destination. It's going to take all day at this rate. But she'll get it in place even if she's here all night. She can most definitely do this.

More sweat trickles down her face and Halo lets go of the pole for a moment to wipe her brow with her forearm, wishing today was one of those rare days when the clouds shield the island from the relentless heat of the sun. Although, those days usually bring storms with them and that doesn't go too well given the flimsy constructions her people call home. The hut Halo shares with her father and brother has already been rebuilt twice in the past six moons despite being the best one on the island. It even has two separate rooms.

Without her hands to steady it, the pole starts to roll backward. Halo dives on it, her hip painfully connecting with the hard metal, jolting all her previous optimism right out of her body.

"Urgh! Poop on a stick!" she shouts, turning onto her back, rubbing her middle with one hand, and shielding her eyes from the sun with her other. This plan had seemed so much easier when it was an idea contained safely inside her head.

"Careful," comes a deep voice. "You'll hurt my ears with that kind of cursing. Almost as much as you seem to have hurt yourself."

She slides her hand away from her eyes and squints at the face hovering above her. It's that guy. The one whose name is a number, but she can't remember which one. He's never spoken to her, let alone approached her like this.

"What do you want?" she asks cautiously, making no move to stand. "Other than to eavesdrop on me."

"Are you sure that listening to someone talk to themselves about bodily functions on sticks counts as eavesdropping?" he asks. "To be fair, I think I might be the one who's been hard done by here. It's a difficult image to shake."

Halo hides the smile that's edging its way to the corners of her mouth as she studies his face. Framed by the bright blue sky, his black hair looks almost like a shadow against his deeply tanned skin. His gray eyes are glinting at her as if she's the most amusing thing he's ever seen.

"It's Four, isn't it?" she asks, propping herself up on her elbows and taking a guess.

He flinches. "Fyve. Foar was my brother."

She grins awkwardly, having no idea if this is a joke. "Well, help me up then, Fyve."

He puts out his hand and she clasps it as he hauls her to her feet a little too quickly. She winces as her bruised hip complains, but this time she refrains from cursing.

"Are you okay?" He seems genuinely concerned.

"I'm fine." She pulls her lips into a smile, not having time right now to be injured. She has a mark to leave. "How did you even know I needed help?"

"We were watching you," Fyve says.

"Okay. Not creepy." She tilts her head and looks around. "And who's *we*?"

A girl steps out from behind a pile of scrap metal several yards away and gives a shy wave. She's a skinnier, fairer, and far less masculine version of Fyve. Halo's noticed her on the island, but just like Fyve, they've never spoken. She looks to be about thirteen, but it's hard to tell from this distance.

"That's my sister," says Fyve.

"Let me guess…" Halo watches the girl approach and laughs. "Her name's Six?"

"Sevin, actually," the girl says, skipping over. "Syx died a while back now."

Halo sobers, realizing Fyve hadn't been joking about his

brother earlier. Death isn't an uncommon occurrence on Treasure Island, particularly with young children, but that doesn't make it any less sad. Halo's own sister died while being birthed, taking their mother with her. Loss is something she can understand.

"I'm sorry to hear that," she says. "I didn't realize."

Fyve nods, his gray eyes hardened to the grief he's been forced to live with. "My sister's kind of obsessed with you."

Sevin punches him squarely in the stomach and he doubles over as he lets out an *oof.*

"Poop on a stick!" Fyve laughs as he rubs his stomach, clearly happier to tease Halo than talk about the loss of his siblings.

Halo throws Sevin a wink. "Aim a bit lower next time. And use your knee. Used to work a treat on my brother."

"I'm not obsessed with you." Sevin crosses her arms and the timid side of her reemerges. "I'm just *interested.* In what you're doing, I mean. You're not like anyone else around here."

Halo narrows her eyes, wondering how she hadn't noticed this girl watching her. "You've been following me?"

"No!" Sevin says just a little too quickly. "Well…maybe a little. I like the things you make. And besides, Fyve followed me here."

Fyve throws out his hands. "I was looking for you!"

"Then come and help me instead of spying on me like a pair of creepy creeps." Halo smiles to let Sevin know she's joking. "I could actually use a little help right now."

"What are you making?" Sevin asks, jiggling on her bare feet. "Is it a boat to go with your motor?"

"You know about my motor?" Unease slides into Halo's gut. She thought nobody knew about the motor she's been building from scrap parts she collects on the shore. Just how closely has this girl been watching her?

Sevin nods enthusiastically at first, then tones it down when she realizes Halo's not pleased. "I haven't said anything to anyone, I swear."

"Told you she was obsessed with you." Fyve puts a protective hand on his stomach, then another on his sister's back. "But she's also harmless. And trustworthy. She means no harm."

Another feeling mingles with the unease in Halo's gut, but this time it's envy. She can't remember a single time her own brother, Ajax, stood up for her like that. He's usually too busy trying to stand up for himself.

"Are you going to build a very tall house?" asks Sevin.

"Maybe it's a rain catcher," says Fyve. "Or a rat catcher."

"No imagination." Halo shakes her head, feeling her long blonde hair tickle the bare skin on her lower back where her tee-shirt doesn't quite reach her shorts. "Nobody seems to be able to imagine building something that isn't practical."

"I can," says Sevin.

Fyve seems confused. "So, you're almost killing yourself moving this pole, just so you can do something totally imprac-tical with it?"

Halo nods. "You got it. Now, if you could just help me move this—"

Fyve hoists the pole off the ground with impressive strength and positions it across his shoulders. This does extremely appealing things to the shape of his upper arms, and Halo looks away, trying not to notice. She needs to focus. On the right things...

"My brother's strong," says Sevin, beaming proudly.

"I noticed." Halo bites down on her bottom lip and glances back at him.

"Where am I taking it?" he asks, balancing himself and step-ping forward.

"Follow me." Halo skips across the flattened rubble to where she'd dug a deep, narrow hole the precise measurements she needs. Sevin is right behind her like a shadow. "Here."

"Which way does it go in?" Fyve asks, glancing at the end of the pole with a hessian bag tied around it.

"The other end goes in first." Halo dashes to the bag and removes it.

Sevin gasps when she sees what's underneath. "I think I know what this is."

Fyve leans forward and lowers the pole into the hole, while Halo drops to the ground and fills in the space around it with the small particles of plastic and sand that line their shores. She has a bucket of slurry ready to go that she made with a stone that she painstakingly ground up into a powder and mixed with sea water. With the sun beating down this hard, it shouldn't take too long to set.

"I still don't get it." Fyve lets go of the pole and takes a step back to survey their work. "What is it? What's all that stuff at the top?"

"You'll see." Sevin is bouncing on her heels now, hands clutched at her chest. "This is going to be amazing."

Halo stands and wipes her dirty hands on her bare thighs. "Watch this." She tugs on her lucky cord that she'd wrapped around the length of the pole. It unfurls a series of thin metal spokes she'd carefully attached to the end. Hundreds of long strips of green plastic dangle down from the spokes as they fan out. It'd taken Halo weeks to collect them all.

"It's a tree!" Sevin claps as she beams up at the branches that are casting much-needed shade around them. "It's so beautiful."

"I've heard of trees." Fyve blinks in surprise. "You actually made one."

"I actually did." Halo tucks the cord into her back pocket and crosses her arms. "I'm going to make a whole forest of them."

"What for?" he asks. "What will we use them for?"

"We'll look at them." She grins so widely her cheeks hurt. "My forest will be a symbol of what's been promised to us by Terra."

Fyve doesn't seem convinced, but Sevin is more than making up for his lack of conviction. She's seeing Halo's invention for exactly what it is. Perhaps having this girl as her shadow isn't such a bad thing.

"But it must be useful for something?" Fyve scratches his chin.

"It is useful!" Halo does a spontaneous twirl, which makes Sevin giggle. "It will inspire people. Isn't that the most useful thing you've ever heard of?"

"You do realize you're kind of crazy, don't you?" Fyve gives her a killer grin, and before her insides can melt, she looks back at her tree. The wind is catching the leaves and they flutter against each other in a dance of victory.

"She's not crazy," breaths Sevin in awe. "She's an inventor."

"All the most wonderful ideas begin with a single thought." Halo clasps her blistered hands together. "Just like every forest begins with one tree."

"Yep." Fyve takes a step back. "Completely and utterly bonkers."

Halo gives him a brief curtsy. "Why, thank you."

"Come on." Fyve slips his hand into his younger sister's and tugs her away. "We have to check the traps. Thanks for letting us help."

"But I want to stay here." Sevin plants her feet on the ground. "It's so shady and pretty."

"It's definitely pretty," says Fyve, his eyes fixed on Halo in a flirtation so obvious it's a miracle his sister doesn't notice. "But we can't eat a tree for dinner. We have traps to check."

"So practical." Halo pokes out her tongue at Fyve as he drags his sister away.

"I'll come back!" Sevin calls out.

Halo nods, not doubting that for a moment. It seems she's made a new friend. Well, two new friends. Although, Fyve seems to be in a very different category of friendship to his little sister. One she hasn't experienced before but is suddenly keen to explore. Although, it's very possible he's like this with

7

everyone around here. Ajax had flirted with just about every girl on this island before he'd finally settled on Cloud.

A sarcastic laugh floats across the rubble behind her and she turns to see the very person she'd been thinking about.

Ajax. Her older brother who she loves with one half of her soul while the other half limps along trying to catch up.

"What in sweet Terra is that?" he asks, clutching his sides as he ambles toward her.

She rolls her eyes, refusing the state the obvious. Ajax is fully aware of the way she obsesses over the laminated calendar their father had given her when she was little. It must have originally been sealed inside another container to have survived the acidic depths of the ocean, as it washed up in surprisingly good condition. Eight of the twelve photographs are still distinguishable as images of a forest. She hung them on the wall beside her sleeping mat even though all she has to do is close her eyes and she can study every inch of them in detail. It had taken her until she was seven to understand that not everyone can see an image and store it in their brain the way she can. Just another thing that makes her different, which she's not sure is a blessing or a curse.

"Dad's going to flip out when he sees this." Ajax shakes his head, sending his blond curls bouncing. "What a waste of resources. You've lost your mind."

Somehow this seems like an insult, whereas when Fyve had said the same thing, it had felt almost like praise.

"I think it's beautiful," she says. "I'm going to build a forest."

"That will take years." He points in the direction of the beach where they sort the trash. "You'll need to find a thousand poles."

"Then it will take years," she says, confident now that she's started her forest, it will get finished. Even if it's her children's children's children who put the final tree in place. "Besides, we already have loads of poles."

"Not a thousand though." Ajax scans the space around them. "Look, you've created a spectacle."

There are people approaching from every direction, all pointing at her tree. Her father is amongst them, which fills Halo with dread. His reaction is going to be everything.

Because he's not just her father, he's the all-seeing Elijah, the leader of this growing faction that claimed this island as their home when the rising seas made what little land remains either too barren or too dangerous. Factions war over whatever scarce resources they can find, with murder and pillaging daily events. Here, they might live on nothing more than an enormous pile of floating trash, but generally it's a peaceful life and with each day that passes, their island grows rather than shrinks.

"What is it?" asks the first woman to approach. "What does it do?"

"It reminds us to dream." Halo smiles encouragingly. "Anything's possible with enough imagination."

"It's a tree," says a man.

"What's a tree?" asks a boy.

"They used to grow on the land," the man explains. "Animals lived in them. Humans breathed the air they made."

"That thing makes air?" the woman asks, finally seeming to be impressed.

Halo quickly jumps in. "It's not a real tree. This one's just for looking at."

Ajax nudges Halo with his shoulder, reminding her she's the fool he believes her to be. Cloud comes to stand beside him, the rounded bulge of her belly now clearly visible beneath her flowing shirt. She smiles at Halo but doesn't speak, holding her judgment so she can keep it in line with whatever verdict their leader might pass down. It's no wonder Halo's father approves of his son's choice of partner so heartily.

More people join them, forming a circle around the tree, craning their necks to stare at Halo's creation. They step aside

9

for her father, just one of the many small signs of respect his people shower on him.

"Elijah," says Cloud. "Halo made a tree."

Halo nods cautiously but remains silent as she studies her father's expression. Her mother was a doer but her father's a dreamer. He gathers his people at sunset to raise their faces to the sky and ask Terra to bring them what they need. Sometimes he delivers prophecies that are whispered in his ear at night. Terra has forewarned them of storms, told them where to find healing plants, taught them how to trap rats. And when someone displeases Terra, she claims them right there on their beach, their life extinguishing along with the remains of the day itself. This makes her a power the people show both gratitude and fear—sentiments that extend to Elijah himself.

Her father scratches the gray bristles of his long beard for approximately eternity, then clears his throat. Halo clasps her hands in front of her chest as she wonders if Terra is whispering in his ear right now.

"My people," he says, stretching his arms out wide as he does whenever he's about to say something important. "Terra is good to us. Our huts provide us shelter. The rain provides us water. Our foraging provides us food. We have everything we need."

The people murmur their thanks to Terra.

Ajax smirks. "Who knew we needed a plastic tree."

"Precisely right, my son," Halo's father says, punching dread into her gut. "Who knew we needed a plastic tree? My daughter did."

Halo's heart swells that her father understands what she's trying to achieve.

"My daughter knew we needed a symbol of hope," her father continues. "Something to remind us of what riches await us when we reach Tomorrow Land."

With their leader's approval, the people let out a cheer and their confused murmurs morph into the singing of Halo's praise.

"I helped her," says Ajax, pulling back his shoulders. "We're going to build a forest."

Halo's eyes widen at her brother's blatant lie, but she keeps quiet, just like she has her whole life when Ajax has taken credit for something he didn't do.

"Terra doesn't want a forest." The all-seeing Elijah caresses his people with a smile. "A tree is a symbol. A forest is a waste. When we go to Tomorrow Land, we will leave all this behind."

Their father wraps one arm around each of his children and his long, flowing hair tickles Halo's cheek. His grip on her arm is firm and she knows it's a warning. He hadn't approved of her tree at all. Nor had he understood the first thing about what she's trying to achieve. He was simply saving face with his people, not wanting them to think his daughter had gone as mad as Ajax had accused her of being. Except, in his desperation for his father's approval, Ajax had thrown himself right on the crazy boat with Halo and now they're sailing out to sea.

"I told you a forest was a bad idea," says Ajax, leaning forward to sneer at her across their father's broad chest.

Halo remains silent, aware she hasn't said a word since her father arrived and hating that the two men in her life have this effect on her. Maybe that's why she comes up with other ways to express herself? Criticism of her ideas doesn't seem to sting quite as much as criticism of Halo herself.

"Will Terra be upset with me?" she asks her father in a whisper as the crowd disperses. "Am I in danger of being claimed?"

Her father shakes his head as he lets his hands fall. "Not if you stop this idea now. One tree is enough. Do you understand?"

"Yes, father," she says, even though she doesn't.

Her father nods and marches away.

Halo's hand slides to her back pocket to take out her lucky cord. She likes the familiar feel of it slipping through her fingertips as she thinks.

But it isn't there.

"Did you take my lucky cord?" She glares at Ajax, knowing that's exactly the kind of thing he'd do.

He holds out his empty palms. "It's just a stupid piece of string. I don't know why you like it so much."

He's got it—she knows he does—but she also knows she won't be able to prove it. She'll have to find herself another lucky cord. Either that or a boat built for one that she can stick her brother on and push him out to sea.

"Ajax is an honest man," says the ever-faithful Cloud with a hand resting gently on her belly. She guides Ajax away, leaving Halo standing alone.

The wind caresses Halo's face and she looks up at her tree, watching the plastic leaves flutter against each in a motion that reminds her of the gentle fingers her mother used to tickle her with when she kissed her goodnight.

"I did it, Mom," she whispers. "It's not a forest, but I picked up my quill, and I left my mark."

Her father let her get away with it, even though he clearly didn't approve. And with the sun getting lower in the sky, it's all she can do to hope that Terra is equally as forgiving.

She's terrified of being claimed.

FYVE

"See, I told you she was nice," says Sevin in a sing-song voice.

Fyve glances at her as they make their way through the village, not sure that's the word he'd use to describe Halo. Intriguing. Clever. Oh, and kooky. "She built a fake tree," he points out.

Sevin's smile, the one that always seems to be waiting to burst across her face, floods her features like a sunrise. "How cool is that? People get to see something apart from decomposed...everything," she says, waving her hand at their surroundings.

Fyve grunts a response. Treasure Island.

Whoever named it, had a sense of humor. All this place holds is a wealth of hardship.

Sevin bumps him with her shoulder. "Although, you weren't really looking at the tree, were you?" she teases.

Fyve shakes his head. There was definitely something more captivating and fascinating than some fake tree, and that was Halo herself. Long, pale hair. Large, expressive eyes. And smooth, clear skin that only comes from being the daughter of the richest man on the island.

"Even Coal's been looking," he grunts, not willing for whatever attraction he feels to be anything more than that. The familiar empty ache in his stomach reminds him he doesn't have time for anything as frivolous as art or attraction.

He has a family to keep alive.

Sevin rolls her eyes. "Coal looks at *everyone*," she says, stretching out the final word as if it can encompass every female on the island.

"Hey," says a new voice. "I don't look at you."

Coal appears from behind a hut that's missing half a roof and loops an arm around Sevin's shoulder, winking at her. Her smile impossibly growing, she squeezes his waist. "That's because I'm your cousin."

Fyve shakes his head at the two of them, finding his own smile hovering on his lips. "Thank goodness. I wouldn't want to whoop your ass again. You ugly cried the last time."

Coal arches a dark eyebrow, flashing the grin that has every female over the age of thirteen tittering. "That's not how I remember it turning out."

Sevin untangles herself from his hold. "I don't know which time you're talking about, but it was a draw. It always is."

Coal leaps at Fyve, who nimbly side steps then slips around to vault on his back. There's a grunt and an oomph as they tussle, the faint tear of material as someone's flimsy shirt gains another hole, then a growl and a chuckle. But neither of them gains the upper hand.

They separate, grinning and jostling good-naturedly. "One day, I'll actually try," says Fyve, shoving Coal once more for good measure.

"One day, you'll find out it's not going to make a difference," Coal shoots back, punching Fyve lightly in the arm.

Sevin rolls her eyes again. "If only ego could feed us," she says on a giggle.

The mention of food mutes the atmosphere a little. It's no coincidence that Coal has just joined them. This is the time they check the traps each day. Not that catching rats needs this many people involved, but it's certainly easier to weather the disappointment of an empty trap if others are there to distract you. There's a camaraderie that comes from bracing yourself for another level of hunger.

Fyve glances at Sevin and Coal as the huts progressively thin, noting the faint resemblance in the dark hair and strong brows. Family. It's the only shred of joy that exists on Treasure Island. The battle to survive kills everything else.

It's all that's worth fighting for.

They walk on through the village, reaching the wasteland that stretches out in every direction beyond its border, and continue on. The island is almost flat, the yards of trash progressively leveling out over the years as they decomposed. The gently undulating horizon is fractured by the odd giant tire or twisted heap of metal, all slowly, inevitably decaying.

Fyve almost shakes his head. Halo probably looks at things like that and sees flowers or birds or something as equally whimsical. While he wonders if they're worth the energy to move so they can have a hut that might stay upright in the next big wind.

The three of them walk quietly, each counting their steps under their breath. The village is little more than a dusty haze behind them when they stop. The two plastic straws pushed into the ground then angled to form an X are just where they left them.

Coal glances over his shoulder to make sure no one's followed, even though they would've heard. The three of them were focused on listening as much as counting. Even if there are three or four rats in the trap, they have two families to feed. If the threat of being claimed wasn't so real, people would kill for that amount of food.

Sevin squats down as Fyve and Coal keep an eye out. She brushes away the granules of plastic that are more numerous than soil particles to reveal the lid of the half-barrel they've dug into the ground. She taps on the trapdoor she fashioned into the lid, and it spins easily around the central wire holding it in place. "Still working," she says, a tinge of pride creeping into the hopeful words.

"Of course, it is. You built it," Fyve says, letting his own pride show. Sevin is clever, just like Halo. It's why his younger sister has followed Elijah's daughter and watched from afar for so long. Although, it turns out Sevin's been doing it far more than he realized. What was that talk of a motor?

Sevin puts aside the lid and peers into the dark hole. Coal squats down beside her, scanning just as intensely. Fyve holds his breath, even as he tells himself he's not going to get his hopes up like they clearly are.

Sevin and Coal's shoulders drop simultaneously. Sevin looks up, the edges of her mouth also turned down. "One."

Coal leans in, waiting as the rat frantically circles the bottom of the barrel. The moment it streaks past his hand, he snatches it. Fyve looks away as his cousin dispatches the scrawny rodent. Not because he can't stomach it, but because he's already doing the math. Out of a brood of eight children, all that are left are him and Sevin. Their father died long ago. But Coal has three younger siblings, Jett, Bloo and Rubee. And their mother, Cee.

At least Fyve's mother's not—

Fyve turns his thoughts away from anything to do with *her*. He's made sure he thinks of his mother as little as possible, and he's not going back on that now. He can't afford to waste energy on anger.

Coal straightens, tucking the meal that needs to feed six

people into his satchel. "It's better than yesterday's haul." When the trap was empty.

Sevin replaces the lid and then scatters the plastic dirt back over it. "We'll collect some cockroaches on the way back."

Fyve scans the uneven horizon, conscious that a handful of bugs is never enough. "Maybe it's time to move the traps further out again."

The number of rats they're catching has been steadily reducing. Maybe it's the location. But maybe it's because they have nothing to use as bait. All their traps can do is wait for unsuspecting rats to fall in.

Coal nods, his dark eyes somber. Moving the trap might mean catching more rats, but it also means more energy to dig this one up, move it, and then to get to it each day. And what if they don't catch more...

"We'll move them tomorrow," he says, glancing at the sun slowly descending toward the man-made skyline. "It's almost time for Gratitude."

They walk back even more silently than the walk out. This time, people are making their way out of the ramshackle homes in the village, walking, shuffling, and limping toward the other side of the village.

Fyve sees their hut up ahead, leaning precariously against Coal's family hut, and pauses. Fyve's aunt, Cee, is usually standing outside, waiting to see what they've brought. But today, she's not. Sevin notes that he's stopped and her gaze flies to the door, knowing there's only one thing that has the power to halt her brother in her tracks.

"She's back?" she whispers, knowing what Cee's absence means as much as he does.

Sevin breaks into a run, her dark hair streaming behind her as she barrels past the sheet of tattered material that acts as a door.

Coal glances at Fyve. "Looks like the rat is now being divided eight ways."

The truth in those words only fuels the anger simmering within Fyve. Anger that's seeped deep into his marrow, becoming a part of him. Sharing their limited food among family is a given. He would never turn his back on that responsibility, no matter how impossible it's becoming. In fact, it's his reason for getting up each day and fighting the invisible enemy that is poverty.

But sharing what little they have with the woman who's barely functioned as a mother, as each year he's had to take on her role and that of his father, has lit a barely banked fire in his bones. There's only so much injustice he can take.

He's just decided there's no way he's entering their hut when his mother appears. She stands in the doorway, leaning on a beaming Sevin. Cee is beside her, the family resemblance between the three females unmistakable. Except his mother looks even worse for wear than Cee and Sevin. As always after one of her absences, her black hair is a wild tangle, her skin a deep brown, her lips are blistered. Her eyes scan the area until they find Fyve, then devour him like she always does after she returns from another of her searches, as she calls them.

Sevin calls them their mother's quests.

Coal calls them his aunt's obsession.

Fyve knows what they really are. A delusion sparked by the loss of six out of eight children, most of them before their second birthday. Fyve and Sevin are the only two to survive, and yet they aren't enough to keep their mother on land for long stretches of time.

As much as he hates himself, Fyve finds himself walking toward her. His inability to cut all ties with this woman only feeds the muted fury licking at his veins. He wants to tell her what her weeks of disappearing out on a fragile raft looking for new land has meant for those she leaves behind. Sevin tearfully asking if she did something wrong and that's why their mother keeps leaving. The glances full of pity as Fyve and Sevin dig, looking for cockroaches. That it was him who had to hold baby Ayt in his arms as he took his last breath.

Instead, he stops in front of her. "Did you find anything?" he asks through clenched teeth.

If his mother was actually doing this for a reason, rather than just being the crazy woman the people of the village think she is, then maybe, maybe, this would've been worthwhile.

Her gaze falls away as her blistered lips tremble. "No." She looks back up. "But I know that Terra will provide—"

Fyve spins on his heel and walks away, not wanting to hear anymore. She's said it all before, and every word has been a lie.

Terra didn't provide. He did.

She hasn't done this because she loves her children. She's done nothing but follow the whims of her crazed mind.

Although the last promise is what's always really fueled the anger.

One day, you'll understand.

Fyve will never understand. Nothing can make what she's done okay.

The need to power his fist through something pounds at him as he passes each hut, but he keeps his clenched hands by his side. Some of these huts will fall in the next gust of wind. His fury would annihilate them.

Instead, he does what he always does. What he has to do. He pushes the anger deep inside until it's little more than embers. White hot embers, admittedly, but no longer flames hungry to become a wildfire. He consciously controls his breathing, saving his energy for when the sun goes down and the cockroaches come out. His family will eat tonight. He'll make sure of it.

Coal appears by his side, his shoulder brushing Fyve's, but not saying anything. He's more of a brother than a cousin, so he knows how Fyve feels about his mother's return. Words aren't necessary. He'd also be feeling the weight of another mouth to feed. It'll be the two of them that won't go to bed until they have enough insects to take the edge off the hunger.

They take their usual place on the multi-colored beach composed of nothing but microplastic. A few yards away from the red-tinted ocean that laps at the edge of Treasure Island, they squint into the dying rays of the sun. The beach quickly fills as people congregate for their daily dose of giving thanks. Fyve registers the moment his mother appears, Sevin still clinging to her. Cee is with them, along with Coal's siblings. They make their way to the front, the area reserved for the more...fervent worshippers. His mother glances over her shoulder, confirming Fyve's where he always stands. She tries for a small smile, but he quickly looks away before it can gain life.

A muted hush falls over the people, telling him that Elijah has arrived. He walks down the beach, his spine straight and head held high, looking every part the messiah of their colony. The breeze plays with his long gray hair and beard, like a fawning wife welcoming him home. The rhythmic waves and tender breeze are all Fyve can hear. Everyone else is collectively holding their breath.

What will Elijah have for them today? The usual prayer to praise Terra? Or some rare, good news? Or another claiming...

Fyve notices Halo a few feet behind her father, her older brother, Ajax, standing beside her with his chest puffed out like it always is. Images of Halo dancing with joy beside her tree, so sweetly genuine and unconsciously graceful, flutter through him. It had been enchanting. Fyve resolutely turns his attention back to Elijah. He doesn't live in a world where words like that survive.

Elijah raises his arms to the setting sun, the robes bleached in the acidic sea fluttering along with his hair. "Great Terra," he intones, a preacher standing at his altar. "We thank you for everything we have. For peace. For each precious breath. For sharing with us your wisdom."

Heads bow as people murmur. "Great Terra, we thank you."

"After everything humans have done. Destroyed your beauty. Desecrated your gifts. Drowned your lands. You have not forsaken us."

"Great Terra, we thank you," the crowd murmurs.

Fyve glances around as Elijah continues, wondering if the ancestors that left them to live in this wasteland had any idea what the world would look like. Oceans stretch for thousands of miles. What little land is left is baked, battered, and barren. And the only way a handful of survivors could find peace was to colonize an island built entirely of their waste.

Elijah turns to face his people, his arms still outstretched. "Terra has spoken to me."

Silence explodes through the crowd. Elijah is the only one Terra speaks to. Fyve normally doesn't have the time or inclination for such whimsy, but Elijah's words are always prophetic. What has Elijah been told this time? Another storm? Or is it where to find seeds to grow healing herbs again?

There's something different about Elijah today, though. A barely contained energy. "A ship will arrive," he announces, his voice loud with adulation. "One that we will use to find Tomorrow Land."

A murmur ripples through the people of Treasure Island. Fyve is as still as Halo's fake tree trunk. A ship? A way to find a life beyond hunger and disease?

"One hundred will come with me," says Elijah, eyes blazing with excitement. "One hundred to find the land Terra has promised us. One hundred to return heroes and lead the remainder of our colony to everything we've ever dreamed of."

Coal shifts his weight. "Everything Elijah's ever said to us has come true," he murmurs, as if he too, is trying to figure out whether this can be believed.

Yet, he's right. Elijah is the chosen spokesperson of Terra. The conduit for the great spirit they worship. A movement catches Fyve's attention, and he finds his mother staring at him. Her eyes shine with the same excitement as Elijah. The same earnest hope.

He looks away. He's seen that look before. Always a day or two before she climbs on her raft and rows away.

Fyve turns his back on Elijah and the red sea that's as damaged as the rest of the planet. He's a survivor. A provider. He's most definitely not a dream chaser.

He has no intention of leaving Treasure Island and everyone he cares about to cross a deadly ocean, searching for something no one's ever seen.

He's not his mother.

HALO

*H*alo stands completely still, trying to process her father's words.

A ship is coming. And it's going to take one hundred people to Tomorrow Land. Then her father will return and take everyone else.

This is his biggest prediction yet. And nobody doubts the all-seeing Elijah, not even Halo herself. Because every one of his prophecies has come true, no matter how outlandish they sounded at the time. This one will be no different.

The ramifications of this announcement are larger than the promised ship itself. Life as they know it will grind to a halt. Without inhabitants, Treasure Island will be wiped from memory like it never existed. This is the only home Halo's ever known. It's the place where she was born. The same place where her mother died. Leaving it feels disloyal somehow.

Her father raises his hands to quieten his people. Terra has more that she needs him to convey.

"There will be five tests known as the Oasis Trials," he says. "They're how we'll choose our strongest and our smartest to lead the way to Tomorrow Land."

Halo nods, wondering if this will include her. And what about Ajax and Cloud? Her family's bloodline is currently blossoming inside Cloud's belly. Halo can't imagine a scenario where they'd be left behind. But, somehow, the idea of being given preferential treatment sits even more uncomfortably with her. She already knows she wants to leave on that ship, just as she knows she's going to make sure she earns her place fairly.

"I call on everyone aged thirteen to nineteen to gather here at first light where the Trials will begin." Halo's father smiles, seeming oblivious to the murmurs this part of the announcement sends across the crowd.

"Why only the young?" a man of around thirty asks. "I'm strong. And smart."

"Hush," his friend beside him warns.

Halo cringes. This man has spoken up at Gratitude before. One day he's going to push his luck with Terra too far. Hopefully that day isn't today. Terra's claimings can feel extremely random at times. Halo's seen lives snatched away without an ounce of it making any sense. And at other times, it's been a clear punishment. Most people choose to follow Terra's rules and not put themselves at risk.

"Terra has spoken." Halo's father narrows his eyes at the man. "It isn't our place to question. Simply just to do."

"But it makes no sense," the man continues, his cheeks pinking up with anger as his friend grips him on the arm, trying to pull him back. "The young are weak. Experience is what makes a person smart."

The crowd falls into silence as the people wait to see if this man has stepped too far. He's voiced his complaints in the past and lived to see a new day, which seems to have buoyed him with confidence. And perhaps this isn't unwarranted, as absolutely nothing happens to him. He remains standing, just as strong as he's making himself out to be.

"I'd like to participate as well," says a woman with silver hair and a shaky voice. "I want to see Tomorrow Land before I die."

"Me, too," a few others mutter, gaining courage in their numbers.

Halo's eyes widen. She's never seen this many people question one of Terra's decisions. But perhaps that's because none of her decisions have ever had such huge ramifications. These people have been raised to believe they'll reach Tomorrow Land —a paradise where food is plentiful and there's space to roam. To learn now that only the young will have that chance isn't sitting well. They're not foolish. What if the ship never returns? Or returns far too late for them? Lives are short on Treasure Island, and it seems there are many who'd rather risk the wrath of Terra than forgo their chance to leave.

This prophecy has changed the game.

"The Oasis Trials will be open to those aged thirteen to nineteen," her father restates firmly. "That is Terra's clear wish. Trust in her wisdom. Terra is always right."

"Terra is always right," Cloud repeats from beside Halo.

But the rest of the crowd doesn't join in. There's desperation and disappointment washing over them. For the first time in Halo's life, she thinks she might be about to witness a full revolt.

Sensing the change in mood, the original man who spoke up steps forward. "Terra is wrong."

A gasp rattles through the crowd as those who stand near the man draw back. His friend who'd held his arm lets go as if his foolishness might be contagious.

"Blasphemy." Halo's father stretches out the word like the roar of a wave.

Halo steps closer to Cloud who takes her hand in what should be a comforting gesture but feels more like a vice.

"Blasphemy," Cloud echoes, her eyes shining with obedience as she straightens her spine.

Halo turns her face from the man, not wanting to see what

she's certain is about to happen. There's no way Terra can continue to show mercy to someone so clearly disobedient.

"We must watch the claiming," hisses Cloud. "Our respect for Terra commands it."

Halo wrenches her hand free but turns to face the man, not wanting to upset Terra. There've been occasions where more than one person has been claimed at once.

The man stands very still for a few seconds before clasping his hands over his ears, his face screwing up and turning purple. A tight band grips Halo's stomach as she accepts this man's good fortune has indeed run out. She resists the urge to run to him and comfort him in his last agonizing moments, knowing she can't. Not unless she'd like to join him to beg for Terra's forgiveness from the sky.

She watches as he collapses to his knees and tears of blood trail down his cheeks and out through his nose. No longer very strong, or smart, the man howls in agony before falling forward, his face connecting sharply with the uneven ground as his body jerks violently, then stills as every one of his nerve endings shuts down.

The scent of death permeates slowly across the crowd in a final farewell. Halo holds her breath as she swallows down her terror.

It doesn't matter how many times she's witnessed a claiming, they're all equally as horrific. She asked her mother once why Terra does this if she's supposed to love them all as her children and had received a sad smile as a reply. She knows her mom had more to say about this. Perhaps if she'd lived long enough, she might have been able to tell her. There's no point asking her father. Or Ajax. And definitely not the ever-faithful Cloud.

It's times like this she feels painfully alone in this world. People are cautious of her, being Elijah's daughter. And she's not like everyone else. She glances across at Fyve, his sister tucked into his side. Sevin gives her a small wave and Halo waves back, hating how much this small gesture means to her.

"My people," her father intones. "We have displeased Terra and another soul has been claimed. Let us learn from this and be her faithful disciples."

The people bow their heads in silent apology. This unfortunate man at their feet hadn't been the only one to disagree with Terra's rules. He was just the only one foolish enough to speak up. Or perhaps the only one who felt he'd rather die than watch a group of teenagers sail away to live his dream.

"If you're of the correct age and wish to voyage to Tomorrow Land, gather here in the morning," Halo's father says. "Our first Trial will begin at dawn, with the results announced at tomorrow's Gratitude."

Halo glances around the crowd, trying to calculate how many teens there are on this island. There must be three or four hundred, at least. But how many will choose to participate? Everywhere she looks there are family groups having hushed and heated discussions. It seems the decision is going to be a contentious one for many.

But not Halo. She already knows she has no choice. Unlike everyone else, for her choosing *not* to participate would separate her from her family. She has literally no reason to want to stay behind.

Her eyes are drawn once more to Fyve, and she shakes her head of the thought that's trying to hold her attention. Yes, he's handsome, and funny, and flirtatious. But she's literally spoken to him once. He's no reason to stay behind. And besides, he'll likely be one of the first to be selected for the ship.

The sun sneaks its way to the horizon and the people lift their faces to the sky.

"Praise Terra," they chant. "Thank you for your kindness. We ask for your blessings."

"Praise Terra," Halo mumbles, finding it harder than usual to participate in Gratitude after witnessing a claiming. She wonders just how many others feel the same.

As soon as the sun disappears and the people turn backs to each other, Halo sneaks away, wanting to make the most of the dying light. There's nothing worse than feeling all alone while surrounded by people.

She scans the coastline as she walks, hoping to stumble across the last few parts she needs for the motor she's been building. For some reason, all the best things seem to wash up at night. Although, she won't get the chance to finish building it now. Just like she'll never get to stand beneath the canopy of her forest. Because when the ship comes, just as her father says it will, all her inventions on this island will be forever paused.

"What are we looking for?" asks Sevin, panting as she catches up to her.

"We?" Halo tilts her head. "I didn't realize we were a team."

Sevin looks aghast. "I'm…I'm sorry."

"It's fine," Halo quickly reassures, wanting Sevin's company more than she's prepared to admit. "I'm not sure what I'm— we're looking for. Anything useful really."

They walk along the man-made beach, the soles of Halo's feet tingling with the prickly feeling of the granules of plastic. She wonders what real sand feels like. Surely, it must be sharp given sand can be used to make glass.

"Does Fyve know where you are?" she asks, glancing back at the crowd.

"He's busy talking to Coal," she says. "He's our cousin."

Halo nods. "Are they trying to guess what the first Trial will be?"

"Fyve said he'd compete over his dead body." Sevin crosses her arms. "Mom's going to kill him when she finds out. Which means I suppose he'll be competing after all."

Halo splutters out a laugh, not having expected Sevin to joke about something so serious. "Maybe he just needs some time to think about it."

Sevin shakes her head firmly. "Not Fyve. When he makes up his mind about something, he never budges."

"Not even to make your mother happy?" Halo narrows her eyes at a small dark shape further down the beach, trying to make out what it might be.

"Fyve doesn't care about making her happy." Sevin says this in a matter-of-fact voice that doesn't belong to someone her age.

"How old are you?" Halo asks, wondering if she's going to be able to compete in the Trials.

Sevin shrugs. "Twelve."

Halo nods, certain she now understands Fyve's stance against the Trials. There's no way he'd leave his sister behind. Which makes it just as well she hadn't pinned her hopes on him. But before she can scold herself for completely kidding herself, her attention is quickly stolen by the washed-up item on the beach. "I think that's a gasket!"

Sevin squints in the dim light then dashes ahead. "Lemme check!"

The younger girl runs ahead, scooting toward what Halo had been looking at. She grinds to a halt a couple of yards too early and picks up something heavy-looking. "It's just a brick!" she calls back.

"Not that one." Halo jogs forward and scoops up the flat, rectangular item of interest and studies the round cut-outs. It's definitely a gasket but the rubber seals have almost entirely corroded away.

"Is that a gasnet?" asks Sevin, having set down the brick.

"Gasket," Halo corrects, holding it out to her. "It's a seal used in an engine. Except this one is probably beyond repair."

"What does it seal?" Sevin takes the long piece of metal and turns it over.

Halo brings to mind the diagram of a motor she'd found, and pictures the section where the gasket was detailed. "It seals the engine block from the cylinder head."

Sevin's brows jump up. "I have no idea what that means. But I *really* want to find out. Will you teach me?"

Halo takes back the gasket and lets out a sigh. This girl is getting far too attached to her. And that never ends well in a place like this. "You realize I'll be competing in the Trials, don't you?"

"But…" Sevin's shoulders slump. "But you can't leave."

"But I want to," Halo softens her voice. "And it's what Terra wants."

"Everybody leaves me." Sevin kicks at the sand. "Except Fyve. But everyone else does. It's not fair."

Halo wonders exactly what this skinny girl has been through in her life but holds back from asking. Sharing secrets is no way to save Sevin from hurting even harder when Halo earns her place on that ship.

"Maybe you can keep my work going while I'm gone?" Halo suggests. "If I get selected, I'm going to need someone to finish everything I started here."

"Do you mean your forest?" Sevin's eyes light up.

"Maybe not the forest." Halo recalls her father's position on this. Although, if he's not here to see it being built, he can't exactly stop it. "Actually…yes, maybe the forest. That's a great idea."

An idea that's certain to keep this curious girl busy and out of trouble for a long time yet.

"I have another idea," says Sevin, the shy girl from earlier this afternoon returning as she avoids Halo's gaze.

"What is it?"

"A waterfall," says Sevin. "We could make one out of broken glass and let the water flow into a pool. It would be a way to clean the water and a safe place to swim."

"Wow." Halo knows better than to criticize such an ambitious plan. Anything is possible if you work hard enough. "I love that."

"You do?" Sevin meets her eye, eager for praise.

"Halo." Her father's voice booms down the beach. "There you are."

"Gotta go!" Sevin darts off into the failing light, tripping on the brick she'd dropped, then continuing down the beach in the direction of the village.

"Dad." Halo walks toward her father, curious as to what he wants to say.

"What's that?" he asks, pointing to her hand.

She'd forgotten she was holding the corroded gasket. "Nothing useful," she answers honestly.

"Halo." This time when he says her name, it's a warning. "Not this again. I've told you there's no need for the things you insist on building here. Our future is in Tomorrow Land. That's true now more than ever."

"What if I don't pass the Trials?" she asks. "I'm not all that strong, you know."

"You will," he says. "You have to."

Halo's brows shoot up. "I don't want favoritism."

"You'll compete just like anyone else." He holds up a hand. "That's what I wanted to tell you. I've had the same conversation with Ajax. Terra doesn't play favorites. I can't put you on the ship simply because you're my daughter. I need you to try your hardest."

She nods slowly, surprised by the urgent tone to his voice. "I always try my best."

"Halo." He reaches out and takes her free hand. "I mean it. You must try. I might be Terra's chosen spokesperson, but I'm also your father. And as much as I don't want to leave you behind, if it's Terra's will then I have no choice."

This kind of statement doesn't surprise Halo. Terra's will

always comes first. "What about Cloud? Surely, she won't get separated from Ajax?"

"If your brother's chosen and Cloud is not, then that is also Terra's will." Her father's eyes brim with sadness and the reality of what he's just said punches her in the gut. Her small family could be torn apart. No matter how many issues they might have, she can't let that happen.

Halo pulls back her shoulders. "Then it looks like we all need to be chosen. We'll pass the Trials, Dad. You'll see."

Her father nods. "Just try your best, Halo. Your mother would want that."

Now Halo's surprised. Her father never mentions her mother. Like, *not ever*. "Would she really?"

"She was certain you were going to achieve great things," he says. "And so am I."

He turns and walks back down the beach, ending any talk of her mom as unexpectedly as he'd started it.

She smiles, pleased with both the memory of her mother and what her father just confirmed. There'll be no advantage given to her. She'll get to prove herself and earn her place on the ship. For the first time in her life, she gets to be just like everyone else.

Bring. It. On.

FYVE

*F*yve watches as the barest hint of dawn crawls over the horizon, tinting the shades of brown that make up Treasure Island with hints of pale gold. He props one knee up as he takes some of his weight off his hut. If he leans too much the whole thing will topple. Resting his arm on the angled leg, he spins the piece of wire he's been fiddling with as he waits for morning to come.

Bringing with it the first of the Oasis Trials.

Not that he intends on entering, but just about everyone he knows who's the right age is planning on stepping up. The promise of getting off this island of trash is just too tempting. Heck, there's nothing Fyve would like more. What would a real tree look like? Smell like? Feel like?

But he has family here. And a loyalty to them that runs far deeper than any selfish need to run. Thank Terra Sevin is still too young to enter. Having to choose between staying back and caring for their aunt Cee and her younger children or following and protecting his last remaining sibling isn't a decision he wants to make.

The sun climbs another inch, chasing away another layer of

night. Time is creeping forward and Fyve is actually glad. He wants these Trials, whatever they're going to look like, over and done with so he can go back to normality. Sure, that means scraping out the chance for those he loves to see another day, but it's all he's known.

There's a faint shuffling sound behind him, and Fyve figures Sevin is awake. She was excited at the prospect of the Trials, asking a million questions on what the ship may look like and when it would arrive. He didn't answer any of them, and not only because he couldn't. But also because he refuses to get caught up in the excitement. Anticipation and speculation won't get rats in traps or bugs on the table.

Nor is he convinced it's coming.

Sure, Elijah's predictions always come true, but nothing is certain in this uncertain existence. One day, Elijah will be wrong. And the promise of a ship might be that time.

The flap of tattered material that acts as a door flutters beside Fyve and he glances up from where he's sitting, any thought of a smile dying when he sees it's not Sevin.

It's his mother. Her face softens as she looks at him, her own smile hovering hopefully on her lips.

Fyve looks away, focusing back on the piece of wire pinched between his thumb and finger. He twirls it back and forth so hard it becomes a blur. If Sevin were here, she'd joke he's trying to take off, which he probably is. He should get up and walk away. It's too late for smiles and soft looks from his mother. They do nothing to take away the pain of her absences.

"You always were an early riser," she says.

The spinning piece of wire becomes his only focus.

"I'm surprised Coal isn't also up," she continues as if they're having a normal morning chat. "He's excited to be entering the Trials."

Which he announced with pride, and no small amount of fervor in his dark eyes. Fyve had been expecting that. He'd even encouraged it. Someone from their family should go and see if there's a chance at a better life out there.

It's just not going to be Fyve.

His mother squats down, although with his unbroken focus on the wire, she's little more than blur beyond it. "I think you should also enter," she says quietly.

His gaze snaps to her. "I'm not leaving."

She must hear the emphasis on the first word, because she winces. "This is what we've all been waiting for, Fyve. This is the chance to find Tomorrow Land." He goes to speak, but she shuffles forward. "You'll come back for the others. That's always been the plan."

"Jett, Bloo, and Rubee need food, Dee," he says, deliberately using her first name. "What's the point of finding Tomorrow Land if they're all dead by the time I get back?"

"You need to have faith, Fyve. Terra will provide, just like she's always promised to."

Fyve's not sure what his mother's definition of providing is, but Treasure Island isn't his. If she wants to disappear for months at a time in the name of faith, firm in her belief there's something out there to be found, no matter how much her children plead for her to stay, then so be it. But he's not doing that to those he loves.

His mother drops to her knees, almost as if she's praying. "I want you to enter the Oasis Trials."

"All the more reason not to do it," he spits back.

Her lashes flicker, the only sign that his words hurt but it's enough for unwanted guilt to flash through his chest. He should've got up and walked away just like he intended. Is he forever going to give this woman one more chance to be the mother he needs? Only to be disappointed and lash out, then feeling worse for it?

Fyve pushes to his feet and flicks the piece of wire away. "It won't matter what you say. I'm not entering the Trials. I'm staying here with Sevin and the others. Coal can be your shining example of faith."

His mother does the same, wobbling a little as she straightens and Fyve has to resist the instinctive urge to reach out and steady her. She's always so weak after her trips away. It'll mean spending extra time searching for food.

She sighs but before she can say anything, Sevin darts through the flap. She stops, her feet skidding and puffing up dust as she sees Fyve and their mother. "Oh, you're still here," she says, her relief evident.

Their mother engulfs her in a hug. "Of course, I am, my heart."

This time, it's a lip curl that Fyve has to suppress. His mother's talking as if her being here is a guarantee. Like they've spent every day of their life being called her heart.

But Sevin looks up, love shining her eyes. "It's today, Mom."

"I know." Their mother tucks a strand of black hair behind Sevin's ear. "It's finally starting."

Around them, people are also exiting their huts and lean-tos, a murmur of excitement rippling through the air. Any dissent about Terra's decision that only those between thirteen and nineteen being allowed to go had quickly been quashed with the claiming of Bor. Not even a frown had flitted over the faces of those who'd agreed with him. Instead, everyone began speaking of the opportunity they've been gifted—their child might be chosen. Their teen could be the one finding Tomorrow Land, then returning to save them all.

Terra had indeed, graced them with her generosity.

Coal appears from the hut beside them, stretching widely. Behind him, Jett and Bloo leap on his outstretched arms, dangling as if he just became their personal climbing frame. Coal makes a show of stumbling under their scrawny weight, and Fyve ducks over, scooping one up, then the other. Squeals of laughter tinkle around them as Fyve juggles two wriggling little bodies. He places them down and he and Coal engage in their usual morning game of tag, allowing Coal's younger siblings to catch them a moment later.

Fyve straightens as his aunt, Cee, appears, smiling broadly as Rubee clings to her leg, and he grins back. It reminds him happiness can be found on Treasure Island. You just have to build it like everything else.

Sevin strolls over, rolling her eyes. "One day you two will grow up."

Fyve and Coal glance at each other. It was only a few months ago that Sevin was playing this game, too. Her sudden need to be all grown up meant she stopped, looking on with Cee as she shook her head, like she'd just aged a decade or two. Fyve and Coal move in unison, no words needed to agree on what needs to be done next. Sevin realizes their intent a second later, but it's too late. Fyve wraps his arms around her and hauls her against his chest while Coal dives in and tickles her mercilessly. Sevin's own squeals and giggles echo those of her cousins only moments ago.

"Stop!" she cries. "I'm too old for this!"

"No, you're not," says Fyve, laughing. "You're a kid. Admit it."

"Never!"

"Then I'm never stopping," announces Coal.

"Okay, okay! I'm just a kid!" says Sevin, already breathless from laughing.

Fyve releases her and Coal steps back, looking at each other triumphantly. Although this had been nothing more than a game, a nugget of satisfaction settles in Fyve's chest. It's too soon for Sevin to grow up. He'd prefer her to hold onto her innocence for as long as she can, even if it means rejoicing in their mother's presence, rather than acknowledging her absences.

Behind him, Fyve feels the warmth on his back as the sun

finally breaches the horizon. The village lights up, the grime and decay no longer hidden by shadows. Everyone sobers.

It's time.

With no breakfast to be had, people begin to move to the beach. Murmurs filter among them, everyone wondering what's ahead.

"So exciting. My boy has barely slept a wink."

"I wonder when the ship will be arriving."

"What do you think the Trials will involve?"

"I'm sure they'll be fun. My Calan is going to excel at anything to do with counting."

"Thank Terra for the opportunity."

"Thank Terra," several people echo, the response almost automatic.

Fyve and his family fall in behind, and he walks a little slower than them. He's content to hold back and watch seeing as he has no intention to take part.

To his surprise, Coal remains with him. They walk on in silence, the growing crowd weaving through the huts. So many feet steadily kick up dust and tiny pieces of plastic, and Fyve keeps his mouth closed, not wanting that to be his first meal of the day.

The scent of the ocean tickles his nose the closer they get, briny, with a hint of sulfur. He wonders, as he has so many times, what it used to look like when it was blue. Before the oceans swelled, swallowing up vast tracts of land. Before it acidified, killing millions of species and dissolving anything with a shell, leaving behind an ocean floor of seared red.

But as it comes into view, he realizes it doesn't matter. He'll never know. In the same way he'll never know what a full stomach feels like. What old age looks like. Or what grass smells like.

The people in front of Fyve begin to murmur as they spread out along the beach, the rows several people deep as hundreds begin to congregate. Fyve and Coal find their families, staring at something sitting on the sand. At first Fyve doesn't see it because there are too many people milling around. But then the people part and he glances at his cousin, wondering if Coal's as confused as he is. He shrugs and Fyve looks back at what has everyone talking among themselves.

A pile of metal poles. But a pile haphazardly stacked on top of each other.

And it's not the only one. More than a dozen piles stretch out down the beach in both directions, large tracts of space in between them, each just as messy and disordered as the next. It's like a giant threw his play sticks down in a huff and stalked off.

Sevin slips in beside him. "What do you think the Trial is?"

"I doubt they're for building a bunch of trees," he says, looking away. Apart from being a bit of entertainment for him and Sevin, it doesn't matter. His only hope is that Coal passes. Judging by the way he's bouncing on his toes and staring at the closest pile as if it's a golden ticket to get on the ship, this is important to his cousin.

"Maybe they have to build a bridge?" Sevin suggests, clearly excited. "Or a frame for a hut that can't easily blow down? Oh, or maybe a tower tall enough to be able to see the ship coming!"

That would definitely take strength and smarts. Sevin angles her head, obviously already calculating how to do that.

"The foundation would need to be strong," she murmurs. "But you'd also want height. It would be all about the angles. And the support beams."

Fyve ruffles her hair. "You can be on my team, any day."

Sevin looks up at him, not smiling like he expected her to. Before he can ask what's going on, the crowd stills and quiets.

"Elijah's here," someone whispers.

Their leader strides down the beach with purpose, his chin held high and face solemn. Fyve finds himself scanning for Halo, quickly spotting her with her brother, Ajax, and his partner several yards behind and already blending into the crowd. Half a dozen young men flock to Ajax, slapping him on the back and thumping chests. He revels in the attention.

Just as many people crowd around Halo, obviously thinking Elijah's children are going to be someone they want to ally themselves with. But while Ajax enjoys the attention, Halo shrinks into herself.

Fyve sighs as he pushes through the crowd to rescue her. "Halo," he says quietly, but loud enough to be heard. "I have a situation. Sevin's talking about building a tower to the moon."

She grins, the action lighting up her whole face. "That would depend on the angles."

He rolls his eyes. "That's what she said."

Fyve takes her hand and leads her back to his family, not allowing himself to register how good it feels to have her palm cupped in his. It's nothing like holding his sister's or cousin's hands. It's…warmer.

Once back beside Sevin, he releases Halo's hand. Halo will definitely be on that ship, which is exactly what everyone else is thinking and why she's about to have a hundred best friends. Unlike them, he's not getting attached.

On the beach, Elijah stops in between two stacks of poles, eyes roaming over the crowd. Fyve has often wondered what makes Elijah so special. What about him had Terra singling him out as being her voice, her conduit to the people? Fyve's never been able to come up with an answer.

"Welcome to the first of the Oasis Trials," Elijah says loudly, and a few people shuffle a little closer, not wanting to miss a word.

"The first of five Trials, each will allow Terra to choose the strongest and smartest to blaze the trail to prosperity."

The crowd murmurs with excitement and Fyve suppresses the need to shift his weight. He agrees with Bor—teens may have youth on their side, but a person's ability to survive is only proven by age, and that's what Fyve considers smart. Not that he's going to say it aloud. He may not be smart like Sevin, but he's wise enough to keep his opinions to himself.

"The chosen one hundred will sail to Tomorrow Land," continues Elijah, lifting his arms out wide. "Our future."

On the ship that hasn't turned up yet.

"Thank Terra," someone shouts, and others quickly repeat the phrase, filling the beach with adulation.

Fyve glances down, noting that Halo isn't joining in. He briefly wonders why before focusing back on Elijah, telling himself it doesn't matter. She probably knows she doesn't need to pray or thank Terra. Her name is already on the list of those sailing away on this mythical ship.

"Now," says Elijah, a weight creeping into his tone. "Will all those between the ages of thirteen and nineteen who would like to participate, please step forward."

Fyve stills. He glances at his cousin, conscious the first step of a possible goodbye is about to be taken.

"I'll bring you back a leaf or something," says Coal, his gaze heavy with wishing he won't be going alone if chosen. "Maybe even a whole branch."

"Make sure it's edible," says Fyve, jostling him.

Coal gives him a crooked smile, then steps forward as dozens of other teens do, too.

Halo's hand brushes Fyve's and he looks down, finding her expressive eyes studying his face. "Just remember, it's all about the angles," he says softly.

She nods, hesitates as if she's going to say something, but then steps forward to join Coal. Fyve straightens his spine, refusing to feel like he's being left behind. In a few days this will be over, and his life will continue as it always has.

A movement beside him has his head snapping to the side. Sevin flashes him a glance, almost one of apology, and then steps away.

Straight onto the beach with the others.

Fyve's after her in a second. "Sevin, what are you doing?" he hisses as he tries to grab her hand.

But she sidesteps him, having spent a lifetime escaping his playful clutches. "I'm joining the Trials," she says loudly.

Coal frowns. Halo freezes in surprise. Dozens of faces turn to see what the commotion is.

Fyve grits his teeth, having no doubt his sister planned to do this all along. "You're not old enough," he grinds out. "You're only twelve."

"My day of birth is today," she says, eyebrows hiking in challenge. "I'm now thirteen."

Fyve opens his mouth to point out that's not true—she was born in the longer months of the cool season—only to find he can't. There are no records of birth on Treasure Island. His sister is lying, but he has no way to prove that.

Her chin lifts as one hand settles on her bony, too-young-for-this hip. "I want a chance to be chosen, Fyve."

"No," he says firmly. He's not going to let her.

And yet, the sea of eyes slowly turning to him are like a tide he can't swim against. Sevin has ensured dozens of witnesses to her declaration.

Slowly, Fyve turns to look at his mother. She's the only one who can stop this. She needs to keep Sevin safe.

Her face hardens with the same stubborn determination settling on her daughter's features. "My daughter is telling the truth. She's old enough to join the Trials."

Every muscle locks as her words cement two things for Fyve.

She ensures the disconnect in their relationship can never be healed. He needed her, and like always, she let him down. In this moment, he almost hates her.

He turns back to Sevin, the next truth settling like a hot stone in his gut. His mother has ensured he must now enter the

Trials. After everything, she's getting what she wants. The bitterness of that is like acid in his mouth.

There's no way he's letting his only sibling do this alone. Everyone is assuming these Trials will be games. Safe and free from danger. But Terra works in mysterious ways. She's shown time and time again how little value she puts on human life. In all honesty, it's kind of fair considering how little care humans gave her in the first place.

Fyve steps forward and joins the crowd of three-hundred strong teens. Sevin beams. Coal grins. Even Halo has a smile dancing at the edges of her lips. All he does is scowl at them.

None of them have any idea what the first Trial involves.

HALO

"*Y*ou told me you're twelve," Halo whispers urgently to Sevin.

"I was." The young girl crosses her arms. "Yesterday."

Halo doesn't believe her for a moment. But now that her own mother has vouched for her, who's going to argue the point?

Fyve mutters something unintelligible.

That's who. But even he must know it's a losing argument.

And now there's three of them, all entering the Oasis Trials along with Fyve's cousin, Coal, making them a team of four. Can Halo dare to think of them as a team? Fyve had drawn her away from the shallow people who'd been suffocating her, somehow sensing her discomfort. That sort of indicates he cares about her, doesn't it? And Sevin's made her feelings for Halo clear. But who's this cousin? Can he be trusted?

"Sevin will be okay," Coal whispers to Fyve. "We'll look after her."

Right. So, he cares about Fyve. That is if feeding him naïve optimism is genuine care. The reality is that none of them really

know if they're going to be okay. These Trials could be dangerous. And the result of passing them could be deadly. Plenty of
people have died at sea, looking for land.

Halo's father spreads his arms wide and the crowd hushes,
keen to find out what these piles of precariously placed poles
mean.

"I'll explain the rules of the first Trial in a moment," her
father says. "But first, you need to choose a set of poles." He
smiles widely. "Choose carefully. Your entire future depends on
this decision."

"How many on a team?" someone calls out.

Halo's father shrugs. "That's up to you. You can all choose
the same pile. Or you can evenly space yourselves out. Terra
would like you to make this decision yourself. Remember, she's
watching every part of this Trial, not just the result."

Halo bites down on her lip as she studies the various piles,
noticing that each one is different. The one closest to them has
been stacked haphazardly, like fire kindling, with poles sticking
out in all directions. The one beside it has been piled up in a
neat square arrangement. There's another she can see further
down that looks more like a tepee, with the poles all on their
ends, resting against each other at the top.

These were the poles she was planning to use to build her
forest. It's kind of ironic they're being used as an instrument
that will lead her to a real forest.

"Which one do we choose?" Sevin asks, ignoring her brother
and cousin who are in a heated discussion.

"Wait," says Coal, turning his attention to Sevin. "I was just
telling Fyve we should split up. Increase our chances of one of
us making it through. Working as a team doesn't make sense."

Fyve shakes his head. "I told you. I'm not splitting up from
Sevin. We either both make it or we're both out."

Halo isn't surprised by this. Fyve's already made it clear his
sister is the only reason he even stepped up. The whole point of

him entering the Trials was to look after her, not to have the prize for himself.

"Well, no offence, but I'm not going on your team," says Coal, frowning. "Our family needs to be represented on that ship."

He stalks off down the beach toward one of the stacks at the end. Halo concedes he made a good point, even if leaving his family was harder than it looked. She saw the pain in his eyes as he'd turned away.

"What about you?" Fyve asks Halo, clearly annoyed with his cousin. "Are you sticking with us, or making your own way, too?"

"I'm not your family," says Halo, not wanting to leave her new friends just yet.

"You sure you don't want to go with your brother?" he asks.

Halo glances at Ajax, seeing Cloud beside him, her face turned to the sky talking to Terra. She shakes her head. "Coal has a point. My family's better to separate."

Sevin claps, pleased to have Halo on her team. "Which stack are we choosing? We don't even know what we have to do with it yet."

"That's the hard part." Halo pushes her long braid behind her back as she concentrates. "We're choosing based on a random set of variables."

"I don't know what that means," says Fyve. "But I think we need to hurry up and make a choice."

He's right. Almost everyone is already standing by a stack of poles. Ajax and Cloud are beside the tepee arrangement. Coal has taken one of the random stacks, along with a large group of people he seems to know from the village.

"What about that one?" Sevin points at an extremely wobbly looking stack that has precisely nobody standing beside it. "We could work alone if we choose that one."

"It looks like it's about to fall over." Fyve's brow crinkles.

"Maybe that's the Trial," says Halo. "Who can bring their tower to the ground the fastest. Honestly, we have no idea if that gives us an advantage or disadvantage at this stage. But the three of us working alone sounds smart. Sometimes making the less obvious choice is the right one. I'm with Sevin. Let's take the wobbly stack."

Sevin beams at her before dashing off.

Fyve puts a hand on Halo's back as they make the decision her father said could shape the rest of their lives. Please, let it be the right one.

"Are you okay?" Fyve asks.

She nods, trying to ignore the way her stomach is cramping with both nerves and the warmth of Fyve's hand on the bare skin of her lower back. "Are you?"

"Not even a bit," he says, anger seeping in underneath his sadness. "Sevin isn't thirteen. She shouldn't be here."

"We're with her," Halo reassures. "I'll help look out for her."

"The way she's following you around, I don't think you have a choice." A smile slips in to mingle with the grief in his eyes and it lights Halo with warmth.

They join Sevin at the stack of teetering poles, ignoring the titters around them as their choice is harshly judged by a group of strong-looking guys at the stack beside them. Their poles have all been laid horizontally on top of each other, forming a compact but sturdy pile.

Sevin's fists are clenched by her sides, and she seems to be gathering her courage to shout back a retort to their laughter. But she remains silent. Maybe the Trials will be good for Sevin's confidence, whether she passes them or not. It's time she started to speak up more for herself.

A girl of about fourteen approaches the group of guys, standing a few feet away from them but having clearly selected their pile as her own.

"This group is full," one of the guys snarls.

"Elijah said to make our own choice," the girl snaps. "He said there was no limit on how many to a group."

"Well, there's a limit on this group," another one of the guys replies.

"You can join us," Sevin pipes up. Despite being so keen to work alone, here she is inviting someone else, simply because she doesn't like to see anyone being excluded. Halo's starting to see why Fyve is so attached to his sister.

The girl hesitates, then plants her feet. "I like this stack. I'm good, thanks."

The group of knuckleheads form a line between the girl and the stack, and cross their arms.

"Do you have a hearing problem?" one of them asks. "We're full up. There's no room for you."

"But this is my choice," the girl says.

"We'll bury you under that pile before we let you join us," the guy sneers.

The girl freezes, and Halo's not sure if she's still holding her ground or if she's too afraid to move.

Sevin dashes forward and slips her hand into the girl's, tugging her away from danger. The girl follows, gripping Sevin's hand tightly.

"We don't know what the Trial is," Halo tells her gently as she comes to stand beside them. "That stack may not have been the best choice."

The girl eyes their wobbly stack with clear hesitation as she nods.

Fyve clears his throat. "I'm Fyve. This is my sister, Sevin. And this here is—"

"Halo," the girl finishes. "Everyone knows Elijah's children."

Halo nods, not appreciating being reminded how different she is when all she wants is to be like everyone else. But the girl meant no offence, so she tries not to take any.

"I'm Justice," the girl says. "Thanks for letting me join your group."

The remaining participants select their groups, a few making last minute dashes when they change their mind.

"Please finalize your decision," Halo's father calls across the crowd. "At the count of ten, wherever you're standing will be your final choice."

As the count begins, Halo holds her breath, hoping she's made the right move. There's no doubt she made this first decision of the Trials with her heart, not her head. And Terra is judging them on being smart and strong, which has little to do with the heart. It's no wonder the knuckleheads didn't want a skinny girl like Justice on their team.

"Ten!" her father calls. "Excellent. You all have a team now. Terra is pleased. The first step of the first Trial is complete."

People look from face to face, trying to figure out if they passed this stage or not. There's simply no way to know.

"Let us begin the next step," Halo's father says. "At my signal, I want you to remove a single pole from your stack. If you fail to remove a pole or your stack collapses, your team is out."

Halo's heart sinks. She closes her eyes, unable to meet the gaze of any of her teammates. There's no question on whatever remains of this desolate planet that they chose the wrong stack. Theirs looks like it's about to fall if they breathe on it, let alone remove one of the many teetering poles.

The knuckleheads hoot and holler. With a stack of horizontally positioned poles, there's no way they can lose.

Halo opens her eyes and finds Fyve grinning, while Sevin kicks at the sand.

"You want to lose!" Sevin wails. "This isn't fair."

"I don't want to lose," says Justice, forlornly. "I really wanted to win."

Halo notices her use of past tense. "We can still win. You

never know. Maybe removing some of the weight off the top will stabilize the stack. It's all about the angles."

Sevin perks up at these words. "It's all about the angles," she repeats.

"As long as nobody sabotages us," Halo adds, looking directly at Fyve. Sevin was right. It's clear he wants to lose. "Just remember we're a team. The decisions we make impact directly on each other as well as ourselves."

Fyve's shoulders slump at these words. It might be true that he wants to lose, but he's still a good guy. He doesn't want to destroy Halo or Justice's chances in the process.

"You may begin!" Halo's father calls as he lowers his hands.

Sevin circles their stack of poles, studying it closely. Halo and Justice do the same, while Fyve waits patiently.

They're going to need Fyve's help to succeed. He's the only one of the four of them who's strong enough to have even a small chance of removing one of these poles without sending the entire stack toppling.

The knuckleheads lift a pole from their neat stack with annoying ease and place it to the side. They cross their arms and turn their attention to Halo's group, not bothering to hide their amusement.

"What about that one?" Justice points to the pole at the very top of their stack. "It's not supporting anything."

"We can't reach it," Fyve says. "Not without some kind of ladder."

"Halo could stand on your shoulders," Sevin suggests.

"Except I won't be able to lift it," Halo points out. "We'll need to find one we can slide out from the bottom."

The group of four turns their attention to the poles resting on the ground.

"This one!" Sevin crouches down and gently taps a pole right in the middle of the stack. "This one will work."

"We're getting old over here!" one of the knuckleheads calls out.

Ignoring him, Halo crouches beside Sevin to study the pole as she calculates the risk.

"What do you think?" Fyve asks. "Will it work?"

Halo sighs. "I'm not sure. I really don't think we can remove any of these poles without a collapse. But this is our best bet."

"Let's do it then." Fyve crouches beside Halo and Sevin shuffles out of the way to stand beside Justice.

"They can totally do this," Sevin tells her proudly.

Halo wishes she had the same confidence. She glances down the beach at Ajax. He looks worried, not taunting her for once, but seeming genuinely fearful. The half of her that loves him grows a tiny bit more. Meanwhile, her father remains unsettlingly calm.

"Are you sure this is the right one?" Fyve asks, placing his strong hands on the end of the pole.

"No, but let's do it anyway," Halo says. "Please, try your hardest."

Fyve tugs gently on the pole and it moves forward an inch. To his credit, he's trying, despite not wanting to succeed. Could this guy get any more appealing? It's almost becoming irritating.

"It's working!" Sevin whispers excitedly. "It's working!"

"Shh," Justice tells her. "Let him concentrate."

Fyve slides the pole out a little more and the stack wobbles dangerously.

Halo puts up her hands, like she can somehow urge the poles to stay in place.

"No hope!" laughs a knucklehead.

Fyve waits for Halo's signal to continue. The stack steadies just a bit and she nods at him. "Go slowly."

He slides the pole out just a little more, but this time it's too much. The stack sways to the left, then right.

"No!" Sevin calls out. "No!"

The entire stack collapses into itself, the poles clattering to the ground while the other teams form walls around their own to protect them from any fallout.

Halo covers her head with her hands as her heart sinks, aware it's the very organ that got her into this position in the first place. But it's not just her heart. Her entire future feels like it's sinking into the acidic depths of the ocean. She won't be going on the ship. She won't be one of the first people to step foot on Tomorrow Land. She'll have to wait here like everyone else and try to live in hope.

As the poles finish their catastrophic fall to Earth, Halo decides she's sick to death of hope. She's sick of fake trees, and half-built motors and living in fear of being claimed. All she wants to do is live.

Right now. Not tomorrow but today.

She lets her hands fall from her head and looks across at Fyve.

"I'm sorry," he says, even though none of this is his fault.

"Me, too." She points at Sevin. "Go and comfort her. I'm okay."

Fyve nods, seeming torn, but goes to his sister and wraps his arms around her. "We don't need that stupid land. We can be happy here. Together."

"We can finish our forest," Sevin sniffs, looking at Halo.

Halo nods, liking the way she said *our*. "At least we have plenty of poles."

This makes Sevin smile.

"Are you okay, Justice?" Fyve asks.

The girl looks stunned, and Halo waits for her to blame Sevin for dragging her onto their team. But she remains silent.

"We did our best," she says, walking away, likely to find her devastated family in the crowd. Halo vows to look for her later. The guilt she feels at what just happened to this poor girl is overwhelming.

"My people," says Halo's father. "Our first team is out, but the Trial is not complete. Round two begins. All remaining teams must remove another pole on my signal."

"Another round?" whispers Sevin. "So, more teams might get cut?"

Halo shrugs as she stands beside Fyve, wanting a better view of the other teams. "It's so hard to figure out."

"Begin!" calls her father, and the knuckleheads efficiently remove another pole. Halo shifts her focus to the other teams. Ajax's group seems to have no trouble removing another pole from their tepee, although their luck is sure to run out soon. The group with the square stack doesn't seem to be having any trouble.

"Coal," says Sevin. "Look, Fyve. Coal's group's in trouble."

Halo locates Coal and frowns. Sevin's right. Coal's stack is wobbling as two of his team members stand paused with a pole pulled halfway out.

"It's going to go," says Fyve, just as the stack comes toppling down. The two people holding the pole let go, but the female doesn't do it in time.

Halo lets out a gasp as one of the higher up poles comes flying down, hitting the girl on the top of her head before she has a chance to get out of the way. She's knocked to the ground and more poles come raining down on top of her.

There's screaming as Coal leaps forward, scrambling to reach her. He moves poles away, sending them sliding over each other and uncovers the girl. He lifts her limp body in his arms, her long hair trailing down toward the ground, once blonde, but now stained with red.

"There's too much blood," says Sevin. "Look at it all."

Halo nods. There's no way this girl will make it if she's not dead already. Her skull is most certainly broken by the way it's caved in on one side. They've achieved many miracles on Trea-sure Island, but medical advances remain stilted, having relied on Terra to look after them, instead. Perhaps, Justice wasn't so unlucky after all. She may not have made it onto the ship, but at least she's not dead.

There was so much at stake already with this Trial, but things have taken a new turn. Because now they're deadly. And the calm way Halo's father is standing there tells her he's not so surprised by this development.

Coal carries the girl to her distressed family and Halo decides he's most definitely a guy she can trust. Although, that doesn't seem to matter now that she won't be going on the ship. And nor might he.

Once the worst of the crowd's distress has dissipated, Halo's father raises his arms. They turn to him, waiting to hear whatever words he might have to say that will make any of this feel okay.

"We mourn the loss of one of our own," her father says. "But we need to remember that this is Terra's will. The reasons don't need to be clear. We need to accept that Terra is looking after us."

Halo's fairly certain these words aren't doing a whole lot to placate anyone here, but nobody speaks up.

"The Trial continues," her father says.

No teams are eliminated in the next three rounds, but on the fourth, Ajax's tepee falls apart, sending both the team members and the poles scattering. Cloud clutches her belly instead of her head as she runs into the crowd.

Her father signals the beginning of the next round, and this time, three teams fail. But thankfully, nobody else suffers the same fate as that poor girl who lost her life. Round after round continues until only the team with the square stack and the knuckleheads remain. Both teams complete the entire Trial, resulting in a tie.

Halo smiles, pleased that such a selfish team can't claim victory on their own.

"Well done," her father's voice booms down the beach. "That completes the first of the Oasis Trials. The results will be announced at Gratitude tonight."

The crowd murmurs their thanks to Terra before breaking up to comfort each other. Others begin to collect the poles to re-stack them neatly on the beach with their other supplies.

"I really wanted to go on the ship," says Sevin quietly. "But at least if I stay behind I have you two. And maybe Coal."

"I wanted to go, too," says Halo.

"Do you really believe it?" asks Fyve. "That there's going to be a ship, I mean."

Halo tilts her head. "Of course, I do. Terra has spoken."

Fyve seems to hold back on something he wants to say.

"Hey there," says Ajax from behind her. "I'm sorry, Halo."

She wraps her arms around Ajax's waist, letting go of all the angst that had passed between them over the years. To her surprise, he hugs her back.

Maybe this day wasn't a total waste. It's possible she'll be saying goodbye to her family in the near future, but at least she has this moment to store in her heart.

Ajax pulls away and presses something into her hand. She looks down to see it's her lucky cord.

"I really am sorry," he says.

She tucks the cord in her pocket and smiles. "It's okay, Ajax. Honestly, it is."

Ajax nods and leaves, and Sevin slips her hand into Halo's.

"You have us now," says Sevin. "You said we're not your family, but we are now. We'll be your new family when your actual one leaves on the ship."

Feeling like she has something in her eye, Halo blinks it away.

"Thanks, Sevin," she says, meaning it. "But can you excuse me for a minute? There's someone I need to talk to."

Sevin nods and Halo makes her way down the beach to her

father. As soon as she reaches him, the people part, knowing after what just happened they're going to need their privacy.

"Dad." Her voice breaks under the strain. "I did my best."

"I know." He puts a hand on her arm. "But Terra hasn't spoken yet. We don't know exactly what she was looking for today. There's still hope."

And there's that word again. The one she'd been cursing only moments earlier.

Hope.

"Do you really believe that, Dad?" she asks. "It's pretty obvious who lost the Trial today."

"There are many ways to lose in this world," he says, remaining calm. "Just like there are many ways to win."

"Do you know the results already?" she asks, lighting with that dreaded word—hope.

He shakes his head. "I'll go and contemplate now, and Terra will speak to me."

"I'm sorry, Dad." She winces, knowing she's let him down. "I wanted our family to stay together. Really, I did."

"And I still do," he says, leaning forward to kiss her forehead. "Believe in Terra."

As he walks off down the beach, Halo tries with all her might to summon what little optimism she has left in her body. Her father's right. Anything could happen at Gratitude tonight.

When everything else fails, there's always hope.

FYVE

There were two rats in the trap today. It's almost as if Terra's celebrating right alongside Fyve. Sevin may have lied about her age and stepped up to join the Trials, but they failed the first test. The knowledge has him stepping a little lighter, his shoulders a little straighter.

He doesn't have to worry about splitting up the one thing he's spent his whole life trying to keep together—his family. He and Sevin are staying on Treasure Island, where they belong.

Not that Sevin is as relieved or happy as he is.

She sniffs for the hundredth time since they set out to check the traps, and Fyve and Coal glance at each other. She's barely said a word, which is even less like her. But Coal looks away, for once, Fyve's partner in the cheer department failing to step up. He feels sorry for Sevin. He knows how devastated he'd be if he failed. And he feels guilty because his team held on for longer.

"Two rats," Fyve points out as they trek back to the village, trying to lighten the mood. "You could have a roasted leg, Sevin."

His sister shrugs, her gaze barely flicking to the two furry bodies hanging from his belt. "Don't care."

"Hey," he says, taking the tail of one of them and flicking her with it. "Keep that up and you won't get any rat tail soup tomorrow."

She shrugs, kicking at the remnants of a plastic fork. "Oh no, I won't be able to extend my existence on this dead-end island."

Fyve drops the tail, having never heard Sevin speak like this. "You're too young to enter the Trials. This is Terra telling you it wasn't meant to be."

That she thinks they should stay together, leaving Coal to be the one to find a world beyond Treasure Island. If there even is one...

Sevin swipes at her cheek, and the sight of the grime smear the moisture has left tugs at Fyve's heart. A little part of him is angry that Terra even instilled this hope. Sevin's never spoken of being unhappy here. It seems the promise of something more, no matter how unlikely it exists, isn't the wonderful news Elijah is painting it to be.

Fyve slips an arm around her shoulder. "In a week or so, this will all be a memory. Things will be back to normal."

That seems to trigger another tear, the single droplet glistening in the afternoon sun as it trickles through the smear the last one left.

Coal steps around Fyve to slip an arm around her other shoulder. "Terra works in mysterious ways. Don't lose hope."

Sevin tears her gaze from the ground to peer up at him. "You really think so?"

Fyve scowls. More false hope isn't what Sevin needs. "We didn't even pull one pole out."

But Sevin tugs away from him, and his arm falls as she slips closer to Coal. "Terra won't want someone like those guys on her ship," she says, gazing up at Coal as if he's Elijah himself. "They may be strong, but they're mean."

"They chose the right pile," says Fyve, glowering at his

cousin even though Coal is smiling down at Sevin. He needs to stop.

"They chose the easiest pile," she responds instantly. "And they didn't let Justice join them, even though she's Zake's sister."

Fyve hadn't realized Justice was related to one of the guys on that team.

"Terra doesn't care about things like that," says Fyve, frustration making his hands clench. "Those guys are just the type she'd want on her ship."

And good riddance, too. Zake and his gang are one of the reasons they have to not only check their traps so often, but also move them. They don't even hide that they're stealing other people's supplies. In fact, they sneer and challenge the person to come and get it back, knowing no one can afford the energy or the chance of being injured.

"Exactly why we'll be on that ship," says Coal.

"Have you two forgotten that someone died in the Trials today?" asks Fyve, stopping as they stand on the edge of the village. He doesn't want anyone else hearing this conversation.

"People die here every day," Coal points out calmly. "My guess is that girl would prefer to give her life to Terra during the Oasis Trials rather than die of starvation or disease."

"Look, Coal, just because you got through—"

"That hasn't been decided yet," he points out. "And even if I don't, even if I died like that girl, I'll be glad I tried, Fyve. It's better than rotting away here, with everything else."

Fyve shakes his head. Coal's always found it easier to believe, possibly because he hasn't lost so much. All his siblings are waiting for them back at his hut. "You have no idea if this ship is coming, or whether Tomorrow Land even exists, let alone whether you'll find it."

"That's what faith is," says Coal, a glimmer of his grin back. "It's the gift of hope."

Sevin nods solemnly. "Yeah. We could still get through."

Anger gnaws at Fyve in the same way the rats would if he lay still for too long—hungrily and mercilessly. There's no way to reason with these two. They're too blinded by that dangerous emotion, hope.

He's about to spin on his heel and stalk away when he stops. A group of people are approaching them with determination.

Zake and his gang.

Fyve and Coal instantly shift closer together, keeping Sevin between them. Fyve surreptitiously moves the rats on his belt so they're sitting in the middle of his back, away from greedy eyes. Unlike hope, those two, slightly warm bodies are a tangible guarantee of a few more tomorrows.

Zake stops a few feet away, that permanent sneer curling his thick upper lip. "Your sister owes me," he snarls, the others around him grumbling their assent.

"I doubt it. She doesn't associate with scum," Fyve asks flatly.

Coal crosses his arms. "Or the scum that grows on scum."

"Shut up!" Zake takes a threatening step forward. "It's because of Nine, or whatever number she is, that Justice failed the Trials!"

Fyve's about to take a step forward of his own when he remembers the rats. Instead, he subtly moves his shoulder in front of Sevin. "Her name's Sevin. She'd be a kid if she was Nyne."

Zake sneers. "I don't care what her name is. Justice is stuck here now because the stupid girl invited her onto your team of losers."

"Only because you wouldn't let your own sister on your team!" shouts Sevin. "That makes you the loser!"

Zake throws his head back and laughs. "We're not the losers. We're the ones who'll be on the ship heading to Tomorrow Land."

"You assume a lot of things in life, don't you, Zake?" asks Coal, his eyes narrowed.

"Yeah, everyone saw you didn't want a girl on your team, even if she's your own sister," says Sevin angrily.

Zake snorts derisively. "Terra knows girls are weaker and stupider."

"Does she?" asks Fyve, putting emphasis on the *she*. Right now, Zake is insulting their creator.

"Yes, she does," snaps Zake, as clueless as always. "And she ain't gonna want siblings on the ship. I don't wanna breed with my sister."

Fyve blinks at that. Zake has actually made a good point. An insightful one. A ship with one hundred teens is best to have them all unrelated. The children of the chosen will be the first ones born in Tomorrow Land. He and Sevin may never have both been able to go.

Thank Terra they're out of the competition.

"Unless Terra wants Justice on that ship," says Coal, amusement tinging his voice. "Because that would mean you sabotaged all your, ah, friends' chances of being there when it sails away."

Zake launches himself at Coal but his gang haul him back. The bully makes a point of struggling against their hold, but he doesn't slip out of their grasp. Fyve suspects it's all for show.

"You'll pay for what you did to Justice," Zake snarls. "When we come back, you ain't getting on my ship."

He spins around and storms away, his gang throwing glares around for good measure before stalking after him. Fyve lets out a long breath. Now the Trials are creating tension among his people. The sooner they're over and done with, the better.

Sevin scowls at their retreating backs. "He's not even making any sense. He wouldn't let his sister onto his team, and it's my fault she didn't pass?"

"He's just looking for trouble for the sake of trouble," says Fyve.

"As an excuse to throw his weight around," adds Coal.

Sevin glances over her shoulder. "We'd better hurry. Gratitude is almost here."

Noting how close the sun is to the horizon, Fyve realizes she's right. He wouldn't be surprised if Zake decided to approach them close to dusk, another way to conveniently ensure no one has time for a physical altercation.

They make their way back to the huts they call home, each caught up in their own thoughts. The sun seems to be dropping faster than Fyve's ever seen, as if Terra's as excited about this as the rest of the village. In fact, most of the huts are already empty as people left for the beach early.

He tucks the two rats under the pile of tattered clothes he shares with Coal, and anyone else in their two families who may need anything. Sighing, he exits the hut, finding his sister hopping from one foot next to the other beside Coal. "Hurry up," she hisses.

He can't help but throw an unimpressed glare at his cousin. All he's done is build her up for one monster disappointment. They make their way through the almost empty village toward the beach, the murmurs steadily becoming louder.

"Praise Terra for such an opportunity."

"My boy, Zake, was as impressive as I expected."

"It's obvious who Terra will pick."

The final comment has Sevin stiffening, and a part of Fyve no longer wants to protect her from it. She's determined to grow up, and with that comes the loss of innocence.

And the realization of how fickle hope is.

They reach the beach, finding the people tightly packed together, as if they're all standing within a held breath. It means they're relegated to the back of the crowd, not that Fyve minds. Once Elijah has made his announcement, he'll be busy picking up the pieces that had hope holding Sevin together. He fully intends on taking her to the pseudo-privacy of their hut so they can put all this behind them.

"Hey."

He glances in the other direction, finding Halo slipping in beside him. The smile that climbs up his face is almost instinctive. "Hey."

He has to admit he likes the idea of Halo remaining behind with him. The thought of exploring the warmth that sparks every time she's close, heck, every time he thinks of her, is something he's looking forward to.

She smiles back, and the warmth spreads, originating somewhere in his chest. Somewhere that's suspiciously close to his heart. But then he registers something else. Her beautiful eyes are carrying more than just pleasure at seeing him. There's a flicker of hope.

She thinks there's a chance they'll pass, too.

He suppresses a sigh as he looks away. What is it with everyone? Can't they see what will happen even if the ship turns up?

A movement on his other side catches Fyve's attention. His mother is staring at them, eyes misty and proud as if they've already passed. Her hair is a crazed tangle. Her lips are blistered. And her sanity is hanging on by a thread after chasing nothing but a dream all her life.

That's not how Fyve sees his future.

The crowd falls silent and Fyve knows Elijah's arrived. Good. It's time to get this over with and done with.

"People of Treasure Island," says their leader in a booming voice. "Terra has spoken once more, and as always, her words are the most beautiful truth."

"Praise Terra," come several, excited shouts. Despite the death of one of their own, the Trials seem to have reinvigorated the people's adoration.

Halo pushes up on her toes as she tries to peer over the crowd while Sevin's hand reaches out to clutch Fyve's. He squeezes it, now no longer looking forward to this. He knows what it's like to have dreams crushed. His mother taught him that at a young age.

"She has spoken about who will continue on in the Oasis Trials," calls Elijah. "Who she wants on the ship that will take the chosen ones to Tomorrow Land."

"Praise Terra!" This time hands rise in the air, palms open to the setting sun.

"She thanks all those who sought to prove themselves to her. She knows we are her loyal followers. She wishes to show us her gratitude."

That has Fyve's attention. Once, Terra promised they'd find food, and the following day a small bag of grain had been found tucked inside a tire. The seeds had been planted, and although it's hard for anything to grow in plastic-riddled soil, that grain provides small amounts of flour for the village.

"But first, the results of the first Trial," says Elijah, sounding a little excited himself. "Terra has chosen that the team with the horizontal stack of poles shall not pass. They are eliminated from the Oasis Trials."

There's a stunned hush.

Then a rush of murmurs.

Fyve blinks. Then blinks again. Zake's team chose the neat stack of poles. They failed the first Trial.

But that means—

"We passed," breathes Sevin. "We'll be taking the next Trial."

HALO

*H*alo hardly dares to believe it.

She passed.

Letting out a long breath, she enjoys the feeling of a heavy weight lifting from her shoulders. Her chances aren't over.

She looks at the knuckleheads who are all standing together. Except the celebration—or rather the gloating—that they'd planned is off the table. Because they've just been eliminated from the Oasis Trials.

"With respect to Terra, our tower was the last one standing," one of the knuckleheads calls out, his voice shaking. "Are you sure this decision is correct?"

"Terra works in mysterious ways," Halo's father replies, smiling gently. "But yes, Terra was extremely clear with her decision."

The knuckleheads glance at each other seeming to be trying to decide if they risk being claimed by speaking up. Not making it onto the ship is devastating. But not making it to tonight's sunset would be far worse.

They choose to stay silent, their scowls doing the talking for them. Halo already knows this won't be the last they hear of this.

Sevin taps Halo's arm to get her attention. "We passed," she whispers, grinning widely.

"We did." Halo smiles back, noticing that Fyve isn't quite as pleased. In fact, he looks even more upset than the knuckle-heads. His face is pale, and his fists are clenched. How can Halo get him to realize that being chosen for Terra's ship is a good thing? It's a chance to start a new life away from the mother he clearly has a complicated relationship with. And on a selfish note, Halo isn't ready to say goodbye to him just yet. He's quickly turning out to be the best friend she's ever had—which says just as much about him as it does her. She hasn't had too many friends.

Looking around the rest of the crowd, she notices many seem confused with Terra's ruling. If winning a Trial gets you eliminated, and losing allows you to stay, then what exactly is being tested? Halo's team hadn't even able to remove one pole without their stack tumbling. Which makes her wonder if the Trial had begun well before they all thought it had. After all, her father had said as much during the test, referring to the team selection as *the first step*.

Which means Terra is watching everything they do. The knuckleheads were an all-male team, which is questionable when talking about starting a new colony. Halo's team had three females and one male, with blood shared between only two of them. Is that what made the difference? They'd also demon-strated teamwork, acceptance of others and flexibility—not one of them had really wanted Justice to join them but they'd taken her in regardless. Are these the qualities Terra is looking for?

Halo lets out a long sigh. These Trials are a whole lot more complicated than any of them had realized.

Her father raises his hands, the picture of calm, and Halo concedes that perhaps he'd already realized. That's why he wasn't worried when he'd spoken to her after the Trial. He knew there'd be more to Terra's decision than whose stack of poles tumbled first.

"Terra is pleased," her father tells the crowd. "And as a show of her appreciation, she asks you to gather again here on the beach at midnight and turn your faces to the western sky. It will be a celebration of the sacrifices you're making, in particular Kite, who lost her life during the first Trial."

Halo raises her eyes to the sky, wondering what exactly this celebration in the sky will be. Surely, the ship isn't going to come crashing down from the clouds? But honestly, nothing would surprise her anymore.

All faces turn to the horizon as the sun begins to slip beneath it, somehow seeming to gather speed the more it disappears. Golden light shoots into the sky in arching beams, reminding them all that even though they can no longer see the Earth's brightest star, it's still there. Just like Terra herself.

"Praise Terra," Halo calls out, her faith in their higher power restored after being spared from being cut from the Trials.

"Ask Kite's mom if she agrees," mutters Fyve, pointing at a frail woman being supported by the man beside her. Her eyes are so puffy from crying that she can barely see through the slits.

"Everything happens for a reason." Halo is aware her voice has become hollow. She wants to believe in Terra, just like she did when she was a little girl. It's just becoming harder the more tragedies she witnesses. Shouldn't life get clearer the more she sees and understands, not the other way around?

"You really believe in this ship?" Fyve raises a brow.

"Of, course, I do," she snaps. "Wait until midnight and you'll see. Something amazing will happen."

"Do you think the ship's coming then?" Sevin's face lights up.

"Maybe." Halo shrugs. "Maybe not. But something's coming

and when your brother sees that, he'll have to believe, won't he?"

"Ummm." Sevin scratches her chin. "Not necessarily. Fyve can be stubborn sometimes."

"Determined," he corrects.

Halo smiles and takes a step back. "I'm going to leave you two to sort out that argument."

"Where are you going?" Sevin asks.

"I need to be alone for a bit." She scruffs Sevin's hair. "I've got some thinking to do."

Sevin's shoulders slump. "But I thought we could celebrate our success."

"We can." Halo gives her a warm smile. "At midnight. I'll meet you right back here. It's only a few hours away. Deal?"

"Deal." Sevin nods reluctantly.

Halo heads down the beach and sighs, glad to be by herself. She's loved making friends with Fyve and Sevin, but all that company is hard to get used to when she's spent most of her life on her own. And Fyve's constant questioning of Terra's motives is messing with her head. He's starting to make far too much sense.

Dusk cloaks her as she walks, and she tries to resist the urge to scan the shoreline for parts to a motor that hopefully she'll never get the chance to finish. Because she'll be far away, starting a new life. She must ask her father what will happen to Treasure Island without him there to pass on messages. How will the people know they're pleasing Terra, or indeed failing her? Will there still be claimings? Because with those knuckleheads running loose around here, she fears for anyone left behind. Another reason to make sure Sevin succeeds. She needs to point that out to Fyve the next chance she gets.

Something hard hits her on the shoulder blade and Halo is launched forward, almost falling but managing to steady herself in time. Just as she turns to see what happened, she's shoved again.

"What the he—"

She crashes to the sharp sand and winces.

One of the knuckleheads is standing over her with his hands on his hips.

"I'm out and it's your fault," he sneers.

Halo's heart hammers as she weighs up her options. This guy is stronger than her. And likely faster. He's also a whole lot angrier. Where's Terra to save her now? Is it too much to hope that she might claim this knucklehead on the spot?

Yes. It really is.

"I had no say in the decision." Halo tries to stand up, but the knucklehead kicks her to the ground again. His foot is like an explosion in her chest as it knocks all the air out of her lungs.

"It was rigged," he says. "Elijah manipulated the rules to keep his precious daughter in."

"That's not true!" she protests. "My father told me himself that I have no advantage."

The knucklehead seems to find this amusing. "We all know that's a lie."

Halo glances around the shadows on the beach, hoping this doesn't mean he's brought company with him. She has a small chance of getting away from this thug, but not if he hasn't come alone.

"I'm telling you the truth." Halo tries to keep her voice steady, glad the failing light is disguising how hard she's shaking. The last thing she wants is for her fear to show.

"Your team lost the Trial," he sneers. "And my team won."

She doesn't point out to him that they actually drew with another team.

"And somehow you get to stay, and we get cut," he continues. "Your father is corrupt. Everything he's ever said has been a lie."

Halo is shocked by this accusation. Nobody has ever questioned her father so openly like this before. "All his prophecies have come true! Terra speaks to him."

"And if you believe that, you'll believe anything." The knucklehead crouches down into a squat. "But it's your lucky day, because you took my sister onto your team, saving her from being cut from the Trials. Which means I'm not going to kill you."

Halo gasps. This knucklehead must be Justice's brother. Then something even more frightening occurs to her. He was going to kill her.

"Look, I'm sorry this happened to you." Halo inches back, trying to get some space between them. "But I think we've said all we need to say for now."

"Now that's something we can agree on." The knucklehead makes a grunting noise and lurches forward, grabbing Halo's arm with one meaty hand and the waistband of her shorts with his other. "Maybe if you've got my child in your belly, your father will have to take me with you."

"No!" She tries to raise her knee to push him off but he's too strong, pinning her to the ground while he maneuvers himself on top of her. Now she's not just afraid, she's terrified. Her limbs are shaking badly, and her stomach turns to stone as she desperately tries to fight back, refusing to accept her efforts are as futile as they seem. He may be alone but even with only one of him, he's completely overpowering her.

"Stop struggling," he tells her. "Or I really will have to kill ya."

A shadow appears behind her attacker, and Halo lets out a whimper to realize that he isn't alone. She really does have no hope of getting away now.

The shadow lifts its arm high, and a metal object catches a glint of moonlight. It slams down fast and connects with the knucklehead's skull.

A loud crack pierces the night air and for a few beats of her racing heart, time stands still. The knucklehead's body goes limp, and Halo pushes him off her. Squinting to see who saved her, she drags herself to her feet

"Halo!" a young voice cries out.

"Sevin?" The word is more like a croak as it tries to escape her throat.

Her new friend slams into her, wrapping her arms around her waist.

"Did I kill him?" Sevin asks, her voice surprisingly calm.

"I don't know." Halo steers Sevin away, not wanting to stick around to find out.

They half stumble, half run down the beach, heading for the village, their hands clutched together in the darkness. Halo's safe. And it was Sevin who saved her. Her body seems to be having trouble catching up with this news as her heart continues to beat at a rapid pace and her breath comes in gasps. Nothing like that has ever happened to her on Treasure Island before. It seems the Oasis Trials really have changed everything, and the ship hasn't even arrived yet.

"Will Terra punish me?" Sevin asks when they eventually slow their pace, having reached a more populated area where a bonfire lights the night sky as the people wait for midnight. "If he's dead, I mean. Will I be claimed?"

Halo's eyes fill with tears as she regains control of her breathing. She wants to say no, but the truth is that she doesn't know anymore what Terra might do. The first Trial has shown just how unpredictable she is.

"You did the right thing," she tells Sevin instead. "If you hadn't come to save me, I hate to think what would have happened."

"Fyve told me not to follow you," Sevin says. "It's just that...I found this."

She holds out her hand, revealing the metal object she'd used to knock Halo's attacker out.

"A gasket." Halo's face lights up as she takes it. "I can't believe you found one. And it's in perfect condition."

Sevin grins, the trauma of what she'd just lived through dissipating for a moment. "Did I do good?"

Halo pulls the girl into another hug. "You did so good."

Justice walks past them, scanning from left to right.

"Are you looking for your brother?" Sevin asks. "Because I saw him walk that way."

She points down the beach, giving that knucklehead much more of a chance of survival than he deserves.

"Thanks." Justice smiles. "We can't find him anywhere. He's pretty upset about being cut from the Trials. Which reminds me...thank you. I owe you big time."

Sevin nods, and Halo's certain she can read her mind. Sevin potentially just killed Justice's brother. The imbalance of who owes who may just have tipped the other way.

"A couple of your brother's friends followed him," Halo says, telling one of the first lies of her life. "So, he has company at least."

Justice runs to her father and the two of them walk down the beach.

"Why did you lie?" Sevin asks, her eyes wide.

"Why did you tell her where he was?" she asks in return.

"I'm scared of Terra," Sevin whispers. "If he can be saved then maybe I won't be punished."

Halo bends down, putting a hand on each of Sevin's shoulders. "Listen carefully. If the blame gets put on you, I want you to say I hit him. Understand? You're not taking the fall for this. Not with Terra and not with anyone."

"But Terra always knows the truth. And I did it," says Sevin. "He was hurting you. I was scared."

Halo swallows. "So was I. But you were brave and now we're okay. Terra will see that. Justice thinks she owes you, but it's me who owes you. *Everything.*"

A shiver runs down her spine as the reality of exactly what Sevin saved her from sets in.

"Can we see if the gasket fits your motor?" Sevin asks, biting down on her lip.

"We can." Halo puts an arm around Sevin. "Midnight is still an hour or so away."

"I hope Terra shows us something good," says Sevin.

"Me, too."

They walk off down the path. Now Halo has an extra incentive to make sure they both pass the Trials, even if it means this is the last part for her motor that she ever gets to fit. Because if they stay behind, it's going to mean a lifetime of dodging knuckleheads on the beach.

Nothing and nobody will be safe.

FYVE

"It's a sign Terra wants you to be part of the Trials."

Fyve spins around to find his mother standing behind him, instantly setting his teeth on edge. He turns to face her even though he was about to check where Sevin darted off to. Although he told her not to go after Halo, his sister isn't so good at following instructions.

His mother takes a step closer. "It's a sign, Fyve," she says again. "You need to stop fighting this."

He pushes his face closer, taking in the aged, wrinkled state of her skin after spending so much time out in the sun. Out on the raft. "And if I leave? What happens to Cee and the others? What about Bloo, Jett and Rubee? Who'll look after them?"

Her face softens, the wrinkles gently relaxing into each other. "I will. Don't you see, I won't have to go away then? You'll be finding Tomorrow Land."

Fyve draws in a sharp breath. He'll be picking up the mantle he never wanted. The mantle he's done everything he can to prove he will never, ever, inherit. He stays and protects, not leaves and forgets.

"If that ship turns up, I won't be on it," he promises his

mother. He glances around, conscious his sister hasn't returned. "And neither will Sevin."

Devastation pulls at her weathered skin, as if this is the first time he's ever said this to her. "Everything I've done is so you could have this opportunity, Fyve. Please don't throw it away."

He flings his hands in the air, having no idea what his mother's talking about. "I'm going to go look for Sevin," he snaps, spinning on his heel and stalking away before he says something he regrets.

"Look to the sky at midnight," his mother calls after him. "You'll see that Terra has a message for all of us."

Fyve keeps walking, ignoring the glances of the handful of people still milling on the beach. His mother is as well known for her craziness as she is for her absences. He's heard the whispers as he passes.

"Poor boy. It's a miracle he's survived."

"No wonder the woman has lost so many children."

"Did you know she named them numbers, as if that's all they are to her—numbers."

It's only the last comment that's not true. Fyve's extended family has a tradition of naming their children according to themes. His mother and his aunt are letters, Coal and his siblings are colors. For some reason, his mother decided numbers were...cute.

"She probably didn't want to get too attached to us," he mutters to himself, echoing one of the sentiments he heard as a child. One that stuck, probably because it felt the truest out of all the comments.

Hunching his shoulders, he continues further down the beach. It's barely illuminated by the crescent moon high above, but Fyve's spent his entire life on this island. Except for the odd hole dug by someone as they see if they can find something useful below the decomposed layers that make up their soil, every inch around their village is familiar.

It means the uneven lump ahead catches his attention. Fyve slows, assuming someone's fallen asleep on the beach, probably trying to get prime position for whatever Terra's going to show them at midnight. When the lump doesn't move as he approaches, he figures they've fallen asleep.

Except the pained groan that trickles into the night air doesn't sound like someone who's just woken up. Fyve rushes over, pushing the man onto his back. "Zake," he hisses as he steps back.

The young man groans again and lifts his hand to the back of his head. He glances around groggily before his eyes shoot open, looking white in the night. Zake leaps to his feet. "Where is the bitch?"

Fyve glances around, realizing that something's happened here. Something that involved a girl. "Who?"

Zake snaps his gaze to Fyve then wobbles a little. Fyve makes no move to steady him, crossing his arms over his chest instead. "That—" Zake stops, snapping his mouth shut.

"Who?" Fyve asks again, his voice harder this time around. Did Zake hurt his own sister? Or someone else?

Zake scans the beach, his eyes narrowed. "I was attacked," he growls, touching the back of his head. He holds his fingers out, blood glistening like oil on his fingertips. "See?"

"By a girl?" Fyve asks, making sure to inject amusement into his tone. "I thought they were weaker and stupider."

"They are," Zake snaps. "Obviously it wasn't a girl who hit me."

"Then who exactly are you looking for?"

Zake looks away. "No one." He winces, touching the back of his head. "I ain't talking sense."

"Zake?" calls a voice. "There you are!"

Zake's gang come jogging up the beach, quickly surrounding him. "Where were you? We just walked straight past here."

Fyve bites his lip. Zake's friends obviously weren't thorough in their sweep of the beach if they didn't think to make up for the lack of visibility.

"I was attacked," Zake snaps. "Someone hit me over the back of the head with something hard."

"We'll get 'em," growls one of the guys.

"Yeah, no one attacks you and gets away with it," snarls another.

"Why?" asks Fyve, wondering what Zake's friends haven't bothered to look at too closely. Why did someone hit Zake not only from behind, but hard enough to knock him out? "Why did someone attack you?"

Zake cuts him a glare. "Because they had something to prove."

"Yeah," says one of his gang. "Zake's number one around here."

Fyve snorts. "Not according to the first Trial."

"I was cheated cause Elijah wanted his daughter on that ship!" shouts Zake. "We all were."

The guys glance at each other, murmuring as if they only just realized this. The mumbles grow as agreement is reached. Their victory was stolen. As was their pass onto the ship.

By Elijah's daughter.

"Stay away from Halo," Fyve warns, stepping in close to Zake. "Or I'll dent your head twice as hard as your attacker did."

"You want to get in her pants, too?" Zake sneers. "Then take a number."

The guffaws around them are what has Zake realizing he just made a joke at Fyve's expense. His grin grows, flashing yellowed teeth in the gloom.

A grin Fyve's looking forward to knocking off the scumball's face.

A hand lands on Fyve's shoulder and he spins, fist ready to strike, only to find Coal looking at him with a raised brow. "This isn't a fair fight."

"I don't care," snarls Fyve. Coal's talking about Zake's injury. "I was planning on rearranging the front of his head."

"No, I mean, shouldn't there be more of them? They won't stand a chance."

That almost has Fyve grinning despite the hot anger scorching his insides. Coal's always been able to do that—find humor in the most humorless situations.

"We'll take him on!" shouts one of the idiots. "We'll take you both on!"

Coal scoffs. "Fyve isn't just his name. It's the number of people he's killed."

The gang glance at each other. "He's lying," one of them mutters.

"Well, then, you throw the first punch," says another.

Zake's hand returns to the back of his head. "You're lucky I'm injured, or I'd finish this."

"Yeah, lucky for us," says Coal drolly. "Maybe another time." He glances at Fyve, waiting to see what he's going to do.

But the barely controlled fury has abated, thanks to his cousin. "Fine. I like the name Fyve. Don't want to have to change to Syx or Elevyn or something."

He turns and walks away, Coal by his side, leading his cousin further along the beach rather than go back to the village. He might not be wanting to pummel Zake anymore, but he's not up for seeing the villagers or his mother yet.

Once they're away from Zake and his gang, Fyve glances at Coal, remembering why he was out here in the first place. "Have you seen Sevin?"

"Yeah, she's back in the village with Halo."

Fyve grunts. Figures. He didn't even need to be out here in the first place. "Then you could've let me at least get one punch in."

"Terra will take care of them. They challenged her choice, not Elijah's."

Fyve doesn't answer. He usually doesn't when Coal goes all Terra The Great on him. If his cousin wants to believe there's someone out there watching everything they do, waiting for the right moment to mete out justice, then he can. Fyve doesn't.

Coal bends over and picks up a shard of plastic. "Have you thought of channeling all that anger into the Trials?"

"No, because I don't want to leave."

There's a soft snap as Coal breaks an edge off. "You can't mean that. Not really."

"I really do."

"It's only because of your mom. Because she wants this for you."

Fyve snaps his mouth shut. "It's not only that—"

"You should be on that ship, Fyve. It's the best thing you could do for Sevin. Just like it's the best thing I can do for my brothers and sisters."

"You honestly believe that, don't you?" Fyve asks quietly.

"I really do. Terra has promised it. This is our chance for each and every one of us to get away from all this." Coal waves his hand to encompass the land mass to their right.

Treasure Island.

A pile of trash first formed by ocean currents, then built on by mankind as they ran out of places to dump their rubbish.

A decaying, decomposing, dying mass.

"Has it really been that bad?" Fyve asks, turning his focus back to the ocean. "We've had good times, you know."

"You think leaving you and the rest of the family will be easy?" Coal snaps another shard of plastic off the piece and flings it out into the ocean, even though it will no doubt float right back.

Fyve's about to respond that family is everything when something catches his eye up ahead. It's small, but almost... glowing. "What's that?"

Coal glances around, now alert. "What's what?"

"Over there." Fyve points but then realizes there's no point. Coal probably can't see whatever it is. He picks up his pace, moving in on the small, barely noticeable blob.

Coal follows, his eyes narrowed as he tries to find whatever has caught Fyve's attention. It's only once they're practically standing on top of it that his face rounds with wonder. "What is that?"

Fyve squats down. "I have no idea."

The small, gelatinous thing sits on the wet sand, the edges of its flattened body flapping. Its center is like a tiny sun, yellow and pulsing. Opaque and luminous, it looks like nothing Fyve's ever seen before. He looks around for something to poke it with when Coal bends over and scoops it up. "I wonder if it's edible?"

"Ah, we're not going to find out."

"Maybe you're not," says Coal, eyes twinkling in the dark.

Before Fyve can say anything, his cousin pops the little jellyfish-looking thing into his mouth. He chews once and his face twists. "Urgh. Bitter."

"And probably poisonous," Fyve mutters.

Coal swallows, his face scrunching up even further. "Or it'll give me the advantage I need for tomorrow's Trial.'

Fyve rolls his eyes. "I thought Terra was looking out for you."

"Or she helps those who help themselves," Coal says with a grin.

"Convenient," he says under his breath, scanning the beach to see if any more of those strange creatures have washed up. But the waves lap at nothing but dark sand, leaving behind pale pink lines of froth.

Coal stretches out his arms and flexes them. "Actually, I think that thing's got me feeling stronger already."

"You know that's because you've convinced yourself, don't you?" says Fyve, unable to keep his mouth closed any longer. The anger is back, fueled by frustration. "Just like all the stuff about Terra. All you're going to be is disappointed."

Coal's smile fades. "I have to believe, Fyve. The other option is knowing that I'm stuck here."

Fyve's about to point out that's not all that bad, but Coal continues.

"It's different for me. Every day I see a little less. You know I do. Right now, my only future is that of my father."

Blind. Starving. Then taken by some unnamed disease they couldn't treat.

The anger fades, muted by the desperate truth on Coal's face. Fyve sighs, the sound dredging from the depths of his chest, already missing the all-consuming emotion.

When he's angry, he's not conflicted.

He's sure, not confused.

The sound of voices have them both turning and watching people arriving at the beach. It must be close to midnight. The hushed anticipation of Terra's gift hangs in the air.

A part of Fyve doesn't want to see it.

Terra's taken so much from him, in the same way she's slowly taking Coal's sight and that of others on the island. And since the announcement of the Trials, all she's given Fyve is turmoil when he finally thought he'd carved a little peace.

Now she has him asking a question.

If the ship comes, should he be on it?

HALO

*H*alo stands with Sevin and waits patiently for midnight. Excited chatter bounces between the people crowded onto the beach normally reserved for Gratitude. A different kind of Gratitude is happening tonight—with the thanks coming from Terra directly to them, rather than the other way around.

The anticipation has been building ever since Halo's father's announcement. Something is going to appear in the western sky. And there's no doubt in Halo's mind that it's going to be spectacular. If that doesn't erase the doubt in any skeptic's mind, then nothing will. Except perhaps the arrival of the ship.

The exact skeptic she was thinking of appears beside her.

"Fyve," says Sevin. "You came."

"Of course." He grins. "I wouldn't miss this. Whether something actually appears or not."

Great, thinks Halo. He's just as excited about the potential of nothing happening as he is of the potential gift.

"You'll see," says Sevin. "It's going to be amazing!"

"Oh yeah, Mom's looking for you." Fyve touches his sister on the arm.

"Where is she?" Sevin squints into the crowd.

Fyve points out their mother who's standing with the rest of his family. She doesn't seem to be looking for Sevin. Perhaps she's just given up for now.

"But I wanted to watch the sky with Halo." Sevin crosses her arms and Halo wonders if she's about to see her new friend have a tantrum.

"It's just as well then that Mom's around so much." Sarcasm drips from Fyve's voice. "You can hang out with her any old time."

"That's not fair." Sevin stalks off, her guilt getting the better of her.

"I could stand near your family," Halo suggests. "Then Sevin could be with us both."

Fyve shakes his head. "Don't do that. I'd rather stay right here."

Halo smiles in the dim moonlight. Fyve pretty much just said they're sticking together to watch Terra's display of gratitude. She likes just how safe she feels with him by her side. Justice's brother would never have tried to pull a stunt like he did earlier if Fyve had been around. She shivers at the memory of just how frightened she'd been. If Sevin hadn't come to her aid...

"I feel bad for Sevin," she says, taking a step away. "We should go to her."

"She's fine." Fyve reaches out and grabs Halo by the shoulder. It's a gentle hold, but enough to have her wincing from the bruises that knucklehead left when he'd pushed her to the ground.

"What's the matter?" Fyve asks, sliding his hand to her waist. "Are you hurt?"

"I'm okay." For some reason, she feels embarrassed about what happened on the beach, which makes no sense given it wasn't her fault. "It's nothing."

"Halo." Fyve isn't buying her protest. "Did someone…oh, my sweet Terra. It was Zake, wasn't it?"

"Zake?" She realizes she doesn't know the name of her attacker.

"Justice's brother," he snaps. "He followed you down the beach after Gratitude, didn't he?"

Halo is relieved the darkness hides the surprise from her face. How could he possibly have figured that out?

"Keep your voice down," she warns, not wanting Sevin to be implicated in Zake's potential death. "We can talk about this later."

"I found him on the beach," says Fyve, pulling her closer so he can whisper. "He was injured."

"But alive?" Halo's heart beats faster as she waits to hear Zake's fate.

"Yes," he says. "Unfortunately."

She's not sure if this news is good or bad. It's good that Sevin won't have to suffer the guilt of his death. But what else is Zake going to be capable of once he's recovered? He'll be twice as angry as he was before.

"What did you hit him with?" Fyve asks.

"It doesn't matter," says Halo, wanting to leave it up to Sevin to tell her brother about her involvement. That is, if she chooses to tell anyone. "All that matters is that I got away before he could hurt me too badly."

Her heart hardens as she realizes Zake hurt her far worse than she's admitting to. And it's not physical injuries she's talking about. She doubts she'll ever experience the magic of walking on the beach alone at night again.

"I swear I'm going to kill that guy," growls Fyve.

"I'm okay," Halo quickly reassures him.

"Look!" several people in the crowd call out at once.

A hush sweeps across them as all faces turn to the sky.

Fyve leaves his arm wrapped around Halo and she snuggles closer to his warmth as she looks up.

"Oh, wow," breathes Fyve.

A star shoots across the night sky, its tip so bright it looks on fire as its sparkling tail streaks behind it. It's so close it almost feels like Halo could reach out and touch it.

She closes her eyes for a beat and sees light streaking across the back of her eyelids. Opening them again, she blinks, trying to take in all the beauty at once. She's never seen anything so bright. So golden. So...miraculous.

Three more stars follow, then four, then an impossible number join the display. Soon the entire sky is lit up with shooting stars. Dozens of them. Possibly even hundreds. It's like Mother Terra swept her hand into the galaxy, gathered her stars, and sent them flying to Earth like a glittering gift.

Gratitude. This brings new meaning to the word. Terra really must be pleased with them to send such a beautiful gift.

Tears fill Halo's eyes. She's seen shooting stars before and always liked to think they were her mother sending her a message. But she's never seen this many at once. Her mother couldn't possibly have this many things to tell her. Although, after everything that's happened in the last few days, perhaps she does.

As the people gasp at Terra's display of greatness, Halo reminds herself these stars are for everyone, not just her. There are enough stars here for everyone's ancestors to be speaking to them all at once. This is truly a gift from Terra, just as her father said it would be.

"Your father was right," says Fyve, positioning Halo so that she's standing in front of him, her back pressed up against his chest as he wraps both arms around her.

She's trapped by him, just as she was trapped earlier by Zake on the beach, and this has her freezing. But as more stars make their journey across the sky, she relaxes into Fyve's warmth with the knowledge that what's happening here is nothing like what happened with Zake.

For one thing, Fyve would release her the moment he knew she wanted to be set free. And...the last thing in the world she wants is that. She's safe in his arms. More than that, she's happy. Happier than she's felt in a very long time. Everything about this feels right.

A star brighter than any of the others begins its journey across the sky and Halo blinks back tears, feeling like that one is there just for her. Her mother is telling her to trust in Fyve. His soul is filled with goodness in the same way Zake's is filled with hate.

She turns her gaze from the sky to Fyve and sees his face is tilted down. He's watching her with the same enraptured look that's plastered to the faces of the people around her.

"The sky," she says, her chest hurting from all the warm feelings swirling inside her. "Look at the sky. It's so beautiful."

"You're beautiful, Halo." He leans down and presses his lips to hers in a way that's far too brief for her liking. In fact, it's so fast that she almost wonders if she imagined it, except for the fact she can still feel the exact shape of his mouth on hers. She's pretty sure if she lives to be a hundred, she'll remember it just as clearly on the day she dies. Because it was the most spine tingling, exciting, promise of a kiss. One that's left her yearning for more.

"I wish—"

She presses a fingertip to his lips, stopping the rest of his words. She knows what he wishes. Because she wishes for it, too. She understands why he held back. He's showing her that he respects her. That he'd never take something from her that she wasn't willing to give. Yet at the same time he was opening a door. Letting her know that the next move is in her hands. That he's just as eager as she is.

Halo looks to the sky once more and sees the last of the stars shooting across the never-ending expanse of darkness. A cheer erupts and the people hold their hands in the air.

"Praise Terra!" someone calls out.

"Terra is great!"

"We are all Terra's beloved children!"

It seems that faith has been restored in Terra, as well as Halo's father's ability to deliver her messages. Because no matter how much anyone might have doubted what her father says is true, it would be impossible to predict that spectacular display in the sky was going to happen without a connection to Terra herself.

Which means the ship is most definitely coming to take them to Tomorrow Land. And Halo has to make sure she's on it. With Fyve by her side. Because now the door between them has opened, she'll never be able to rest until she's stepped through and basked in whatever's waiting for them on the other side.

"Hey!" Sevin appears beside them, her arms still firmly crossed. "Mom wasn't looking for me. You tricked me!"

Halo tries to subtly step away from Fyve, feeling self-conscious of how cozy they'd gotten during Terra's display of gratitude. He unwraps his arms from her shoulders and tucks his hands in his pockets.

"Oh," says Sevin, beaming widely. "I see. You two are... Umm. I think maybe Mom *is* calling me."

Before either of them can answer, Sevin dashes away.

Halo and Fyve laugh, and he pulls her into another hug, this time with her chest pressed to his. She thinks she could just about cope with being eliminated from the Trials if it could mean spending the rest of her life like this.

"Well, isn't this sweet?" sneers a voice that sends a shiver down Halo's spine.

Zake. King Knucklehead. Or more accurately, King Swollen-head as he has a rather large lump that looks like it has a pulse in it.

Fyve lets go of Halo and tucks her partially behind his back as he raises one of his fists.

Zake laughs. "Trying to make sure you pass the next Trial are you, loverboy? This one's definitely up for it. You might want to wear a helmet though."

"You asshole," growls Fyve, clearly better at swearing than Halo is. "If you put one finger on Halo ever again, I'm going to smack you so far into tomorrow you won't even remember these Trials happened."

"Tomorrow was exactly where I was trying to go," says Zake. "Until my chances were ruined by the likes of you and your pathetic team who couldn't keep your tower together to save your lives."

"That wasn't the real test," says Halo, stepping out from behind Fyve. "Except you were too dumb to realize that."

Zake points a finger into Fyve's chest. "It was you who hit me, wasn't it? Such a coward, attacking from behind like that."

Fyve looks to Halo, clearly confused. But he quickly recovers, his hand flying up and grabbing Zake's wrist and twisting it backward. Zake's arm is forced behind his back at a painful angle.

"Let go," he howls. "Terra can see you!"

"I hope so," Fyve hisses in his ear. "Because that means she can also see you."

Fyve lets go of Zake who hobbles a few steps away.

"Keep away from us," Fyve snarls.

"You watch," says Zake when he's at a safe distance. "Your girlfriend will make it through to the end no matter how pathetic she is."

"That's not true!" Halo protests. "I'll earn my place on the ship."

"We'll see then." Zake walks away, doing his best to hold his head high.

"It's not true," Halo says again, this time to Fyve. "My father wouldn't lie to me. We all saw tonight that what he says is the truth."

Fyve nods, but even in the dim light of night, Halo can see that Zake's words sparked the same doubt inside him as they did within herself.

Is she really competing in the Trials just like everyone else? Or is she the biggest fool Treasure Island has seen yet?

FYVE

*D*espite the crowd congregating at the beach the following morning, Fyve spots Halo almost immediately. Maybe it's because Elijah just arrived and she seems to appear just a little before him, as if by turning up separately their connection isn't obvious.

Or maybe it's because there are only two things that kept him awake much of last night—what to do about the second Trial. And the kiss they shared.

The kiss he should never have instigated.

Halo's gaze roams the crowd, finding him almost as quickly as he found her. Even at a distance he can see the flicker in her eyes. The same flicker that sparks in his chest. It has him smiling before he can stop himself. A smile that only grows when she reciprocates.

"You've got it bad," mutters Coal beside him, chuckling.

Fyve tears his gaze away to scowl at his cousin. "Zip it."

"Hey, I think it's a good thing. Whatever keeps you invested in these Trials is most definitely good."

A muscle twitches in Fyve's jaw. That's exactly why he

should never have kissed Halo. He gave her the wrong idea, just like Coal.

Sevin grins up at him. "I think it's freaking fabulous."

"Language," he admonishes, channeling all his frustration into that one word. "Nor do I agree with the term 'fabulous' right now."

"What's fabulous?" asks Halo, appearing through the crowd.

His heart flip-flops, but Fyve ignores it. "The weather."

She squints up at the cloudless sky that the sun is barely illuminating. "Feels like it's going to be another hot one."

"All the more reason for Sevin to be sitting in the shade of our hut," he grumbles, throwing his sister a glare.

She grins. "I'm not brown enough," she says, holding up a skinny arm that's the same shade of chestnut as his.

Fyve sighs. He already tried to talk her out of being here on several occasions last night, and several times this morning. But the more he mentions it, the more determined she becomes. He can't fight against the draw of Tomorrow Land. It hasn't helped that their mother supports Sevin. Her public lie about Sevin's age is proof of that. Her words will forever stain his mind. They were irrefutable evidence—the final straw on the pile of disappointments she's accumulated—that he can't depend on her.

And now, he has to decide what that means for him. Does he participate in the second Trial? Does he go with Sevin, or stand back and hope she fails?

The crowd hushes as Elijah makes his way to a podium that's been built on the beach. He climbs up several stairs regally, stroking his beard in thought. Fyve wonders if Terra is talking to him now. Or do her words come only when he's deep in prayer? Or only as decrees, rather than conversations? He glances at Halo, watching her watch her father. Her face is guarded, her body tense, and Fyve's not sure what that means. It reinforces the conclusions he came to before the sun had touched the horizon.

He barely knows Halo. Sure, she's beautiful and he's drawn to her, but they have little in common.

She's Elijah's daughter, for starters. She's a believer. And if that ship actually turns up, she's guaranteed to be on the thing. So will her brother. Terra has smiled on Elijah and his family from the beginning.

Which means she hasn't had to fight for their survival, or for her own. Her belief in the value of a fake forest only shows that. To her, these tests are nothing more than an opportunity to find something better. She doesn't have to risk her heart being torn apart by leaving anyone behind.

"People of Treasure Island," Elijah calls out. "Welcome to the second Trial."

"Praise Terra," someone shouts on the other side of the crowd.

"Praise Terra," echoes everyone else, including Fyve's mother.

But there's no echo from the girl to his left. Fyve glances down, registering that Halo hasn't spoken. In fact, she seems to tense, as if she's bracing herself against the words. He determinedly returns his gaze to Elijah. She's probably just being a silent worshipper.

"As you know, only a hundred of us can be chosen to leave for Tomorrow Land. Terra wants only the strongest and smartest to fulfil her promise. The second Trial allows you to show her why you deserve the chance to be one of the first to set foot in paradise."

More 'Praise Terras' circulate and Fyve wishes Elijah would just get to the point. Then he can show Sevin why this is a bad idea. He hasn't given up trying to talk her out of this.

"Today, Terra wants you to demonstrate your endurance and determination. You will run laps of the village. With each lap, the last twenty to finish will be eliminated from the Trial."

Murmurs move around the crowd. Some look confident,

others shuffle uncomfortably. Endurance takes energy, and energy needs food, a scarce commodity on this island.

"But this isn't just a test of stamina," Elijah continues. "Each lap you will be required to remember a number. Those who fail to recollect it will also be eliminated."

"How many in total won't pass this Trial?" someone calls out, then quickly blends in among the others and disappears from view.

Coal snorts quietly. "Terra can still see them."

Elijah raises his hands. "I do not decide this. Terra will tell me who will not be continuing onto the next Trial. In the same way she told me of the gift she was sending us."

People nod, the memory of last night's shooting stars sparkling in their eyes.

"All those who wish to prove themselves worthy, please join us at the starting line." Elijah waves his arm toward a thick line drawn in the sand beside the podium.

Excitement ripples through the people of Treasure Island as almost three hundred teens break away from the crowd and hurry down to the starting line. Fyve reaches out and grabs Sevin's hand before she can move but she turns a fierce scowl on him as she sidesteps his grip. "I'm entering. So, are you coming with me, or what?"

He sighs, noting that both Coal and Halo are watching and waiting. Fyve wouldn't be surprised if his mom is, too, but he's not going to glance up to find out. "I don't really have a choice, do I?"

"Sure you do," says Coal, slapping him on the shoulder. "I can look after her."

Halo grins. "Me, too."

Sevin skips forward a couple of steps. "Awesome! We're going to nail this!"

Fyve watches a little slack jawed as the three of them walk over to join the back of the growing throng of teens. Halo even glances over her shoulder, a hint of challenge in her green eyes.

Not giving himself time to think this over, Fyve trudges after them. "She's my sister," he mutters to himself. He's the one who's always looked after her, and he's not going to stop now.

He swears Halo and Coal are suppressing a smile as he joins them, although Sevin is openly grinning. She wraps her arms around Fyve's waist and squeezes. "Best brother in the whole entire world."

He squeezes her back, not pointing out he's the only sibling she has left.

A man steps up beside Elijah, holding a large, flat piece of red plastic and everyone goes silent.

"On this board is the number you must remember," Elijah calls out. "If you do not remember the number at the end of the lap, or you are one of the last twenty to cross this line, you will not take part in the next lap. But do not lose hope! Terra is always watching."

Elijah's talking about the fact Fyve's team was the first to be disqualified in the last Trial, and yet, they're here, competing in the second one. Although, surely things will be much clearer this time. Finishing last in this Trial should be a clear sign of failure.

A few teens smile at each other, but Fyve knows it can't be that simple. The last Trial showed that. In fact, someone died. His hand tightens on Sevin's shoulder at the thought.

The man with the red plastic hauls it up over his head. The number three has been etched on it with charcoal.

"Begin!" Elijah shouts.

The crowd of teens jolt forward as one, the muted thud of hundreds of feet on sand echoing around Fyve. Sevin tries to sprint to the front, but Fyve tightens his grip, having expected her to do that. She yanks on her shoulder, trying to get away as the space around them grows. A bunch of boys and girls have set off to establish the lead.

But Coal grabs her other shoulder. "We need to pace ourselves," he says, just loud enough for her to hear.

"Exactly," agrees Fyve. "We don't have to be first. Just not last."

Halo nods, seeing the truth in their words. "You heard my father. This is about endurance."

Sevin huffs, but her body unwinds. Collectively, they break into a jog as they pass over the now obscured line in the sand.

Fyve's officially taking part in the second Trial.

They run past the spectators, and he sees his mother and aunt there, each holding their clasped hands to their chests. He closes his mouth to the growing cloud of dust and looks away. Unfortunately, his gaze then lands on Zake.

The thug is at the forefront of the crowd, sneering at everyone who runs past. Fyve wonders how the guy hasn't turned green with jealousy. A girl runs past him, and he reaches out to shove her.

"Don't you let me down, Justice!" he shouts.

His sister easily sidesteps him, obviously used to ducking his violent fists and increases her speed. Fyve can hear her faintly repeating one word. "Three, three, three."

Sevin rolls her eyes. "Three is easy. She was Mom's first daughter."

Fyve nods curtly, having already thought the same. Won and Too were both sons. Threy was the first girl. Three is also the number of days she lived.

Zake sneers as he sees them approach, hot hatred focused on Halo. Fyve extends his stride, so his body breaks their line of sight. Zake's gaze snaps to his. "I've got a surprise for you," he snarls with relish.

"Sorry, can't talk," Fyve says lightly. "I have a Trial to take part in."

Coal waves from the other side of Halo. "Wish you could be here."

Zake's face twists before storming away, his hands thick fists at his sides. It's the first time Fyve's glad he took part in this madness.

"Hurry up," Sevin says urgently. "We're falling behind."

Fyve glances over his shoulder, seeing only a handful of stragglers behind them. "Come on then."

The four of them fall into a steady jog and Fyve can already feel the sweat beading on his forehead. Halo's prediction of a warm day is about to come to fruition. They angle left, following the hundreds of footprints in the colored dust surrounding the village. It takes about twenty minutes to circle it and Fyve wonders how many laps they'll have to do. This will drain them all. If the rat trap is empty tonight…

Around the other side of the village are more spectators. They watch silently, no doubt saving their energy. His mother's there, an encouraging smile on her face. One that falters a little when she looks past Fyve. He glances over his shoulder, seeing the stragglers are even further behind. What's more, they're breathing as if they've done fifty laps. One girl's feet barely lift off the ground, scuffing up dust that swirls around her legs. From the strain on her face, it looks like it's a cloud of tar, not dirt.

Fyve moves a little closer to Sevin. The selection process is already happening. On his other side, Halo's breathing has picked up, but she's coping. A glance at Coal has him grinning and winking as if he could do this all day.

Another gentle curve left and they're jogging around the other end of the village. The teens ahead are now spaced further apart and Fyve and the others catch up to Justice. She's still murmuring under her breath, the number three punctuating each of her footfalls as she fiercely focuses on the ground.

"There's the line," Sevin calls out.

A man steps from their right as they approach it. "Number please."

"Three," she announces proudly and Fyve, Halo, and Coal echo her.

The man nods and steps back. "Continue on."

"This is easy," Sevin says quietly. Almost excitedly.

Fyve isn't sure if he's happy about that. Realizing that has him admitting a part of him hoped they'd fail. Then he doesn't have to choose to leave the Trials, and Sevin won't hate him for trying to stop her from succeeding.

Ahead, Justice is nearing the freshly drawn line. Her spine straightens and her feet pick up a little. Then she glances up.

Three numbers are now being held up on the podium. *319.*

"They're increasing the numbers we have to remember each lap," Halo observes as they cross the line to start their second lap.

"What does it say?" asks Sevin and Fyve can see Coal is also squinting at the numbers.

"Three, one, nine," says Fyve.

Three. The baby girl who lived as many days as her name. And now one. The first child his mother birthed. Fyve remembers him. Won introduced Fyve to loss when he was only young as he had to watch his oldest brother die of an infection after cutting his foot.

This time it's Sevin who grips Fyve's hand. "We'll have to remember them all."

Before Fyve can answer past the lump in his throat, Elijah speaks as he lifts his arm to point back along the track. "You are eliminated."

A glance over his shoulder shows about twenty teens scattered along the trodden sand. A few simply collapse on the sidelines, not bothering to finish. Some have already fallen and aren't getting back up, as unmoving as if they're...dead. The closest guy falls to his knees with a wail.

"We need to move ahead," Coals says.

They can't be the last over the line in this next lap or they're out. Which still sounds like an excellent option to Fyve.

"Come on," says Halo, picking up her pace. "We're strong and smart. We can pass this Trial."

They fall into place beside her, already overtaking someone else who's breathing hard and lagging. Yet Fyve doesn't share Halo's optimism or confidence. How many laps before they collapse, too? And how many numbers will they need to remember?

Just as he suspected, passing this Trial won't be simple.

Or easy.

And he has no idea what he wants the outcome to be.

HALO

The second lap is so much harder than the first. Which Halo supposes is the whole point of this Trial. They could hardly expect it to get easier as they go on.

She sees the red plastic sign in her mind's eye, almost as clearly as when she'd seen it for real. She can read the numbers off the image. The strange way her brain works, she'll probably still be able to read them after a decade has passed.

319

The memory component of this Trial isn't going to be a problem for her. But the endurance component—she drags in a ragged breath—yeah, that's a little harder.

Fyve is jogging beside her, making sure he keeps up with Sevin. If his sister had planned to dart ahead of him, she has zero chance. He makes sure he keeps her within arm's length, able to grab her by the shoulder at any moment if he needs to. They'll either both pass or both fail. It's endearingly sweet and Halo is quickly learning that Fyve is equally protective about all those he cares about. Including his cousin, Coal. And, it would appear, now her. That promise of a kiss they'd shared had proven that.

"Are you okay?" he asks, as if breaking into her thoughts.

She nods, wanting to save her air for breathing rather than words.

They pass two teens who are clutching their sides as they walk ahead.

"Slow down." Coal drops his pace.

"We can't be last," Sevin complains, not seeming to be struggling at all.

"We're not going to be last," Fyve points out as they pass a guy bent over and heaving. "These guys have gone too fast too soon. The key to this challenge is to pace ourselves."

Sevin slows to match Coal's reduced speed, and Fyve and Halo follow suit.

"Do you remember that story my mom used to tell us when we were kids?" Coal asks, seeming to be doing the best out of them all, as they pass another competitor. "You know the one… it was about a snail and a rat."

"I love that story." Sevin beams.

"Tell it to me," huffs Halo, needing the distraction. Nobody's told her a story since her own mom died. Unless prophecies from Terra count. She needs something—anything!—to take her mind off this torturous Trial.

"Good idea," Sevin says. "Tell us, Coal."

"Once upon a time…" Coal pauses to pat his younger cousin affectionately on the back as they walk. "There was a snail who challenged a rat to a race. The rat laughed and laughed saying that the snail never stood a chance."

"He sounds like Zake," mumbles Fyve.

Halo nods. That guy is definitely a rat. Although, given they'd all be dead without the protein from those delicious creatures, that's too much of a compliment for a guy like him.

"He's more of a snake," says Halo.

"Yeah, full of poison," Sevin readily agrees.

"Hey!" Coal protests. "I'm telling a story here."

They pass two more competitors who've also dropped to a walk, and Halo focusses on Coal to distract herself from the way her legs are aching. The desperation in their faces as they watch themselves be overtaken is a reminder of what's at stake.

"So, the race begins, and the snail sets off on a slow but steady pace," says Coal.

"Do snails really leave a magical trail of silver behind them?" asks Sevin. "Or did Aunty Cee make that bit of the story up?"

"Dunno." Coal shrugs. "Made it up, I think. No animal could do that."

"I think it's true," says Halo. "At least, I hope it is."

"Me, too," Sevin agrees. "It's definitely true."

"Meanwhile," Coal huffs, struggling to keep the attention of his audience. "The rat decides he has plenty of time to find himself a snack and make it to the finish line to be waiting for the snail."

"So, he goes to the big apple tree in a field of green grass," adds Sevin. "And he sees a juicy red apple near the top of the tree."

"That's right," says Coal, his idea of walking pace a little faster than Halo's but she's keeping up. "He scurries up the tree and across a branch and gobbles the apple right up."

"But now that his belly is full, he gets all tired." Sevin pats herself on her stomach and Halo smiles sadly, wishing this skinny girl knew what it felt like to eat so much it made you want to sleep. That's not a luxury anyone on Treasure Island has ever felt.

Which makes it all the more important that they succeed in this Trial. They're halfway through the village now and making good pace. Halo's legs aren't hurting nearly as badly now that she has something else to focus on.

"The rat decides to take a quick nap in the shade of the tree before he finishes the race," continues Coal. "After all, he has plenty of time."

"This is the best bit of the story," Sevin tells Halo.

"Let Coal tell it." Fyve shoots his sister a grin.

"When the rat wakes up, he starts making his way to the finish line," says Coal. "He's shocked to find a trail of silver ahead of him."

"He slept too long!" Sevin explains unnecessarily, but Halo does her best to look surprised.

"That's right," Coal says. "He runs to the finish line but it's no use. He arrives just in time to see the snail cross over the line proving that slow and steady wins the race. The end."

"Did you love the story?" Sevin asks.

"I did." Halo says, but now that the distraction of the story is over, she's already filling with dread. "Maybe we should walk a little faster just in case? I'm not sure anyone in this race is about to sneak away to eat an apple."

"We've passed twelve people so far," Fyve reports. "That's good progress."

"But not enough." Halo's heart picks up pace. "We need to move faster."

"Okay," Coal agrees. "Are you all ready to channel your inner snail and give this lap a final burst?"

They all nod, breaking into a jog.

"And can everyone remember the number?" Coal asks.

"Three, one, nine," Fyve and Sevin say in unison.

The group of four fall into silence and concentrate on developing an even rhythm. Halo's chest complains after only a minute, but she ignores it. The sun is even hotter now which means they'll need some food or water very soon if they intend to do another lap. Had they not slowed down and distracted themselves, she'd be already lying by the side of the road. Coal was right. This is all about pace. And who even knows if elimination from this Trial means final elimination at Gratitude tonight. After all, they'd been eliminated from the first and still made it through to the second.

They approach a group of spectators and Halo sees Fyve's mom, aunt and younger cousins jumping up and down and calling out to them to hurry up.

"We're being snails!" Sevin calls out, but her voice is lost in the crowd. Perhaps that's just as well. It's not the most encouraging thing she could have told them.

They curve to the left, passing two more teens who are traveling at little more than a slow walk, their faces contorted in agony.

Fourteen. It's not enough. They need to pass six more competitors if they're going to make it through to the next lap. But there's a large group in front of them who still haven't crossed the line. There's still hope they can make it.

Halo sees Cloud at a standstill with one hand on her pregnant belly. She slows down when she reaches her. "Where's Ajax?"

"I told him to go on ahead," Cloud puffs. "No point both of us being eliminated."

Fyve mumbles something beside Halo that indicates he begs to differ, but she doesn't ask him to repeat it.

"I can help you," says Halo, not wanting her future niece or nephew to be left behind.

But Cloud shakes her head. "I can't do it, Halo. It's no good for the baby. It's too much in this heat."

Halo's friends have paused beside her, which is making her anxious.

"Keep going," she tells them.

"Go with them," Cloud urges. "Don't ruin your chances for me. That's what I told Ajax. If it's Terra's will for me to pass, then I'll be fine."

Sevin tugs on Halo's tee-shirt. "She's right. Come on."

Halo is still panting, trying to find the energy to protest. This doesn't feel right. How can she possibly leave Cloud behind? How did Ajax? Maybe Terra goes easy on pregnant women...

Fyve slips his hand into Halo's and pulls her forward. "This is what you want, remember? Don't give up now."

She shoots Cloud an apologetic look and goes with Fyve, even though she knows winning this Trial isn't necessarily what he wants. But he's right about one thing. It's what *she* wants.

There's a shout from the group running ahead, then another.

"Something's happening," says Coal, squinting.

They move forward and soon the teens in front are scattering in all directions and crying out to each other.

"Rats!" says Fyve. "They've released some rats!"

Halo's eyes widen. Dozens of rats are scurrying onto the path. More juicy rodents than she's seen in the one place in her whole life. There's enough there to feed a family for a month.

"We need to catch some." Fyve darts forward.

"No!" cries Coal, pulling him by the back of his shirt. "It's a distraction. Fyve!"

"It's our chance to pass everyone," says Sevin, watching the teens who are more focused on their next meal than the next lap as they throw themselves on the scurrying rodents, trying to grab hold of them.

Halo's heart breaks all over again. Sevin could use a feed more than any of them. And still, she's choosing the Trials, smart enough to have learned that living for tomorrow is so much more important than the now.

"That's it!" cries Halo, as the realization slides over her. "Terra is testing us. She wants to know we can resist temptation to secure our future. That's who she wants in Tomorrow Land."

Fyve doesn't look convinced, his eyes tracking the rats as he tries to pull away from the grip Coal has on him.

"Please, Fyve!" Sevin begs, her voice etched with desperation. "Please! Don't ruin this for me. Halo's right. It's called Tomorrow Land, not Today Land. I really want this."

Pure anguish crosses Fyve's face. He loves Sevin more than life itself. Which means he has a choice to make. One that he's been struggling with since the Oasis Trials began. Does he choose his sister or himself?

"Okay!" he cries out, and the four of them surge forward with renewed energy, the finish line their focus. They pass their frenzied competitors, Halo even needing to jump over a rat at one point.

Two men step forward as they get close to the finish, blocking their path.

"Number please!" they call out.

"Three, one, nine!" they shout in turn.

The men step back and allow them to pass over the sweet, sweet finish line.

Relief pours through Halo as she slows to catch her breath. There are far more than twenty teens behind them. They did it! They passed the second lap.

"We can't stop to rest," shouts Coal. "Remember the snail. Come on! Let's move."

"Urgh!" Halo pushes forward, wishing she was leaving a magic silver trail behind her instead of dry choking dust.

A man holds up the red sign as they begin their third lap. This time, three numbers have been added. Halo studies it closely, taking an image of it in her mind.

319075

Fyve reads the number to his sister and cousin, leaving Halo wondering if it's their literacy or their eyesight he's concerned about.

"Beware of the trapdoor," the man holding the sign says. "The two hundredth person will trigger it."

"What trapdoor?" Halo asks.

But the man is already holding up the sign for the next competitor and telling them the same thing.

"Come on!" Coal calls. "This is our chance to break away."

Halo steadies herself and focuses directly ahead, ignoring the cheers and jeers of the crowd gathered at each side of the path. Her throat burns. She needs water. Another lap is going to be impossible without it. But Terra doesn't seem too keen on providing them with anything to drink. And what was that trapdoor thing all about?

"Hey, Halo!" a deep voice calls from the crowd.

Great. It's the big rat. Also known as the knucklehead. Or the snake. Halo ignores him, focusing on pushing her feet forward instead.

"Halo, I'm talking to you!" Zake calls again from somewhere just ahead of her.

She keeps her gaze forward as she passes him. He will not be getting her attention today, or any other day.

There's a flash of movement to her right and she instinctively glances over just in time to see Zake swinging a bucket, sending a torrent of liquid heading directly for her. She dodges but is nowhere near fast enough and the water connects and soaks painfully into what feels like every screaming cell of her body.

Seawater.

That giant poop on a stick has thrown seawater at her!

Seawater from an ocean that has progressively acidified as it rose and grew warmer, forever changing the face of Earth. It burns her and she lets out a gasp, instantly regretting it when a trickle of water runs into her mouth and stings the back of her throat.

Fyve curses loudly as he rips off his shirt and starts madly dabbing at her skin, trying to soak up the water.

"I'm okay." Halo bites down on her bottom lip. The water hurts but it's not going to kill her. The biting sun will evaporate it in minutes, and she'll be left with nothing more than a rash.

"I swear when this is over, I'm going to get that guy," says Fyve, still dabbing at her with strong, caring hands. If she weren't in so much pain, she might enjoy being fussed over like this. She's barely in a position to even notice the way his chest muscles are rippling. Barely...

"I'm okay," she repeats, pointing at Coal and Sevin who are waiting a few paces away. "We need to catch up to the others."

She stumbles ahead, desperate not to let Zake ruin her chances. Terra will see her courage. Her determination. Her ability to focus on what's important no matter what.

She can do another lap, even if her skin feels like it's caught fire.

319075

If the number wasn't as clear as an image in her mind, she doubts she'd be able to remember it. Behind them, someone cries out as another bucket of water is thrown.

Fyve ties his shirt around his waist and falls into step beside her, putting a steadying hand on her waist.

"Where's the trapdoor?" Halo asks, glancing down at the ground.

"I don't know," Fyve says. "But I'm starting to think these Trials are nothing more than one elaborate trap."

"Lap three," says Coal when they catch up to him and Sevin. For the first time in the Trial, he's starting to look a little nervous. "Everyone sure they want to continue?"

Halo frowns, wondering if she should be nervous, too.

Sevin takes the opportunity to break away from Fyve and run off ahead, making her decision more than clear.

Fyve chases after her.

"Come on," Coal calls as he breaks into a jog.

Halo follows, telling herself that whatever happens at least she won't end this lap in as much agony as she's starting it.

Unless...well, unless she's the two hundredth person to cross over the trap.

FYVE

Fyve's starting to resent the sweat he's carrying, even if it cools his hot skin with any hint of a breeze. For the first time in his life, he appreciates being lean—right now, every gram he has on his body counts.

Except being lean means less energy to complete this lap. And any others they'll have to do.

Beside him, Halo's breathing is harsher and choppier. Even Sevin doesn't have the lead she's been trying to maintain since she streaked ahead. They're all starting to feel it. Except Coal, of course. He looks like this is his first lap, not his third.

Ahead, a group of three teens are scuffling through the multi-colored dirt, kicking up dust and microplastics. It means that if they want to keep their lungs supplied with oxygen, then grit comes with it.

And all for what? The promise to go on some mythical ship to a never-seen land?

The tallest, and skinniest, of the group suddenly drops. He reaches out a desperate hand to the nearest teen, but they side-step it without even glancing down. The pair, a guy and a girl, continue on as if nothing happened.

Fyve slows, the uncertainty he's supposed to be here only multiplying. Is this what Terra really wants? Winning at any cost? Halo glances back at him as a few feet grow between them. Someone even overtakes them.

For the first time, Fyve wonders what Sevin will do if he drops out and risks failing the Trial. Will she really continue on without him? Or has she been betting on his loyalty winning out? He slows a little more. Will his sister choose to remain here if it means staying with him?

Fyve's steps falter. Can he really force that kind of decision on her?

"Fyve?" Halo asks, frowning.

"This isn't worth it, Halo," he says through panting breaths. "Not only are we draining ourselves of energy we don't have, what about the trapdoor?"

"But Tomorrow Land—" she stops even though he hasn't said anything. It seems she knows there's no point arguing with him.

He never really wanted to be here in the first place.

Sevin glances over her shoulder, her face streaked with sweat, and she registers that Fyve's dropped back. In fact, another teen overtakes him, one who doesn't look much older than Sevin herself.

Her own frown scrunches her strained face. She nudges Coal who looks back to see what she has. Fyve allows his apology to leach from his eyes. He knows he's about to disappoint them and that's never what he wanted.

All he wants to do is keep his sister safe.

To his surprise, Coal slows and falls into step on Fyve's other side. "Halo, could I have a word with my cousin, please?"

"You can't talk me out of this," Fyve mutters back.

"Sure," Halo passes him a disappointed glance—one that hits harder than he'd like it to—then determinedly jogs a little faster to catch up with Sevin.

Fyve wipes the dust from his eyes as another participant shuffles past, breathing hard. "Save your breath, Coal. You'll need it to pass the Trial."

"Actually, I don't feel as bad as you look."

A quick glance to his right reveals Coal's not lying. Sure, he's as sweaty as the rest of them, but his shoulders are higher, and his feet leave footprints, not scrape marks. "You been hoarding rats or something?"

"Bloo would sniff them out," scoffs Coal. "I think it was that squishy thing I ate last night. I'm telling you, it was an energy shot."

Fyve sighs, although it's lost between his panting breaths. Coal is a clear example of the power of faith. He believes that jelly-thing has made him stronger, so it has. Fyve doesn't have that luxury, and he's not sure Sevin does, either.

He returns this gaze forward, noting the way his sister's skinny little body looks so wired with determination, yet weak enough to snap any moment. "This isn't right. Sevin's life is fragile enough as it is." The statistics of their siblings is proof enough of that.

"Have you considered what it would look like if we all made it through?" Coal asks quietly.

Fyve almost trips as his cousin's words hit him. Coal's arm shoots out but Fyve rights himself before he needs it. "The chances of that are—"

"Higher than her life expectancy on this island," finishes Coal.

The words are another blow to Fyve's already depleted body. "But Jett, and Rubee—"

"I'm looking after them by competing in the Trials. I'm fighting for a better life for them."

"You're also leaving them behind to die."

"If your mom didn't do what she did," Coal asks quietly,

undeterred, and obviously not finished with the sucker punches, "would you be fighting this so hard?

Fyve falls silent as they continue to jog. A quick glance over his shoulder tells him they're progressively falling last. Definitely in the bottom twenty.

Yet Coal is still right beside him. It hadn't occurred to Fyve that Coal would throw the Trial just as he hoped Sevin might. Can he really take this away from both of them?

And what if his cousin is right? What if they could all pass? What if they did forge a path to a new land, where their family could not only survive, but thrive?

Sevin glances anxiously back at them. What would it be like to see her rub a full stomach? To know she has a chance to have gray hair?

Fyve realizes there's only one way to find out...

He flashes his cousin a grin, only something Coal could draw out of him at a time like this. "You could talk a starving guy out of his last scoop of rat eye soup."

Coal grins back. "If it was for my family, I would." He picks up the pace. "Come on, we have some catching up to do."

Fyve tries to keep up, but his muscles are trembling and cramping. "Hey, not all of us had some pseudo pep juice."

Coal turns around and jogs backwards a few steps. "We'll go looking for more squishy things tonight. You'll see, they're like an energy shot."

"Show off," Fyve mutters good naturedly, then concentrates on catching up to Sevin and Halo. All he has to do is pretend his lungs aren't self-combusting.

It takes several minutes, but when he does, Sevin's smile makes it all worth it. "I...love...you," she says between pants.

"Love you back," he says, his chest tight. A glance to his other side reveals just as big a smile on Halo's face, making it doubly worth it.

"And I love both of you," says Coal loud enough to startle the teen they're slowly gaining on. "And you, too, Halo. Sevin's right, you're now part of this family."

Halo giggles, demonstrating the power that is Coal—he can bring a smile to anyone's face, anywhere.

They fall into a steady rhythm, their feet thudding out their progress down the trodden track. They pass one teen. Another fallen one. Then two more.

"We just need to keep this up," says Coal, enough determination in his voice for all of them.

Except the sun is higher now. Hotter. More bent on sucking every drop of moisture out of their bodies. Sevin is the first to stumble. Fyve catches her, not letting either of them break stride. She glances up with a flutter of a smile and continues on.

A couple of minutes later, or maybe it's a couple of hours, Halo gasps. "The line."

She's right. The podium is ahead, Elijah standing atop it like a regal statue.

"What's...the...number?" Sevin croaks.

Sweet Terra. The number.

"I know what it is," Halo says, frowning as she focuses on the dusty ground.

But what if they have to quote it themselves?

Fyve digs past the layers of pain, trying to remember. Threy, the little girl whose number predicted the amount of days she'd live. Won, the first of many deaths. Nyne, the boy who actually made it to ten years. Zero, the number of children his mother should've had. Sevin, the smart, dream-filled girl he's doing this all for. Fyve, the poor fool left carrying all of this.

The man from last time steps forward. "Number?"

Fyve and Halo quote it together. "319075."

The man grunts and steps past them. "Number?"

"Ah, 3...2, 9...0, ah...7, 5?" pants a girl, the skin of her exposed shoulder a little mottled from where acid water must've been thrown on her.

"That is incorrect. You're eliminated."

She falls to the ground, either not bothering or unable to move another step. A woman rushes over and drags the girl off the track and Fyve wonders how many others have fallen that they haven't seen. There's no way of telling how many teens are still left in the Trial.

A movement on the podium catches his attention. A new number has been raised.

3190752618

"Beware of the trapdoor," the man holding the sign says. "The two hundredth person will trigger it."

"Just focus on remembering the number," Coal orders, not slowing down.

Fyve's about to read it aloud for them when the man with the sign still hasn't finished. "And no talking permitted in this round. It will result in automatic elimination."

Coal's shoulder blades twitch as if someone just struck his chest. Sevin muffles a gasp. Halo passes Fyve a concerned look. Neither his sister nor his cousin probably saw the number.

Coal launches forward with a little more speed, communicating he has no intention of stopping. Fyve and the others follow, varying shades of frown across their faces. They made it to the final lap, but the likelihood of all of them passing just significantly decreased.

Behind them, a guy grunts. "I'm out," he says, not even bothering to be quiet. "I can't remember the number."

"Thank, Terra," gasps a girl, followed by a muffled thud as she drops to the ground. "I ain't dying of exhaustion or falling down no trapdoor."

"Me neither," says the guy. "It's just not worth it."

The words echo the very thoughts that have taken root in Fyve's mind, despite the way his mother is urging him on from the sidelines. He opens his mouth just as Coal looks over his shoulder. His cousin doesn't say a word seeing as he can't, but he doesn't need to. His unblinking, unflinching gaze says it all.

It's worth it.

A scream has them all spinning around. The guy is on the ground, back arched like a bow as he grips his face. A garbled moan breaks from his lips as every tendon on his body resembles a taut rope. Red seeps from between his fingers, quickly turning into a rivulet of crimson onto the dirt.

Halo's hand clamps to her mouth, her eyes so wide they're more white than green.

The guy's body arches impossibly higher then collapses, limp.

Claimed.

Because he spoke.

The girl beside him is as pale as a translucent sky hovering between dawn and day. Then she's scrabbling away, at first on all fours, then onto stumbling feet. She disappears into the village, as if Terra won't find her there.

Coal's face is carved from stone as he waves his arm, indicating they need to continue. Sevin dutifully breaks into a jog. Halo hesitates, her stricken gaze finding Fyve's. Even if he could talk, he doesn't know what he'd say.

The guy was right. This isn't worth it.

Setting her jaw, Halo follows Coal and Sevin. Fyve follows her, leaving behind the proof of Terra's swift justice.

And the cost of taking part in these Trials.

Coal establishes a steady, almost cruel pace as they round the village. Sevin stumbles often enough that Fyve holds onto her shirt at the shoulder and doesn't let go. Halo's feet scrape the ground with each step, leaving jagged lines scratched in the dirt.

As they round the final bend, Fyve no longer has any idea how many competitors may have already passed the line or how many could be behind them. Plus, what if there are twenty back there, but they all collapse and don't make it? Does that eliminate Halo, Fyve and his family?

Then again, so many have already been eliminated. Surely, they've passed. In fact, from what he can tell, Coal is in the lead. He's only a few yards from crossing the line.

Fyve glances up at the sun-scorched sky. Terra probably decided who passed before they even started and she's just watching this for entertainment. She's wondering how far these humans will go to please her? How much do they want this?

Is it really worth it?

Fyve's so tangled up in his thinking that when the light glances off something ahead, he doesn't pay any attention at first. But the flicker of something bright definitely catches his attention the second time.

He peers closer, trying to focus past his harsh breathing and screaming muscles. There it is again. A faint line stretching across the track.

A wire!

The trapdoor!

And Coal is running straight toward it!

Yet, Fyve can't yell out. Images flash through his mind. The guy's abnormally arched back. Pain stretching every nerve taut. Blood flowing from his ears. Death is the only thing that ended it.

Fyve injects energy he doesn't have into his trembling muscles as he vaults forward. "Coal, no!" he screams, not caring about the risk of being claimed.

His cousin looks over his shoulder, humor glinting in his dark eyes. He shakes his head as he sees Fyve running toward him, then points to his chest. He's coming first.

But this isn't a joke.

"No, stop!"

The panic tidal waving through Fyve must be apparent

because Coal slows, the grin fading. But he doesn't slow down quick enough. Nor does he stop.

His right foot presses against the wire, stretching it into a tight curve. There's a *click*. A *whoosh*.

Then, he disappears.

"No!" screams Fyve, a new burst of desperate energy flooding his system.

He reaches the edge of the hole that Coal fell into and falls to his knees. "No." This time, he moans the word.

Coal lies at the bottom of a six-foot crater, unmoving. His head tilts at an unnatural angle. His chest is as still as the dirt he's surrounded by. He's dead.

Another sacrificial lamb for Terra in these deadly Trials.

A choked sob sounds beside Fyve and Sevin appears in his peripheral vision. A hand falls onto his shoulder on the other side and somehow, he knows it's Halo. Their presence helps.

And yet, the pain is overwhelming. It's coiled around every cell of Fyve's body, and viciously clenching. Coal can't be dead. He's too…alive. There's no future Fyve's ever imagined without his cousin in it.

But the eyes staring up at the cloudless sky are blank. Unseeing. Devoid of life.

Terra didn't save him.

She took him.

Fyve pushes to his feet, his body feeling like the grief has riddled his very bones.

Sevin wipes her cheeks then steps forward, Halo going with her. They take a handful of steps before realizing Fyve hasn't moved. He watches, stunned and still, as they look back, confused.

They're going to finish the race?

Sevin indicates with her hand to join them. She points to Coal, then the finishing line.

His sister's words echo in his mind as clearly as if she'd said them. *He wanted this.*

"This has to stop," Fyve grinds out through clenched teeth. "I won't lose you, too, Sevin."

She shakes her head and indicates more desperately. Fyve doesn't have to look over his shoulder to know others are coming. They need to get over the line or they fail.

"No, I'm not passing that line." Terra can take these Trials and blaze them into non-existence in her too-bright sun.

He knows he's making her choose, but he doesn't care. This needs to end. Now. Just like Coal's life has.

Sevin's lip trembles and she bites down on it. A flutter of lashes later, her face hardens. She takes Halo's hand, turns and walks away.

Within a handful of painful heartbeats, Sevin slips over the line, taking Fyve's heart with her. He stands, immobilized by a fresh wave of pain.

He just lost Coal and Sevin in one Trial.

Fyve spins on his heel and stalks toward the village, tempted to walk straight out to the wasteland on the other side and never stop.

He should never have entered the Trials.

It was far from worth it.

HALO

*H*alo grips Sevin's hand, unsure who's shaking the most.

They're thirsty.

They're exhausted.

But most of all, they're devastated by the loss of Coal.

Forbidden from speaking, they walk on. There's no need to discuss their pace because neither of them can move any faster. It will be a miracle if they can cross the finish line at all. Halo's skin is still burning from the seawater the knucklehead had thrown at her, although she's barely aware of it given how much every other part of her body hurts.

Fyve has given up, and Halo can't say she blames him. She'd wanted to as well. The only thing that had kept her going was knowing she had to step in for Fyve and look out for Sevin, just like she'd promised.

Wishing she could talk, she wants to tell Sevin that Fyve hadn't abandoned her. He left, hoping his sister would follow him. He was calling her bluff and is likely just as shocked as Halo is that Sevin took it. She wants to succeed in the Oasis Trials just as badly as Fyve doesn't.

Halo wants to succeed too, of course. But not at this cost. Coal had been a spark of light in their dark world. He'd only just told them all that he loves them—Halo included, and he'd only just met her. That was the kind of person he was. The kind who saw the best in people. The kind who loved everyone until they gave him a reason not to, when almost everyone else operates the other way around.

Why did he have to be the two hundredth person to cross the line? How could Terra take a life so randomly? Did she need to see how much they all want this? To see who was prepared to continue despite the danger...

They round a corner, and the road stretches out ahead. Sevin tugs on Halo's hand and points. There are teens lying on the side of the road at regular intervals. It seems this is the lap that's going to separate the pack. Anybody who pushed themselves too hard on the first three laps won't have the energy to complete the fourth, let alone remember a ten-digit number at the end of it.

Can Sevin remember it? Halo isn't sure Sevin actually saw the number in the first place. And Fyve didn't get the chance to tell her what it was.

Letting go of Sevin, Halo holds up her left hand in front of them with three fingers extended.

Sevin looks puzzled for a moment, then nods, holding up three fingers of her own, then folding down two.

Halo nods. *Three, one.*

Together, they hold up nine fingers to represent the following number, then bunch their fingers into a fist to represent zero.

Three, one, nine, zero.

Sevin then points to herself for seven, then toward the village for five. Halo smiles as she mimics the action.

Three, one, nine, zero, seven, five.

But now Sevin looks completely blank. She shrugs at Halo.

Halo holds up two fingers, then six, then one, then eight. She does it over and over as they walk, Sevin now the one to mimic her. It becomes like a game, their fingers like dancers as they repeat the set of numbers until Halo's confident Sevin has it right. There are many ways to talk without using any words. Halo just has to hope Terra doesn't see it like that. The way she'd claimed that guy right before Coal died had been horrific to witness. Yet she hadn't claimed Fyve when he'd spoken... Had she not heard him? Or is Terra selective in who she chooses to make an example of? None of it makes much sense.

Halo and Sevin pass dozens of competitors, their steady pace and dancing hands distracting them in the same way Coal's story of the snail had during their first lap. If things keep going like this, it's possible this lap will take them to the top one hundred competitors. Which Halo has to hope is enough, because she's not doing another lap. She can't. And perhaps, more to the point, she won't. She'll drag Sevin off the course if she has to. Only one hundred people are going on the ship. They've proven themselves enough. It's time for Sevin to find her brother and grieve the cousin they just lost.

A familiar shape is hunched over in the middle of the path in front of them and Halo hurries her steps. It's Ajax, her own brother who'd left Cloud behind in order to fulfil his dreams. Halo isn't sure if he deserves her help, but she can't pass him by. Not after what she just witnessed with Coal.

Placing a hand on his back, she urges him forward. He shakes his head, his blond curls plastered to his scalp with sweat, as he tries to tell her something with his eyes. He's lost hope. But he's still standing! He can make it if he tries. Step by step, they'll reach the finish line eventually.

Sevin taps Ajax on the arm to get his attention and holds up her fingers, showing him the numbers, and Halo realizes what this younger girl had instinctively known. Ajax had given up hope, as even if he managed to reach the end, he couldn't remember the code to be allowed to pass the line.

It takes Ajax a moment or two to understand what Sevin is trying to tell him, but when he does, his eyes light up, and he starts copying her hand actions.

They walk forward. Ajax in the middle and Sevin and Halo on each side, stepping him through the sequence.

3190752618. 3190752618.3190752618. 3190752618...

Something lights up deep inside Halo that she eventually recognizes as pride. Her ability to take images of things with her mind and recall them later is the only thing that's getting any of them through right now. She only wishes that both Fyve and Coal were with them, then she could allow some happiness to mingle with her pride.

Turning the final corner, they stumble ahead, not having spoken a single word during the entire lap. Forgetting about the hand actions now that the numbers are clear in all their minds, they forge on.

As they get closer, Halo can see the trapdoor has been covered over and she wonders if Coal is still at the bottom of that hole. She's not sure she'll ever get the picture of him with his neck twisted at such an unnatural angle out of her mind. Unlike the welcome image she holds of the sequence of numbers written onto the red plastic sign, that image is one that will haunt her for the rest of her days.

But then she sees Coal's mother and siblings bent over a crumpled form and realizes he's been lifted out. Fyve's mother is with them, although her eyes are on her daughter, watching Sevin move forward. Halo finds it strange she hadn't gone after her son, but then again, the dynamics of their relationship isn't something she's been able to unravel so far. She knows Dee goes out to sea on a raft for weeks at a time looking for Tomorrow Land and can only imagine Fyve has resented her absence over the years. Halo's not sure what's worse—having a mother who fought against having to leave you through her death, or one who's alive but willingly walks away?

With no time to answer such questions, Halo focuses on the finish line and reminds herself that each step is bringing her closer.

Step. Step. Step.

Legs burning. Lungs screaming. Skin scorching. Heart breaking.

Step. Step. Step.

Nearly there. Not long now.

Step. Step. Step.

Three men jump in front of them on the path.

"Number please!" they demand, leading each of them away from each other so they can't hear each other's response.

"Three, one, nine, zero, seven, five, two, six, one, eight," says Halo, glancing over at Sevin, who is using her hands as she tells the man her number.

The man nods at Halo and she waits for both Ajax and Sevin to be given the all-clear. She takes their hands and together they limp over the finish line, every cell in her body screaming for water. Her head is spinning. Even just standing up straight is a challenge.

"Are we allowed to talk now?" whispers Sevin, pointing at the red sign.

Five digits have been added for the fifth lap, making the number impossibly long for anyone, except perhaps Halo. But that doesn't matter. Because… She. Is. Done.

"I can't go on," she tells Sevin. "And nor should you."

"I can," says Ajax.

"There's no point." Halo takes his arm, almost toppling over as she makes contact. "There's no way one hundred people are making it over this line. You've proven yourself already. The next lap could kill you. Think of Cloud. Think of your child."

Ajax hesitates. It's obvious he wants to listen to her. What she's saying makes sense. But his stubborn streak is strong. Too strong.

He breaks away and takes off in an impossibly slow run.

"Halo." Sevin tugs on her hand. "I need you to tell me the number."

Halo remembers the way Sevin had stopped short of the gasket on the beach the other night. And how Fyve had been the one to tell her the numbers in this Trial from the start.

"How much can you actually see?" she asks, aware that failing eyesight is becoming a growing problem on Treasure Island.

Sevin shrugs. "Usually enough. But not for this."

"Sevin!" Fyve shouts from the edge of the crowd. His face is twisted in anguish. It must've hurt him to come back. Almost as much as it had hurt him to leave. "Sevin!"

"Please, Halo," Sevin begs, ignoring her brother. "Just tell me the number. I want to go on."

Halo is torn. Denying Sevin what she wants goes against everything she's been raised to believe. Terra is *asking* them to put themselves through this. They should go on until they can't. That's the whole point of this Trial. But another lap could be the last thing Sevin ever does. Which makes Halo question what the point of all this is. Surely, there has to be another way to choose who goes on the ship! This isn't right. Coal should *not* be dead.

She looks at Fyve who shakes his head at her. His handsome face fills with worry lines, and she knows that telling Sevin the number would be a direct betrayal of him. And as much as she's grown attached to his feisty, intelligent sister, her connection with Fyve trumps everything. Her heart lies with him.

"I can't," she says to Sevin. "I'm sorry. It's time to stop."

Sevin glares at Halo, not seeming to find the words she needs. She runs forward, catching up with Ajax who hasn't gotten very far, and tugs him on the arm. He shakes her away like she's an annoying mosquito.

Halo already knows he won't tell Sevin the number, even if he can remember it. He's too competitive for that. Telling Sevin could result in her beating him.

Sevin tugs on his arm again and Ajax increases his pace. But the strain is too much for him and after only a few steps, he collapses to his knees, then the ground. Cloud emerges from the crowd and rushes to attend to him.

Realizing her last hope of finding out the number has just been extinguished, Sevin runs into the crowd. Fyve takes off after her. Halo stays exactly where she is, not just because it's her brother who Sevin needs right now, but because she can't move another inch.

The world spins faster and Halo falls to the ground, lying there for what feels like hours but may only be minutes, until eventually the shadow of a person appears above her.

She attempts to blink her eyes open as a woman crouches down, tilts up Halo's head and pours water into her mouth. She drinks in the cool liquid, trying not to spill a drop of whatever she's lucky enough to be offered.

"Go slowly," the woman says.

Halo lifts her gaze and sees who's come to her aid. It's Fyve's mother, Dee.

"You helped my daughter pass," she says, in answer to the question Halo never asked. "So, I'm helping you."

"I didn't help her," Halo chokes out, her throat feeling like it's full of gravel.

"That's not true." Dee puts a damp cloth on her forehead. "She would never have passed that last lap without you. Nor would either of you have survived another lap. You were right to put an end to it now."

"You really want her to pass." Halo takes another sip of water.

"More than anything," Dee says. "I want her to see tomorrow. My son, too. Why else do you think I've spent so long searching for it? I love my children. All of them, including the ones I lost."

Halo searches this weary woman's face. She looks far older than her years, her skin beaten by both the elements and her grief. Her life's been built on suffering. It's only natural she wants better than that for her surviving children.

"I'm sorry about Coal," says Halo as she feels the first effects of the water hydrating her depleted body.

"Me, too," says Dee, with the hardened voice of someone who's well acquainted with loss. "He was a good boy."

Dee feeds Halo the last of the water.

"Thank you," she says, licking her cracked lips.

"Will you do something for me?" Dee asks. "Maybe in return for the water…"

Halo had thought the water was already in return for helping Sevin with the final lap, but she still finds herself nodding, unable to deny Dee anything right now.

"I need you to talk to Fyve." Dee looks Halo directly in the eye. "I need you to convince him to continue with the Trials. He'll listen to you."

Halo feels her world slipping away. How can she convince Fyve to take part in the Trials when she's not even sure she wants to continue herself?

FYVE

*F*inal goodbyes happen quickly on Treasure Island. Fyve's not sure whether it's for practical reasons— to send people to their watery graves on the same day they die— or if it's to save those left behind from the physical reminder of what they've lost. The infant son. The mother who was claimed. Or the cousin who was more of a brother.

As Fyve stands on the sand just beyond the reach of the waves, he reflects this isn't the first time he's stood here, watching this. Nor is it likely to be the last. Final farewells dot his life almost as often as his birthday.

But for some reason, Coal's hurts more than the others. Probably because he's the one person Fyve has spent all his life with. His father died when he was twelve, handing over the mantle of eldest male. His mother has been absent. There was always the worry Sevin would suffer the same fate as all their other siblings.

But Coal was always there. A fellow eldest sibling. Someone who understood.

And now, he's dead.

Fyve's mother is stoic as they lower her nephew's body into

the red ocean, but the sobs wracking Aunt Cee mean she can barely stand up. She cradles Coal's head as the gentle current tugs at her waist, looking like she's about to topple any minute.

Maybe that's what she wants. To sink along with her son as the stones tied to his body draw him under the surface.

Suddenly, Bloo breaks into a run, but Fyve catches her before she's more than a few steps away. The moment his arms clamp around her, she crumples, twisting around to curl up in his chest. He holds her tightly as he walks out of reach of the acid water, stroking her scraggly hair.

"Shh, I've got you."

The moment he stops, Jett and Rubee wrap themselves around his legs. Fyve crouches down so he can hold them all as best he can. They contract together, like a heart constricted by grief.

And yet Sevin doesn't move from her place a handful of feet away. She stands, immobile, watching as Coal's body disappears from view. She doesn't seek comfort, even though her entire body is etched in agony. She's hurting as much as Fyve and her cousins. But she's determined to carry it alone.

Fyve blinks rapidly, trying to wash away the sting in his eyes. The Trials have put a wedge between them. The knowledge means white hot anger clashes with the cold shards of grief. One moment he feels like his veins are frozen, the next as if he's burning from the inside. It's as chaotic as it is painful.

Fyve's mother steps back, her spine so straight it looks like she might snap. Cee's shoulders are hunched as she cries loudly, and her sister has to grab her before she collapses under the weight of her grief.

"We need to get out of the water," Fyve's mother says gently.

The acid would be stinging their skin. If they stay too long, it will turn an angry red. Then begin peeling. Given enough time, the sea water will progressively devour it, layer by layer.

Cee allows herself to be led out, glancing over her shoulder repeatedly even though Coal is no longer visible. Hopefully the acid will eat his flesh and dissolve his bones long before the leatherskin sharks find him.

Once Cee is out of the water, her children extract themselves from Fyve and run toward her. She collapses to her knees and clasps them, their tears blending as faces are pressed against faces.

"He's with Terra now," Fyve's mother murmurs as she places a comforting hand on Cee's shoulder.

Fyve draws in a sharp breath. "Then I hate Terra," he growls.

Cee gasps, clutching her children tighter as if to protect them from the words.

"Don't say that," his mother admonishes with a hiss. "Terra has always looked after us."

The anger explodes, burning away the cold, numbing grief. "How can you say that?" he shouts, throwing his arms out wide even as he notes the way Sevin flinches.

The desperate search for Terra's bounty took his mother away for weeks at a time.

Terra sat back as his siblings and father died, some far more slowly and painfully than the others.

And now Terra has stolen his cousin and best friend.

Fyve's mother takes a cautious step forward. "Fyve, I know you're hurting," she says gently. "But Terra is looking over you. I know she is."

The absolute certainty in her eyes only fuels the fury. "Terra hates me," he throws back at her.

"No," says Sevin, rushing closer. "She's looked down on you from the beginning. On both of us. That's why we're here, taking part in the Trials."

Fyve's mother's face softens as she regards her daughter. "Terra will always bless you with her protection."

Sevin glances at her, nodding as her shoulders straighten. "I won't let her down."

Fyve jams his fingers through his hair and presses his palms into his temples. Hard. As if that can keep his fractured feelings contained.

He stalks forward until he's in front of his mother. "Can't you see the damage you've done?" He points to Sevin. "You've poisoned her mind. She believes as blindly as you do."

Meaning Sevin could die in these Trials, just like Coal.

"Yes," she says, her gaze unwavering as it holds his. "I've given her hope, no matter what tests come our way."

Fyve spins around and strides away before he does or says something he'll regret. He wants to tear his entire world apart with his bare hands. He wants to shred the sky, dredge the bottom of the acidic ocean, expose exactly how much Terra cares.

If she even exists...

Shocked by his own thoughts, he takes a sharp left and circles the outskirts of the village as he practically runs from the secluded beach. His tired body can't keep up with the storm in his mind, though, and he stumbles to a shuffling gait far sooner than he'd like. He curses under his breath, hating that the Trial has taken just as much of a physical toll as it has a mental one.

Despite the exhaustion tugging at his very soul, Fyve angles out toward the wasteland. He'll check the rat traps. If they've caught anything, then at least Sevin can nourish her body and replace the precious energy these awful Trials are depleting her of.

As he turns his back on the village and prepares to trudge out to the barren, decomposing land that is Treasure Island, Fyve hesitates. He's never checked the traps on his own. Sevin usually accompanies him. Coal has always been there.

Now, Coal's dead and Sevin is determined to follow in his footsteps. Leaving Fyve to watch the fragments of his family slip through his fingers, no matter how hard he tries to hold on. He's never felt more alone.

"Hey," says a soft voice behind him. "I've been looking for you."

Fyve turns to find Halo not far away, watching him with eyes full of compassion. "We were farewelling Coal," he says, the words coming out more sharply than he intended.

"I figured as much," she says, not seeming to take offense. "I know that would've been hard."

Fyve looks away, not sure what to do with the softness in her gaze. "I'm going to check our rat traps," he says, indicating toward the expanse of nothing beyond the village. "I'll see you at Gratitude." He almost chokes on the last word. Feeling thankful is as far away from how he's feeling as Tomorrow Land.

Halo takes a step forward. "I could come with you?"

For a moment, he almost says yes. But then he remembers who Halo is—Elijah's daughter. That she wants these Trials as much as Sevin and his mother. "You should stay here," he says, looking away. "You need to rest and recuperate."

"I had a piece of bread." She smiles a little. "And your mom gave me water at the end of the Trial."

That surprises Fyve, even if it shouldn't. His earliest memories of his mother are those of nurturing and care. It's why it hurt so much when she left. He'd actually believed she loved him.

Then, a thought strikes him. "She wants you to convince me to join the Trials, doesn't she?"

Halo doesn't hesitate as she nods. "I know it seems manipulative, but I think she really cares about you." She takes another step closer. "And that's not why I'm here. I'd like to come with you."

Fyve blinks as those words sink in. Halo's green eyes are pools of honesty, but also something else. Vulnerability. Despite his determination that they have nothing in common, it echoes something deep in his chest. "Fine, but it's a bit of a walk."

She arches a brow even as her smile grows. "I'm not as weak as I look, you know."

He already knew that—her completion of the last Trial is proof of that—but Fyve just turns and starts walking. "Hopefully the trap has caught one or two rats. It'll make the walk worth it."

Halo falls into step beside him, the sun glinting off her pale hair. "The trap may have caught some of the ones that were released during the Trial. There could be more than two."

Fyve grunts although he doubts he'll be that lucky. No matter what his mother believes, Terra hasn't taken a shining to him.

They walk in silence and Fyve's glad. It allows for the storm within him to calm a little. He notes the sun is steadily dropping, meaning it'll be Gratitude soon. Those who failed today's Trial will be announced. And he'll probably be among them.

The realization has relief flowing through him. The decision will be made for him. Except it's quickly replaced by guilt. Will Sevin ever forgive him?

"See that over there?" she asks, pointing to the outline of a hulking pile of metal.

"Yeah?" Fyve says, squinting.

"That could be a children's climbing area. Just for fun."

He looks at her strangely. "Or a shelter."

Halo angles her head, studying it a little more. "It kind of looks like a great big, spiky creature. One with a super long nose."

"Or a shelter."

She throws him an unimpressed look. "Or your hair."

Fyve finds himself reaching up to pat it down before he's stopped himself. He passes her his own unimpressed glance. She shrugs, looking as if a smile is playing at the corners of her soft mouth. "I like your hair. It makes it easy to think of beautiful things."

Fyve has no idea what to say to that, so he doesn't say anything, but he finds his hand brushes hers. He hadn't realized he'd moved closer.

"And that pile of tires?" Halo continues, pointing to their right. "They could—"

"Be used to make shoes?"

She grins. "I was going to say little ponds to collect water, but it seems you do have an imagination after all."

He flushes before he can stop himself and he quickly focuses on where he's going. "You're trying to distract me," he says.

"I am," she responds. "Sorry. I find it helps whenever I feel bad."

He glances at her. "You're right. It does." Fyve's not sure, but he thinks Halo blushes. For some reason, he likes that. He stops, seeing the two crossed forks jabbed into the ground. "Here we are."

Halo glances around then scans the flat ground. "We are?"

Fyve squats down and brushes away the fine layer of dirt and plastic, revealing the lid of the trap. Halo joins him, running her finger over the little trap door. "Sevin's idea?"

"Yep."

"Clever. She's using their weight against them."

"She sure is," he says as he lifts the lid. Except she's not so smart when it comes to what's best for her.

Any other thoughts are cut off when Fyve sees four rats scurrying around the bottom of the trap. "Wow. We usually get one or two. Sometimes none."

Halo beams. "These must be the ones that got away from the Trial."

Fyve reaches in and grabs the first one that runs past his hand as it desperately tries to escape. "At least one good thing came out of today," he mutters.

He holds the wriggling rodent and is about to twist its neck when Halo's hand shoots out. "Wait."

He pauses, his stomach clenching. He'd love to give Halo one, but that means less for Sevin and his cousins. He was hoping he wouldn't have to make another tough choice today.

"Have you thought of breeding them?"

The question is so unexpected that Fyve almost drops the rat. "What?"

"Breed them, so you have rats whenever you need them," Halo says. "You could eat two now, then keep a pair to breed."

Fyve looks down at the rat. "Where would I do that?"

Halo looks around before her face lights up. "In a tire? You could build quite the home, in fact."

His stomach rumbles, quietly objecting to the idea of not filling it right now. But his mind can see the merit of Halo's idea.

She shrugs. "It would feed your family far beyond just today."

"Is it really fair that you're both beautiful and smart?" he asks, shaking his head. This time, a blush definitely creeps up Halo's cheeks. He lifts the rat, and it squeals as he turns it over. It's a male. "We just need a female."

Halo reaches in and scrabbles for a few seconds before pulling out another rat. "Another male." She smiles. "Also known as dinner."

Fyve grabs another and checks it. "A female!" he crows as if he just pulled out something the size of the long extinct dog.

Halo claps her hands then snatches the final one. "Dessert!" she says triumphantly.

"Here, hold these," he says, passing the live rats to Halo. She takes them, frowning with concentration so she doesn't lose them.

Fyve yanks his shirt off, glad for his dark skin as he instantly feels the sun bite at his shoulders, even this late in the day. He ties up the neck hole and sleeves and then holds it out like a sack. "Put them in."

Halo does and he quickly ties up the top as they squeal and scramble inside. He just has to hope the thin material will hold. "Done."

She stands up, smiling. "Now, they just have to make babies."

Fyve pushes to his feet, too, suddenly conscious of the space between them. Of the way her smile fades, yet her mouth remains soft. Of the way Halo's made today bearable.

Of the way it felt when they kissed...

They gravitate toward each other, their arms slipping around to clasp tight. Fyve breathes in the comfort she's giving him, the pain in his chest subsiding rather than writhing. He tightens his hold, wondering if he can stay here with Halo forever.

A squeak and a wriggle has them leaping apart, reminding Fyve that he has two rats to bring home. Hands slipping away reluctantly, they turn and make their way back to the village, the sun almost hugging the horizon.

"I'm sorry about Coal," Halo says, the words said so softly and gently that they seem to slide straight past Fyve's defenses.

"Yeah, me too," he mutters. "He really wanted a chance to get out of here."

Halo squints at the horizon. "But you don't."

Fyve doesn't answer as he mulls over the question. "It never occurred to me there was another option, to be honest." His whole life has been this island. Survival. His family.

Halo nods as she chews her lip in thought. "What do *you* want, Fyve?"

He stops. "What?"

"You heard me," she says, moving to stand in front of him. "I know what your mom wants."

Compete in the Trials.

"I can also predict what Coal would want you to do."

Also compete in the Trials.

To leave everything he loves behind.

"But what do *you* want, Fyve?"

His answer is almost immediate. "To do the right thing by those I care about." He steps around her. "And yes, sometimes that means doing things they don't like."

There's a faint huff and then Halo's catching up to him. "You sound like your mom."

"What did you say?" he demands as he comes to a sudden stop.

Halo's lashes flutter, but then her chin comes up ever so slightly. "Isn't that what she did? What she thought was right, even if you didn't want her to?"

Fyve spins and stalks away. "I knew you were here because of her," he throws over his shoulder. Next thing she'll be saying his mom did the right thing.

There's a flutter of footsteps. "I'm sorry," Halo says, grabbing his hand and pulling him to a stop. "I shouldn't have said that."

To his surprise, he doesn't let go. "I've spent my whole life trying not to be like my mother," he says, even more surprised that he's explaining himself. "I won't leave them."

Especially now that Coal's gone. Who will provide for his family?

Halo nods sadly as she steps back. "Then you should stay." She glances down at the rats wrapped in his shirt. "In fact, that will be easier now."

Her green eyes heavy in a way he hasn't seen before, Halo steps around him and walks away. Fyve blinks as he watches her, realizing she's right. Breeding rats will mean a regular food supply. He can feed Cee and her children. Sevin. Even his mother.

His breath catches.

Halo has inadvertently given Sevin a reason to stay. His sister doesn't need the Trials.

And once he fails, she'll see that she's better off remaining here, with him.

HALO

ratitude. Halo turns the word over in her mind as she stands on the beach, waiting for her father to start the formalities. She knows the word means to be thankful, but to the people on Treasure Island it's more of a ritual than a feeling. Not to say they don't appreciate all Terra does for them, of course. It's just that since the Oasis Trials began, the word *gratitude* has been laced with other emotions.

Anticipation. Excitement. Fear.

The air is abuzz with chatter about who will be eliminated tonight.

Halo looks to Fyve, confident she and Sevin will make it through. But she's unsure about him. Not only had he spoken out loud when Coal died, but he'd quit before the final lap. Terra won't be happy about either of those things.

She reminds herself that the outcome isn't as simple as that. Terra's elimination in the first Trial had taken them all by surprise. Perhaps she's looking for people who stand up for what they believe is right. Maybe Fyve's protest will be seen as a positive?

"You'll be fine," Sevin tells her brother. "Terra won't leave you behind."

"You still don't get it, do you?" he grumbles.

Sevin huffs, not seeming to have the energy to argue further. Every teen who took part in today's Trial is holding on by a thread, their physical exhaustion trumped only by their mental wipe-out. It's been a day of speculating, scheming, and strategizing. And not one of them can be certain if all their efforts will lead to success.

"My people." Halo's father has a way of projecting his voice so it carries over the crowd without sounding like he's shouting.

Everyone falls instantly silent, keen to hear Terra's verdict.

"Congratulations to all who took part in today's Trial," he says. "It was a true show of strength and intelligence. I would like to take a moment to remember someone who made the ultimate sacrifice today." He bows his head and Halo does the same. "Coal showed his respect for Terra by continuing with the Trial despite knowing the risks. Many of you standing here did the same. And Terra is grateful for your loyalty and commitment."

Halo notices he doesn't mention the loss of the guy who was claimed right before Coal died, but this is no surprise. People who are claimed aren't recognized for anything. They're forgotten like they never existed, only spoken of in hushed tones by those who loved them most. Sometimes not even then, just in case Terra decides to extend her reach.

"Terra has provided me with the names of those who will continue in the Oasis Trials," Halo's father says. "Please step forward if you participated today."

Sevin slips between Halo and Fyve, taking each of their hands and pulling them forward.

"Tonight, fifty of you will be eliminated." Halo's father smiles at the hopeful faces before him like this is good news. It's a larger number than Halo was expecting and once again she wonders why she expects anything at all. "Please stand still. If I tap you on the shoulder, then you have been eliminated and are required to step back immediately. Remember, Terra is watching over us."

"How does he know who to tap?" Sevin asks. "Does he really know all our names?"

Halo nods. "He does." It's a point of pride with her father. Each time a child is born, he visits the family, burning the name into his memory and using it as often as he can over the coming years. Halo's witnessed the way he walks through the streets of Treasure Island greeting people by name as he blesses them with Terra's love. It's just one of the reasons he commands such respect. Everyone likes to be remembered.

Halo stands with her spine straight, holding her breath as her father makes his way through the crowd. She's not sure if it's better or worse that she'll be receiving this news from someone she loves. He walks directly to two girls who appear to be sisters and places a hand on each of their shoulders. The girls nod stoically like they were expecting this news before clasping hands and returning to their family. Halo's father seems relieved. He might be their leader, but she knows he hurts and bleeds just like anyone else. It's not easy to deliver news like this. Although, perhaps not quite as hard as receiving it.

Proving her point, her father moves to an older teen and taps him on the shoulder. The guy's face crumples as his posture sags like the weight of his leader's hand has crushed him. It's certainly crushed his dreams of a life beyond the plastic shores of their island.

Halo leans forward and watches her father approach Ajax and Cloud.

"They'll be okay," Sevin whispers, noticing the anxious way Halo's wringing her hands.

She wishes she was as certain. Ajax had done well in the Trial, but Cloud surely hadn't done enough to make it through.

But after a brief hesitation, her father walks right past them, touching the girl beside them gently on the shoulder.

"No!" the girl whimpers. "I did two full laps!"

"Are you questioning Terra?" Cloud hisses, making Halo uncertain if her warning is to keep the girl safe from a claiming or her absolute devotion is unable to be contained. "This is Terra's will."

The girl falls silent as the boy beside her pulls her to his chest, holding her close as he waits to see if he's about to be eliminated as well. He looks like he's wishing for it, which makes Halo realize how much more complicated these Trials are getting with each round that passes. How many people standing here are still willing to set foot on the ship without those they love beside them?

"Please return to your family," Halo's father says to the girl, making no move to eliminate her friend.

He then turns and Halo's heart stills to see an expression that only those who know him best would recognize. He's preparing himself to do something difficult. Something he really doesn't want to do. Is he about to walk toward her? Was her confidence in making it through misplaced?

He takes a quick step back and places his hand on Cloud's shoulder, a war raging in the depths of his eyes.

Halo gasps. This can't be happening! Cloud is carrying the great Elijah's own grandchild. Surely, Terra can't be eliminating her. That baby is the future of their family's bloodline.

Fyve moves closer to Halo, but she edges away, forcing her tears to stay locked behind her eyes. Why had she been so foolish to let herself start caring about Fyve and Sevin? These Trials had seemed fun to begin with. But now hearts are hurting. Dreams are being dashed. Lives have been lost. Terra is starting to feel...cruel.

Halo wipes the traitorous thought from her mind immediately. Her father's told her on many occasions that Terra can read their minds, not just view their actions.

"Are you certain?" Ajax asks their father.

"This is Terra's will," says the boy beside them, still holding his devastated girlfriend. The sarcasm in his tone is unmistakable.

Cloud doesn't seem to like hearing her words repeated back to her as much as she'd enjoyed delivering them, but to her credit, she doesn't argue. She straightens her spine, gives shell shocked Ajax a curt nod, then walks stiffly away.

Halo goes to her brother, slipping her hand into his, willing him to stay strong. Ajax squeezes her hand, holding onto her like a lifeline. She should have been standing by his side this whole time. Not with her new friends. Friends who are unlikely to play a role in her future, just as much as they hadn't played a role in her past. Family is what's important now. She doesn't want to be like either Ajax or the devastated guy beside them, mourning the loss of the one who stole her heart. She's stronger if she keeps her emotions caged, just like Fyve's breeding rats.

Their father looks at both his children for endless seconds and Halo forces herself to stand tall as she awaits Terra's verdict. He moves away, sending her breath whooshing from her lungs. They both made it! Terra has spared them yet again.

Her father eliminates three more people before reaching Fyve and Sevin.

Now it's Ajax squeezing Halo's hand, knowing how much this means to her.

"I don't care," she says, trying to convince him as much as herself that it's of no consequence to her if they get through.

Their father nods at Sevin with a small smile as he passes. Halo finds herself nodding in return, knowing this would happen. He moves onto Fyve and gives him the same nod, tapping the girl on his other side on the shoulder instead.

It takes Halo a moment to process what just happened.

"He's safe," she says as Fyve's fists clench by his sides. He looks exactly like the other teens who were just eliminated. Devastated. Except...he's staying. At least he's still with Sevin. Surely, that's good news?

"Terra really does work in mysterious ways," Ajax says through gritted teeth.

Halo turns to him so fast she hurts her neck. This is the closest thing to blasphemy she's heard from her brother's lips. But then again, he just watched Cloud—Terra's most loyal servant—get eliminated while someone who'd openly defied her made the cut. This really is impossible to figure out.

"We'll talk to Dad when we get home," says Halo, wanting more answers than she knows she's going to get at Gratitude.

"He won't tell us anything," Ajax spits out. "He never does."

"But this is different," she insists. "He might be Elijah, but he's still our father. We need to talk as a family. We have to decide what to do next."

Ajax drops her hand as he shakes his head, his blond curls falling into his eyes. He's a handsome guy, a fact he's unfortunately very aware of. Although, it would be hard for him to be oblivious given the number of girls who throw themselves at him. Even Cloud's protruding belly hasn't been enough to scare some of them away.

"There's nothing to decide," Ajax says. "We both enter the third Trial. Cloud doesn't. Simple."

"It's not simple," she hisses, falling into silence as their father continues to thin out the group of prospective teens. She notices Justice makes it through, which is one consolation. Her decision to team up with them on the first Trial opened up a whole range of opportunities for her. With the bonus of it likely to annoy Zake. No bully likes to be outdone by his little sister in a game of strength and smarts.

When the elimination concludes, Halo's father stretches out his arms once more. "The sun is about to set on another day.

And as we give our thanks to Terra for her generosity, I want you to gather your strength. The third Trial will begin in the morning."

Halo looks to Ajax in surprise. She'd thought they'd have at least a few days to recover from today's ordeal.

"The ship must be getting close," he says. "Terra's in a hurry."

Halo looks to the ocean, half expecting to see the form of a ship edging its way toward them. But the sea is as clear as it is vast. The golden orb of the star that keeps their dying planet alive sinks to the horizon, sending rays of light into the gathering clouds.

"Praise Terra," someone calls.

"Terra is great," someone else adds.

Halo listens for Cloud's voice in the sea of worshippers but hears nothing. She tugs on her brother's sleeve. "We need to look for Cloud."

Ajax nods. Together, they leave Gratitude, and head toward the village.

"Where do you think she'd go?" Halo asks, realizing she doesn't actually know Cloud very well.

"Our new place," he says. "It's where I always find her."

"Of course." Halo knows the hut Ajax has been building to raise his young family is nearly finished. It makes sense that's where Cloud would choose to go.

But when they reach the crooked hut made from sheets of tin and plastic, Cloud is nowhere to be found.

Ajax runs his fingers through his hair and curses. "This wasn't supposed to happen. I really thought Terra would keep us together."

"So did I." Halo goes to reach out for him but lets her hand fall. She's not the one he needs comfort from. "Which is why we need to talk to Dad."

"Maybe she's at our place anyway," he says on a sigh. "She might be looking for me there."

They walk home in silence, Halo wishing there was something she could say to make any of this better. Fyve's face slides into her mind's eye and she pushes it away, determined not to feel this same pain her brother's experiencing. Besides, relationships are trouble on this island. Mainly because they usually lead to children and that only leads to more heartbreak and despair. When she makes it to Tomorrow Land, she can allow herself to think about a future. Right now, she has to focus on getting herself there.

Some gifts for their father have been left in front of their hut, and Halo and Ajax gather them up. This isn't unusual in itself, but Halo's noticed the quantity of these offerings has multiplied since the Trials began. Do people really think that will make a difference to the result?

Ajax pushes open the door and the first thing they hear is sobbing.

They rush inside and Halo blinks in the dim light, seeing Cloud crumpled on Ajax's sleeping mat as she clutches one of his shirts to her face.

"Cloud!" He puts down the gifts he's holding and crouches to sit beside her, stroking her hair off her forehead with the kind of tenderness Halo's only ever seen him use with her. "I'm so sorry."

"I should have done more," she sobs. "I should have tried harder. I disappointed Terra. I let her down."

Halo goes to the separate room her father sleeps in, wanting to give Ajax and Cloud some privacy in this impossibly small space. Their house is simple, like all the houses on Treasure Island, although the addition of a second room for her father is something not afforded to other families around here. But he needs a quiet space to receive Terra's messages, so it's a necessity more than a luxury.

She tries not to eavesdrop but that turns out to be impossible and she ends up wringing her hands as she listens to Cloud and Ajax trying to come to terms with their future.

"I want you to continue with the Trials," says Cloud, pulling herself together. "It's Terra's will."

Ajax pauses before responding. "I think so, too. But what about—"

"I won't be the first woman on Treasure Island to raise a baby alone," she says. "I'll raise him to know all about you. And then you'll return for us. Terra said it would be so. You'll find Tomorrow Land, then you'll come back. And we'll be waiting for you. It's not forever, just for a little while."

Halo's eyes fill with tears. None of them can be certain that a return to Treasure Island will eventuate. The ocean is an extremely dangerous place. Perhaps in some ways it's better that Cloud stays behind. At least if something happens to Halo and her family, the future of their bloodline is safe.

Her eyes open wide as a sick feeling wraps itself around her insides. Is that why Terra eliminated Cloud? Is this a blessing in disguise?

No! A voice in her head shouts. Nothing about this is okay. Babies are meant to grow up with both their parents. She knows firsthand exactly what it's like to lose one of them and it's not what she wants for her niece or nephew.

There's the familiar bang of their front door and Halo emerges from her father's room to see him entering their home. He walks right past the gifts that were left for him, goes to their table and lights a candle, filling the room with a soft glow. Candles are rare and saved for important occasions, which Halo supposes must be exactly this.

Cloud and Ajax get to their feet and the four of them sit around the table on smooth lumps of concrete that act as stools. They wait for someone to break the silence. Halo already knows that will be her father.

"My children," he says. "It gave me no joy to deliver Terra's decision tonight."

They all nod their understanding.

"Terra works in mysterious ways," he continues. "Ways that we don't always understand at the time, but her intention is clear. One day we'll make sense of why this is the way it must be."

Frustration bubbles deep in Halo's chest.

"I live to serve Terra," says Cloud, returning to being the devout follower Halo's always known her to be. "She looks after us."

A thousand curse words enter Halo's mind, and she settles on the one she's heard Fyve favor, enjoying the way it makes her feel as it rolls off her tongue. It's certainly more satisfying than *poop on a stick*. She bangs her fists on the table for effect.

"Halo," her father admonishes. "What's bothering you?"

"You are!" she says, looking at each of them in turn. "And you. And you."

"Be careful with your words," Cloud warns, glancing around like Terra might claim her here and now. "Terra is watching us."

Halo lets out a sigh. "I'm tired of not being able to say what I really think in fear of being struck down. I mean, you're sitting here saying that Terra is looking after us, but where was she when Coal fell down that trap? Was she looking after him then?"

Ajax and Cloud look aghast. But surely, they must've had similar thoughts when Coal died? Was she the only one to question the reason behind it?

"Life is a series of traps." Her father takes her hand and squeezes. "We encounter obstacles numerous times a day and Terra is there to guide us. But we still have free will. The power to make our own decisions. We can't burden Terra with blame when the decisions we make don't turn out well."

"Coal didn't choose to die." She pulls back her hand.

"No." Her father gives her a gentle smile. "But he chose to continue with the Trial after being warned there was a trap. That was his decision."

"And what if it had been me?" she asks. "Would you still accept this so calmly?"

Her father nods. "I would. I'd be upset, of course. You're my daughter and I love you. But I would accept Terra's decision, just like we have to accept what she's decided for Cloud."

"I don't understand." Halo hangs her head. "How can separating families be for anyone's good?"

"We don't know," says Cloud. "All we know is that this is how it must be."

"But what if there's another way?" Halo gets up from the table and goes to the corner of the room where her sleeping mat is positioned along with her few precious possessions, including her fading photos of the forest stuck crookedly to the wall. She returns to the table with her sketchbook and flicks to the diagram of the motor she's been trying to build.

"Not this again." Ajax rolls his eyes.

Halo taps her finger on the diagram. "Treasure Island floats. We can move it with a motor if we build it right. We could *all* look for Tomorrow Land. We don't need these Trials because we don't even really need a ship."

"Heresy!" Her father's fist slams on the table with far greater force than Halo's previous show of defiance. The entire hut shakes and Halo breaks out in a sweat. "Terra has been very clear, and I have indulged you for too long. No more work on that ridiculous motor! Do you hear me?"

Halo stands and walks from the hut before her burning tears get a chance to fall. Ajax had been right. She'd been a fool to think she could talk to her father as a parent and not a leader. Being the leader of Treasure Island isn't a role he plays, it's who he actually is.

Terra's mouthpiece.

Which leaves Halo having to decide if she's willing to continue to listen. Or is it time to start thinking for herself?

FYVE

*F*yve squats down as he looks in the half-barrel inside their hut, trying to make out the two furry bodies inside despite the pre-dawn gloom. He squints, then frowns. He can't see them.

Surely, they haven't lost the one thing he was going to use to convince Sevin to stay.

"I put a small metal box I found in there," a voice whispers behind him, making him jump. "So they have their own little hut."

Fyve grins up at his sister as she braces her hands on his shoulders so she can peer over the top. "Seems they like it."

"I also put in a little bowl of water. And the husks from the millet mom used to make the flatbread."

He nudges her. "Next thing they'll have some blankets."

Her eyes catch what little light there is, twinkling. "You know that shirt of yours that had more holes than material?"

Fyve's eyebrows shoot up with surprise, before slamming down in mock outrage. "That was my favorite shirt!"

Sevin covers her mouth to suppress a giggle. "Each one of those holes was a testament to that."

There's a soft groan from the corner of their hut where their mom's sleeping mat is. Fyve grabs his sister's hand and pulls her outside, a finger over his mouth for her to be silent. Although it looks like he wants to ensure his mother gets as much sleep as possible, what he really wants is time alone to talk to Sevin.

Outside, the first groans and grunts are drifting from nearby huts. Everyone will be awake soon, no doubt excited to head down to the beach for the next Trial. Fyve presses his lips together, his chest tightening.

He won't be one of them.

Sevin stretches as she does a slow pirouette. "I slept so well last night."

Because they were all exhausted from the last Trial. And now Terra wants them to almost kill themselves again.

Or die, just like Coal did. Something Fyve can't let happen to his sister.

He takes a step toward her as she comes to a stop, facing him. "You've done a wonderful job setting things up for the rats."

"Thanks," she beams. "It's kinda fun thinking of what they'll need to survive."

"You're a natural," he says warmly. "And now we have a way to feed our family."

Sevin nods, even as she goes still. "Yeah. As long as the rats survive."

"Which they will under your expert care," he says, half teasing, mostly serious. "And we'll provide for Mom, Aunt Cee, Jett, Bloo, and Rubee. Heck, once we have enough, we could trade them."

She blinks. "I hadn't thought of that."

They'd be richer than Elijah himself. Even better, everyone else will be able to feed their families.

Excitement jostling through his muscles, Fyve grabs Sevin's upper arms. "Don't you see? We don't need Tomorrow Land."

Sevin frowns. "But—"

"We wouldn't have to leave anyone behind. We'd have everything we need here."

She steps back, removing herself from his grip. "You don't get it, do you, Fyve?"

"No, it's you who doesn't get it. I'm trying to keep us together."

"Coal got it," she says, glaring at him. "He knew there's no tomorrow here on Treasure Island. We have to leave for our family to have a future."

"No, we don't," he growls, then lowers his voice. There are shuffling sounds from within their hut. "We can forge every one of our tomorrows, right here on Treasure Island." He straightens as something strikes him. "Halo showed us that when she raised her tree."

"It was fake!"

"It's more real than Tomorrow Land," he snaps back. "Besides, I thought you loved that tree."

"Fyve?" says their mother, exiting the hut. "Sevin?"

They both clamp their mouths shut as she makes a half-hearted attempt to tame the wild mane that is her hair. She sighs, giving up. The strands were long ago matted by the winds of the ocean, never to be untangled again. "What's going on?"

Fyve clenches his jaw even tighter. He has no intention of answering the question.

Sevin crosses her arms. "Fyve wants me to pull out of the Trials."

He throws her a glare. Fine, if she wants to do this, so be it. "The same Trials that killed Coal."

"The Trials are our one chance of surviving," his mother says, shaking her head. "Terra has given us this opportunity because she knows that."

Fyve huffs out a frustrated sigh. "Of course, you'd say that.

You've almost killed yourself countless times chasing that same empty dream."

"It wasn't an empty dream," his mother snaps.

"You don't know that!"

She moves so fast, Fyve doesn't get a chance to stumble backward before his mother's grabbed his arms in the same way he'd grabbed Sevin's. "I know!" Although the words are hissed, she may as well have shouted them, they contain so much conviction. "I know without a shred of doubt. Why else would I let my only remaining children take part in these Trials?"

Fyve blinks. He can barely remember the last time he was close enough to his mother to feel her touch, let alone the steel grip she has on him. It feels…good. And she looks so sure.

He yanks himself away before that realization can sink too far into his consciousness. He needs to stay strong right now. Sevin's life might depend on it.

"Coal knew, too."

Fyve spins around at the new voice. A soft one. His aunt Cee's voice.

She smiles, her lips trembling at the edges as she walks to him, lifting her hand. "He knew this was worth dying for. It's all a mother can ask for her children."

Fyve doesn't move. He's not sure he can. His entire family have surrounded him. There's an imploring face no matter where he looks.

Sweet Terra. Do they know what they're asking of him?

What if Sevin dies in this Trial? How could he live with himself? His heart stutters as he realizes his next greatest fear. What if he dies? With Coal gone, who will look out for the faces desperately beseeching him?

Will his mother's faith be so steadfast then?

At the same time, he's tired of fighting for this. The unblinking gazes, almost as if Sevin, his mother and Cee are all holding their breaths, tell him they won't be swayed. They truly believe Terra will gift them with everything Elijah's promised.

Fyve has to make a choice.

And in a blinding moment of realization, he knows what that is.

He sighs, his shoulders sinking. "Fine. I'll enter the next Trial."

Sevin whoops and leaps on him, wrapping her arms and legs around and holding on tight. He can't help the chuckle that escapes. He hugs her back, looking up to find a lone tear tracking down the lines of his mother's face.

And yet, he's never seen her happier.

In fact, her expression is what he'd always imagined she'd look like if she found her elusive Tomorrow Land after her endless months out on a raft at sea. The softening of her weary lines, the way her eyes glow with emotion, is downright beautiful. Without realizing what he's doing, Fyve smiles back. His mother looks like she's about to melt into a puddle of joy.

Fyve looks away and clears his throat. It will be the only time he'll see that expression in his lifetime. It will disappear forever once she discovers what he's really decided.

Sevin does a little skip on the spot then takes his hand. "Come on. We don't want to be late."

Cee steps forward, pulling out two rat drumsticks from the folds of her sleeves. "Here. You'll need your energy."

"Thanks, Aunt Cee," says Sevin, taking hers. The small morsel of meat is instantly sucked off the thin bone.

Fyve is about to refuse, but then he takes it like anyone who has committed to the Trials would. "Thanks," he says, his stomach growling a demand that he eat it even faster than Sevin.

Instead, he waves at Rubee tucked around her mother's leg. Just like he knew his little cousin would, Rubee runs at him and throws her arms around his waist. He hugs her back, surreptitiously slipping the drumstick into her pocket, then presses a kiss to her forehead. "I won't let you down," he whispers.

Fyve straightens and takes his sister's hand again. "Come on. Let's do this."

Sevin practically skips the whole way to the beach, and each jolt and tug on his hand echoes in Fyve's chest. He hadn't expected her to be quite this happy.

"We're going to ace this Trial just like the others," she chirps.

Fyve glances down at her, but his gaze barely settles before he looks forward again. It's too painful to see Sevin glowing the same way his mother was.

The beach is already crowded as the sun tries to peek through gray clouds. "Looks like rain today," he mutters, more for something to say than anything.

Sevin shrugs, her smile not dimming. "We won't be hot, then."

Fyve squints up at the sky. "Let's hope Mom and Cee remember to put out the water containers." If he were home, that's exactly what he'd be doing right now.

His sister shrugs again. "We have more important things to think about."

Fyve's shoulders tighten as he sees Elijah has arrived. This is the problem with the Trials. Everyone's so excited about what they promise that they're forgetting basics like food and water.

They're forgetting there are those who won't pass. Those who will stay behind.

That's assuming the ship even arrives.

Elijah climbs back up on his podium but Fyve finds himself scanning the crowd. Halo's golden hair is easy to spot, although he suspects he could find her even if she was wearing a head-scarf. Her height is already familiar. The way she stands impossibly still so she isn't noticed, yet holds her chin up just in case someone does. The way her gaze always seems to find his, like she can sense him watching.

Halo smiles as if she's glad to see him here, but then she quickly looks away. Fyve does the same, telling himself her reaction was a good thing. He can't handle any more expectations or joy.

"Welcome, my people, to the third Trial," Elijah booms, his voice full of warmth and welcome. "Today is a short Trial, but a significant one. One that will decide the fate of each teen who takes part."

Fyve swallows, wondering how Terra always seems to know just what to say.

"All those who want to take part, please step forward."

Somehow, Sevin's smile is a thousand times bigger than any of the others this morning as they join the growing crowd on the wet sand. Fyve estimates a little over two hundred teens step forward, and for the first time, he wonders what the Trial will involve. Elijah said it would be a quick one, which means no more punishing laps around the village. The teens here have proven their endurance.

What will they have to prove next?

Elijah raises his hands. "Terra spoke to me last night. The ship is on its way." The crowd gasps. "It will arrive soon," he promises.

Sevin clasps her hands under her chin, almost as if she's praying for it to arrive today. Fyve wonders what the people of Treasure Island will do if the ship doesn't turn up. The Trials have stirred their faith to fever pitch.

It feels like no one has prepared themselves for the possibility of disappointment. Unlike Fyve, they haven't protected themselves for that almighty crash.

Or their families.

"Today, you will form teams of three," says Elijah, beaming. "Each team will be required to carry their collective weight in water to fill a barrel. You must fill your barrel to capacity as quickly as possible." Elijah waves an arm to the left, and Fyve notices a seesaw-like contraption with metal buckets stacked beside it. "Choose your teams and step forward to be weighed."

There's a murmur as the teens glance amongst each other. Some people instantly form a trio, while others frown, considering their choice.

"This Trial is about strength and strategy," Sevin says thoughtfully. "Having light people means less water to carry, but less muscle power to carry it."

Fyve nods even though it makes no difference who is on their team. Against his will, his eyes stray to Halo. She's standing beside her brother, obviously forming two of their team. Even if he wanted to, they couldn't work together.

A boy who must be close to nineteen walks over to Ajax, smiling. He says something, then flexes his tricep. Ajax nods and it's clear they've just completed their team. The guy moves to stand next to Halo, a little too close for Fyve's liking.

"Can I join your team?" Yanking his gaze away, Fyve finds Justice standing before them. "I'm light, but strong. Just what you want."

Sevin looks up at him. "She's right."

"Go and find another team," growls Fyve, the reality of what he's planning tightening his throat.

Justice raises her chin. "You need to have a team of three to compete."

"And she's light," adds Sevin, looking at Fyve as she wonders what his problem is.

Fyve nods again, this time his throat too tight to talk. Having a team of three means one more person just became part of his plan. And he knows enough about Justice to appreciate why the Trials are so important to her. Her mother died a couple of years ago, leaving her and Zake to be raised by their brutish father. Zake inherited the violent tendencies. Justice is trying to escape both of them.

She'd be wishing for that ship with every shred of her being.

Fyve chokes out an agreement as he pushes down the guilt. He's doing this for Sevin. His family. He has to be their safety net, no matter what. Even if it means Justice will be spending the rest of her life on Treasure Island alongside her awful brother.

Because Fyve fully intends on sabotaging this Trial.

Neither he nor Sevin will pass.

HALO

*H*alo's new teammate smiles at her. It's a brilliant smile that lights up his blue eyes and produces a dimple in one cheek that she's certain would make most girls swoon. She's seen him around. He's the kind of guy impossible to miss, partly due to his good looks, but mostly because of his swagger.

"I'm Halo." She smiles back at him.

He laughs. "So, you're funny as well as beautiful."

"Huh?" She feels lines stretching across her forehead as she frowns. "How am I funny?"

"Because we've met…a few times actually." The guy's smile falls as he realizes there's a female on Treasure Island who doesn't know his name.

Ajax lets out a belly laugh and slaps him on the back. "Halo, this is Striker. We used to hang out. Remember?"

"Of course." Halo nods, feeling a flush rise to her cheeks. "I remember now."

"Don't take it personally," says Ajax. "My sister's more interested in connecting wires than connecting with people."

"That's not true!" She jams her hand in her pocket, feeling

for her lucky cord and grasping it tightly. *It is true, though.* She's never really been good at relationships. Not even with her own brother or father. Until she met...

She looks across at Fyve, cursing that her eyes keep getting drawn to him no matter how much she doesn't want them to. Justice has joined his team. Smart kid. With two team members who weigh virtually nothing, and another with muscled strength, they're sure to smash this challenge. Maybe she should have teamed up with them instead of Justice.

Pushing this thought away, she glances at her team members, trying to summon the family loyalty to Ajax that she'd decided was her best way forward.

"We've got the balance wrong," she says. "You two are heavy. And no offence, Ajax, but you're not all that strong."

His eyes flare as he puffs out his chest. "Look who's talking!"

"I'm not saying I *am* strong." She pulls her hand from her pocket and raises her palm. "But I don't weigh much either. The team to win this Trial will be high on strength and low in body mass. And that's not us."

"I disagree," says Striker. "The team to win this will be the one where each member can handle their own share of the weight. I know I can. Can you, Halo?"

He locks eyes on her as she considers the challenge he just threw out.

"Of course, I can," she snaps.

There's movement in the crowd as teams move forward to be weighed by standing on one end of a wide plank that's been placed over a pointed plastic structure positioned in its center. Halo's father's volunteers are placing pre-filled buckets of seawater on the other end of the plank, making a note of how many it takes to tip up the plank to balance out the combined weight of the team standing on the other end. Each team is given their number and asked to choose one of the barrels lined up on the beach.

Halo's team joins the queue.

"What do you think?" asks Ajax. "We'd be about eight buckets at most."

"More like ten," she replies, biting her tongue from adding that it could even be eleven to account for the size of Striker's head.

Fyve's team steps up and as the seventh bucket is positioned, the three of them rise a few feet in the air, hovering as the plank finds its balance.

"Seven's my lucky number!" Sevin squeals in delight.

Halo's heart swells to see such joy, knowing that her determination to protect herself from getting too close to Fyve and his sister has failed. The two of them have already wormed their way into her heart.

Fyve doesn't celebrate with his sister. He keeps his eyes cast down, seeming reluctant to look at anyone. Halo's actually surprised he even turned up today after walking out on the previous Trial. What had Sevin said to him to get him to participate? Whatever it was, it must've been convincing.

The buckets are removed from the plank, and Fyve, Sevin and Justice step away, disappearing back into the crowd.

Ajax and Striker shuffle forward as the next team learns how many buckets it's going to take to fill their team's barrel. Eight or nine is the average, which thankfully doesn't seem too daunting. Every muscle in Halo's body is still aching from yesterday's Trial.

When their turn comes, they step up to the plank. Halo stands between the two males and Striker puts a steadying hand on her back.

"I'm okay," she tells him, deciding that as cocky as this guy is, he doesn't have a dark heart. He's miles away from that creep, Zake. But he's also an equal number of miles from Fyve with a smile that lights up his heart as well as his eyes.

She shakes her head, trying to eject Fyve from her brain,

concentrating instead on the buckets being raised and placed on the other end of the plank.

Ajax grins at her as the eighth bucket is positioned. "Get ready for it."

But the plank remains firmly stuck in the sand. Two more buckets are added before any kind of movement is felt. It's the eleventh bucket that really gets things moving and the plank rises into the air. It seems Striker's head needed to be accounted for after all.

"Eleven's easy," Striker boasts. "You just watch. I can carry twice as much as some of these skinny runts."

They step down to allow the next team to get their weigh-in started, and Halo is forced to acknowledge something that's been nagging at her since her father announced this Trial.

What does any of this have to do with who should go on the ship?

The first two Trials she could understand. They've been tested on their strength, their smarts, their endurance, their ability to work as a team, and alone. But what is this Trial testing that hasn't already been assessed?

Letting out a sigh, she follows Ajax and Striker to the long line of barrels that have been set up several yards back from the shoreline, each with two buckets beside it. Halo didn't even know so many buckets existed on Treasure Island, making her wonder just how long Terra has been planning these Trials.

"Why only two buckets?" she asks.

"Maybe we didn't have enough." Ajax shrugs.

"There has to be more to it than that," Halo muses, deciding this must be the new part to this Trial—negotiation. She can already see teams arguing over the buckets, with most competitors keen to prove their worth. Surely, Terra's not looking for people who are willing to stand back and let others do all the work? Or...maybe that's exactly what she's looking for? In some ways, that's what a leader does. The very way her father is standing on the shoreline watching over this Trial is proof of that. He's the only person here who's guaranteed a place on that ship without having to lift a finger to earn it.

"Ajax and I will do the first run," says Striker, taking a bucket and handing the other one to her brother. "It'll take five runs with one of the buckets, six with the other."

"They're going to be heavy when full," says Halo.

"If you don't think you can carry it, we can do it." Striker pulls back his broad shoulders.

"It's not that." Halo shakes her head. "I'm wondering if we're better to half fill the buckets? It will mean more runs, but we can move faster."

Ajax and Striker shake their heads.

"That's what the weaker teams will do." Ajax tilts his head toward Fyve's team who seem to be deciding between Justice and Sevin for the first run. "They have fewer buckets to carry. If we do that, we'll lose for sure."

"I suppose so." Halo nods. Each bucket is a little less than a third of their body weight. If Ajax and Striker think they can do that in one trip, that will set them up well.

The final team finishes their weigh-in and joins them at the barrels while Halo's father stalks up and down the beach in front of them, making sure everything's going to plan. When satisfied, he raises his arms to quieten the crowd.

"Thank you for your cooperation," he says. "Terra is pleased. The rules of today's Trial are simple. Terra would like you to fill your barrel with your combined body weight in seawater. You all know how many buckets it will take to achieve that. But I should warn you there's more to it than that…"

Halo's ears prick up. She knew there was something she was missing. "Once your barrel is full, you must take it to the scales so it can be weighed. If it matches your team's combined weight, then you have successfully completed the challenge. Does anyone have any questions?"

People look at each other, too afraid to speak.

Halo clears her throat. "How much does the barrel weigh? How do we account for that?"

Her father nods slowly. "The weight of the empty barrel is approximately equal to the weight of eight empty buckets. You may need to make some adjustments to take that into consideration."

"Lucky you asked," Striker says quietly.

"Lucky for everyone else, too," Ajax complains. "That could have given us an advantage."

"Does completing the challenge keep us safe from elimination?" asks a guy, plucking up the courage to speak. No doubt, the leader's daughter asking a question bolstered his courage.

Halo's father looks to the sky. "That's up to Terra, of course."

"Great," mutters Striker.

Ajax shoots him a warning glare. There's still every chance of someone being claimed before this Trial even begins. Losing a team member now would be catastrophic. Especially someone as strong as Striker.

"What?" Striker hisses back. "I said it was great."

"Nice try," Halo mutters. "But Terra knows what you really meant."

Striker rolls his eyes as he clutches the bucket to his chest.

"How do we move the barrel to the scales?" asks a young girl in a team of similarly young friends. They must only weigh five buckets in total. Even so, moving their weight all at once is going to be a challenge.

Striker leans into Halo. "Still think the lighter teams have an advantage?"

"Your strategy is entirely up to you," Halo's father explains, walking to the end of the beach to clear the path. "Let the Trial begin."

The empty beach is stormed by desperate teens who surge toward the crimson ocean. Halo waits beside the barrel, noticing Fyve's team has left their barrel unattended. That must've been Sevin's idea. The buckets don't have handles, making them awkward to carry. Rather than choosing between Sevin and Justice on this first run, they plan to share the load of one bucket while Fyve takes the other.

Smart.

But then again, that does seem to be Sevin's middle name. The rules didn't say anything about how many can carry a bucket at once. This Trial is testing their assumptions as well as their negotiating skills.

Noticing what Sevin and Justice are doing, some other competitors leave their barrels to dash forward. But Halo stays where she is. Striker's ego would never allow her to help. And she already injured Ajax's ego enough when she said he wasn't strong. Besides, it's important at least one of them doesn't wear themselves out. They still have to figure out how they're going to move the barrel once it's full.

She adds a few more attributes to her list of what Terra might be looking for in this Trial.

Forward planning. Reserving strength. Thinking outside the square.

As each layer of the Trial is uncovered, it's making more and more sense. It seems Terra knows what she's doing after all.

Striker is one of the first to fill his bucket and make his way back up the beach. It's clear from the strain on his face that it's not just an awkward shape, but it's also heavy. He's filled it to the top with every drop of water it can take.

There's a girl beside him moving slightly faster, having opted to make more trips with an emptier bucket. Halo still doesn't think that's such a bad strategy. Ajax is in the middle of the pack, yet strangely Fyve hasn't appeared. She can just see his dark hair on the shoreline and realizes he's insisted on filling both buckets for his team to save Sevin and Justice from having to dip their sensitive skin into the water.

Halo shakes her head. Seriously, would it be possible for that guy to get any more appealing? Ajax has never once taken care of her like that.

She thinks back to when she built her tree, which was only several days ago yet feels like several lifetimes. Fyve hadn't laughed at her even though he hadn't understood what she'd been doing. Ajax had laughed, though. And he'd taken her lucky cord. So why then does she feel more loyalty to a person who treats her badly over someone who's only ever been kind? Is blood really that much thicker than water?

She looks to her tree, the top of it visible in the distance. The leaves are swaying in the breeze, and it's still the most beautiful thing on this island.

Fyve moves up the beach with his bucket. He's removed his shirt, which is wise for someone who doesn't own more than a couple of them, and his biceps are rippling under the strain of the weight he's carrying.

Perhaps the tree might have to settle for second place...

She tears her gaze away and notices the piles of poles stacked up at the end of the beach from the first Trial. The same poles that were supposed to be her forest. It's a shame they ended up like this. She would have liked to have seen these shores lined with trees.

Striker reaches the barrel, panting heavily, and pours the water in, careful not to lose any.

Halo puts out her hands to take the bucket, ready to play her part, but Striker disappears back down the beach without so much as glancing at her. She tries to feel disappointed, but looking at the strain on everyone's faces, she finds herself feeling more relieved. Does that make her a bad person?

She pulls back her shoulders. No, it doesn't. It makes her smart, just like Sevin. She adds another attribute for Terra to her list. *Play to your strengths.*

Not everyone can be strong, just like not everyone can be

clever. She can bring something else to this Trial that nobody else would think of.

She walks off down the beach toward the pile of poles and inspects them, deciding she's going to need four of them for her plan to work. And unlike her tree, the shorter the poles, the better. Scanning the selection, she chooses four that are only a few feet long, the rest of their length having corroded away, leaving a jagged end that's pockmarked with holes.

Reaching into her pocket for her lucky cord, she threads it through a hole in the end of each pole and ties a knot to form a loop. Then getting to her feet, she drags the poles behind her, heading back to the barrel.

Onlookers are staring at her like she's gone completely mad, but she doesn't care. This is how they'll move something that's the combined weight of the three of them. They'll roll it. Nobody will be staring when they figure it out for themselves—they'll be tripping over each other to get some poles for themselves.

Puffing for breath, she moves as fast as she can. The sooner she can get back, the easier it will be to position the poles.

She arrives just as Ajax is returning with what she guesses is his second bucket.

"What are you doing?" he barks at her. "We don't have time for you to build any of your stupid trees."

Ignoring him, she squats down and unties her lucky cord, shoving it deep in her pocket where Ajax can't steal it.

"Help me tip up the barrel," she says, rolling one of the poles to the edge.

"What for?" he asks.

"What do you think?" She rolls her eyes. "Hurry up."

Realization lights his face just as Striker returns.

"Wait!" Ajax shouts at him. "Don't pour it in just yet."

"What's going on?" Striker is red in the face, not seeming at all pleased for his rhythm to be interrupted.

"My sister's a genius, that's what," says Ajax, giving Halo possibly his first compliment in her life. "We're going to roll the barrel when it's full."

Striker's jaw drops and he sets down his full bucket. "Beautiful, funny *and* smart."

Halo doesn't remind him he'd decided she wasn't all that funny when he'd realized she was being serious about not remembering his name.

Between the three of them, they maneuver the barrel to position both poles underneath. The other teams look on, a few of them entering deep discussions as they try to decide if this is a strategy worth mimicking. Does Terra award points to copycats?

"How will it work?" Striker asks. "Won't the barrel roll right off?"

Halo shakes her head. "It will roll off one pole, then we'll pull it out and move it forward. Then it'll roll off the other. And so on."

"So, why do we have four of them?" asks Ajax. "Won't two do the job?"

"Yep." Halo drags the other two poles over to Fyve's unattended barrel. Sevin will know what to do with them. She returns to Ajax who's shaking his head in disapproval.

"Terra rewards kindness," she tells him.

"I thought you said Coal was kind," Ajax points out.

She opens her mouth to argue, but realizes she has no comeback, so remains silent.

Ignoring their bickering, Striker lifts his bucket and dumps it into the barrel. "That's three from me. How many from you, Ajax?"

"Two. But I was helping Halo," he says quickly, which isn't strictly true given he'd been helping for all of about a minute when Striker had approached.

"Six more to go." Striker dashes back down the beach.

"Maybe only five and a half to account for the weight of our extra buckets."

"I can do the next one." Halo reaches for Ajax's bucket.

He doesn't hesitate to hand it to her, and she runs toward the water. Would it have killed Ajax to have pretended for a moment to have wanted to spare her? He's twice her size. Not that she'd have let him, of course. She wants to play her part in this challenge by carrying at least one bucket.

He's not Fyve, she reminds herself as her feet hit the acidic ocean, making her skin sting. She can't expect the same level of protectiveness from him as Sevin gets from Fyve.

She dips the bucket into the water, wincing as the sting becomes a biting pain. She needs to do this quickly before she burns. Her skin has always been more sensitive than most people's, but she should still be able to do this.

"Urgh!" she cries, filling the bucket and trying to lift it to her chest. But it slips out of her hands halfway there, forcing her to start again. She's not actually sure she's going to be able to lift this. Maybe that half bucket Striker suggested will have to do.

A warm body pushes her aside and takes hold of her bucket.

Fyve.

Of course, it is.

"Get out of the water!" He turns his back to her as he scoops up more water. "Your skin is pink already. Go! Now!"

Her mouth opens to protest, then realizing it's futile, she wades back to the plastic sand and tries to shake the water off her legs.

Fyve emerges from the water, with the bucket held to his chest and she puts out her hands to take it from him. But he doesn't pause, running right past her and up the beach. If she didn't know him so well, she'd think he was stealing it from her.

She races to catch up to him, hating that he's still beating her despite her hands being empty, and reaches him just in time as he tips the bucket into her team's barrel.

"Shame on you," he says to Ajax who's standing there, mouth agape.

"It's called equal opportunity," retorts Ajax.

"You mean you'd watch your sister lose the skin from her legs, just to prove a point?" Without waiting for an answer, Fyve dumps the bucket at Ajax's feet and runs back to the shoreline where Justice and Sevin are waiting for him. Helping her has cost his team precious time. Thankfully, the poles she got for them should make up for that.

Ajax grumbles something unintelligible and picks up the bucket, heading for the shoreline.

Striker appears out of nowhere and empties another bucket into the barrel. "That's eight."

"I thought it was seven?" Halo tilts her head as she counts.

"I've done two since we put the poles under." Striker is panting heavily, and his shins are bright pink. They're not as angry looking as Halo's, but bad enough. "Three more to go."

He's gone before Halo can offer to take another turn. As she watches, she wonders if Ajax had a point. Is it sexist to let the males do the bulk of the lifting? Or is it just practical? They're doing a far better job than Halo can. And she's contributed in a different way.

Play to your strengths, she reminds herself.

Her attention is quickly stolen by the team beside her who are celebrating having filled their barrel with the required number of buckets. However, their victory is soon quashed by the realization that their barrel is far too heavy to lift.

"We'll drag it," the male of the trio says. "Here. I'll pull and you two push."

With great effort, they manage to move it about an inch and some of the water sloshes out.

"That's not going to work!" one of the girls cries out. "We need to do what Halo did."

They all turn their attention to Halo's barrel, before nodding to each other and dashing down the beach toward the poles.

Halo shifts her gaze to the weighing station, noticing a few teams had elected to move their empty barrels over there before filling them up. It's further to carry the buckets but an impressive idea. Perhaps even better than Halo's. She smiles, knowing that Terra has room on her ship for all kinds of clever. About half the teams have full barrels now and she can hear debates about whether they ditch the contents, move their barrel, and start again. Or if they need to try out Halo's idea with the poles.

Striker returns at impressive speed and pours in the ninth bucket.

"One more from me," he puffs. "Assuming Ajax makes it back this century."

"You're doing an amazing job," Halo tells him, trying to give him an extra boost. Plus, it's true. His strength and stamina are incredible. It seems he has that swagger for good reason.

"Maybe we can celebrate later?" He flashes her a flirtatious grin, adds a wink, then runs back down the beach.

She shakes her head and smiles. There's no chance of that. He may be confident and handsome and strong, but on this occasion Striker has *strikered out*. Her head is too full of Fyve to look at anyone else.

Ajax groans as he returns with his bucket and tips it into the barrel. "Please tell me we're done."

"Almost," says Halo. "As soon as Striker returns. Unless you think we should collect one more to account for any wastage as we move the barrel?"

"No chance." Ajax bends forward with his hands on his thighs. "I'm done. Besides, if Striker brings a full one then we're about half a bucket overweight anyway."

"Let's start moving it then," Halo suggests, noticing that Sevin has worked out how to use the poles and is rolling their barrel already.

They grip the barrel at either side and roll it forward on the compacted sand. It moves with ease.

"I'll get it!" Halo shouts as the barrel rolls off the pole at the rear. It's heavy but on its own she can manage it. She takes it to the front of the barrel and inserts it underneath while Ajax pushes it forward.

They complete this step four more times before Striker returns with a full bucket.

"Should I tip it all in?" he asks.

Halo shakes her head. "We seem to be stable moving it like this. Tip in half, like you suggested earlier."

Striker pours in half the bucket, then goes to tip the other half onto the sand.

"Wait!" says Halo. "See if one of the other teams needs it."

Ajax uses a word their father wouldn't be pleased about but Striker grins at her. "Beautiful, funny, smart, *and* kind. My list is growing."

"Hurry up," she tells him, ignoring his praise.

He dashes away to ask the nearby teams if they need a top-up while Ajax and Halo push the barrel forward. Once Striker returns, they make quick progress reaching the scales. They're the first to be weighed. Even the other teams who filled their barrels nearby are finding it impossible to move their load.

Halo's team rolls their barrel onto one end of the plank, leaving their poles on the sand.

"Here!" Halo calls to one of the nearby teams she noticed struggling to move their barrel. "Take our poles!"

Her offer is eagerly accepted.

Making sure their barrel is stable, Halo's team walks across to the other end on the plank. As they cross the middle, it starts to move.

"Not too fast," Ajax warns, and they slow their steps.

The crowd watches as the barrel rises and the plank finds its balance, settling perfectly with both the barrel and Halo's team hovering in the air.

"We did it!" Striker punches the air in victory and Ajax wraps an arm around Halo.

"We make a good team," he tells her.

Halo searches the crowd for the set of gray eyes she's been trying unsuccessfully to avoid all day. She finds Fyve and he gives her the smallest of nods. Just enough to show her that he's happy for her, even if just like her tree, he doesn't understand exactly why.

Sevin tugs on her brother's sleeve to gain his attention and he gets back to work, removing a pole from the back of the barrel and placing it at the front.

Halo's team crosses the plank once more to reach their barrel. When it touches the ground, they carefully tip it over and remove it to allow Fyve's team to take their turn. She's thrilled they're going to come second. There's no way either of their teams will be eliminated now. Maybe she can dare to dream of a future with Fyve after all.

Sevin and Justice push their load forward while Fyve removes the pole at the rear as the barrel touches the edge of the plank. He moves to the front and stands to grip the barrel by its rim and ease it forward so it can be weighed.

"Careful!" warns Sevin. "It's tipping!"

"I've got it," says Fyve.

But as soon as he says the words, his hands slip from the edge of the barrel and it lurches forward as Sevin and Justice push from the other side, unaware it's not being held. Fyve tries to steady it by throwing himself in front of it, but momentum has taken hold and the barrel continues its inevitable trajectory toward the earth. Sevin grapples with it, desperately trying to stand it back up while Justice cries out in distress. But their efforts are too late and Fyve has to dive out of the way as the barrel crashes over, spewing its contents over the plank and onto the sand in a giant acidic puddle.

"Fyve!" Sevin screams as her dream of leaving this island is snatched away. "Fyve! What have you done?"

"It was an accident," he protests. "I'm so sorry."

Sevin lets out a whimper and Halo's hand flies to her mouth in shock. Because when the barrel tipped, just for a moment, she saw a glimmer of something on Fyve's face that Sevin hadn't.

Satisfaction.

He tipped that barrel on purpose.

Fyve just threw the Trial.

FYVE

*F*yve pushes himself up, dusting plastic and sand off his chest and arms, finding it a whole lot harder to face Sevin than he expected. The flash of triumph when the barrel tipped had been short-lived. His sister's cry had cut it abruptly off, killing it.

He finally forces himself to look up, already dreading what he'll see. Except Sevin isn't where he expected to find her. A heartbeat later, he finds her crumpled on the sand, shoulders drooped in a way he's never seen before, head hanging down even lower. Justice is shaking her own head, silently mouthing "no" over and over.

Fyve takes a cautious step closer to Sevin, her pain unbearable to watch. "Sevin, I'm so sorry."

And he means it. Right now, she looks...broken. Uncertainty flickers through him, undermining his belief that he had to do this.

"Sevin?" he asks again, his voice strangely hoarse.

She shoots to her feet in a blur of movement. "Stay away from me!" she screams. "I never want to speak to you again."

"I'm sorr—"

Sevin shoves past him with enough force that he staggers back a step. Fyve watches as she runs from the beach and toward the village, her sobs trailing behind her. The crowd divides as she streaks through them, and Fyve sees his mother near the front. She looks at him, for some reason not looking as devastated as he expected. She shakes her head then follows Sevin, the crowd compressing together as they watch with a mixture of sympathy and curiosity.

"We can't have lost," Justice whispers behind him. "I can't stay on this island."

There's the sound of rapid footfalls and she also runs past Fyve, her hand over her mouth and tears wetting her cheeks.

He just broke two hearts with a single choice.

Another team arrives, jostling their barrel and Fyve rolls their empty one out of the way. The one he tipped over. Deliberately. Doing what he thought was right for his family.

He straightens, finding Halo with her brother and the guy only a few feet away. Her eyes are wide, looking almost as hurt as Sevin or Justice. She shakes her head, 'how could you?' stamped across her features.

Fyve stiffens. It's like she knows...

No. There's no way she could. He wasn't even sure he had the gumption to do it until the opportunity arose. He knew as they were loading that barrel onto the plank it was now or never. And he'd been very sure to make it look like an accident. Losing his grip on the edge of the barrel could've happened to anyone, especially after carrying all those buckets filled with seawater, then pushing the full barrel to the weighing plank.

But Halo's gaze doesn't waver. The betrayal and hurt don't fade. The knowledge doesn't leave her eyes.

She knows.

Feeling suddenly trapped, Fyve spins on his heel and stalks away. She'll see. Sevin will get over this. Not to mention the disappointment was probably going to be inevitable. He actually saved his sister even more hurt by stopping before they got to the final Trials.

The crowd parts for him, too, even though he wishes they wouldn't. He wants to disappear into obscurity. Although sabotaging the Trial was the right thing to do, he's never felt more awful.

The village is eerily quiet and empty as everyone is still watching the rest of the Trial. Fyve trudges to their hut, trying to think of what he can say to make this easier for his sister. Maybe he can distract her with the rats they'll breed, show her there's still hope for the future. Didn't she say something about thinking up ways to ensure they survive? Maybe they could go scouting for things to build a cage for them. By the time they're finished, the rats will be living better than they will.

There's no one outside the hut, but Fyve expected that. The front flap is back to let light in and he slips through the open doorway, still needing a second for his eyes to adjust to the gloom. When they do, a fist clenches around his heart and squeezes. Hard.

Sevin is on her knees beside the half-barrel they were using to hold the rats, their mom beside her, her arm wrapped tightly around her shoulders as they heave. Sevin tucks her face into their mom's neck, a soft, keening wail curling through the harsh sobs.

"We won't need it, you'll see," their mother croons, pressing her lips to Sevin's hair.

Fyve isn't sure why his mom's changed her tune and is now telling Sevin just what she needs to hear, but he doesn't care. She's right. They don't need the Trials. And making his sister feel better is all he wants.

"Sevin," he says quietly, his voice tight. "I'm so sorry. I know this was important to you."

She doesn't answer, just burrows further into the crook of their mother's neck.

Fyve enters completely and folds to his knees. "We'll be fine. We always are." No matter what's taken from them. He reaches out only to stop when she jerks back. "Sevin?"

"Things will never be okay again," she says, not untucking her face.

"They will," he promises her fervently. He'll make them. "We still have the rats to breed. Maybe this is what Terra wants us to do," he adds, even though he's not totally sure he believes that. People forge their own futures. Terra prefers to sit back and watch. Or to end them.

Sevin finally uncurls enough to look at him, and the devastation carved in the lines of her face takes his breath away. Her eyes are as bleak as Treasure Island itself. Not breaking their gaze, she reaches into the half-barrel and pulls something out.

Two rats.

Two dead, skinless rats.

What's more, lengths of wire have been skewered through them, ready for them to be cooked.

Fyve leaps to his feet. "You killed them?" he roars to his mother.

She nods, as always failing to look apologetic even though she just killed, quite literally, any shred of hope he could've instilled in Sevin. "You need your strength for the Trials."

But the rage dies as quickly as the rats would've when their necks were snapped. Fyve shakes his head, his own despair finally finding a chance to flourish. "You said... You said we don't need it."

"I was talking about breeding the rats," his mother says gently, yet with determination. "And you don't. Because you won't be here."

Sevin tucks her knees up, then drops her forehead onto them as if her head is too heavy. "Except we failed the Trial."

"Hush now," says their mother, tightening her arm around

Sevin's shoulders. "Terra works in mysterious ways. You'll be on that ship, I just know it."

Fyve's tattered emotions completely unravel. "You don't!" he shouts, his arms exploding outward. "You can't promise her that when you have no idea who will be on that ship!

His mother holds his gaze levelly, her eyes as hard as steel. "I do know that."

His hands clamp onto his head. How can he argue with blind faith? How can he hope Sevin won't be totally crushed by this if their own mother keeps talking like that? "Just stop it! You're only making things worse! Sevin was too young to enter, anyway. She was never meant to on some ship that no one's even seen!" He presses the heels of his hands into his temples, trying to contain the anger. "We're not meant to leave. We never were!"

To his surprise, Sevin's head snaps up. "Which is exactly what you believe, isn't it?" She unfolds and comes to her feet. "That's what you've always wanted."

"I'm being realistic—"

"Were you even really trying, Fyve?" she demands, the tears evaporating under the heat of her own anger. "Because you never wanted to be part of these Trials."

Fyve snaps his mouth shut. Sevin is getting dangerously close to the truth. If this is how she's reacting, thinking he made a mistake, how will she feel if she knows he failed on purpose? "I just want what's best for you," he says, hoping that some part of her might understand that.

"No, you don't," Sevin screams. "You want what's best for you!"

For the second time that morning, she shoves past him then runs out of the hut. Fyve whirls back to his mother, his world feeling like it's imploded. "You did this!"

His mother shakes her head. "I have a lot to be held accountable for, Fyve, but this isn't one of them."

"You killed the two rats that were going to give us a future!"

His mother scoops up the lifeless, skinned bodies and almost cradles them to her, as if she's protecting them. "I told you. You both need your strength for the Trials. And the trip to Tomorrow Land."

"See what I mean?" Fyve accuses. "You keep lifting her up, not caring how far or hard she'll fall."

"No." She snaps out the word so sharply that Fyve blinks, unused to the harsh tone. He can't remember the last time his mom has been angry with him. She's usually feeling too…guilty. "You're the one who let Sevin down this time," she says, sparks of conviction flickering in her eyes.

Fyve opens his mouth only to find there's no response waiting to explode out. Does his mother know, like Halo does?

Not wanting the answer to that, he spins around and stalks out. It's not like she was going to listen to reason, anyway. Her unfailing belief is too deeply entrenched. Plus, it's Sevin he needs to talk to. She's the one who really matters in all of this.

But she's not standing a few feet away like he was expecting her to. Nor is she in the adjacent hut that houses their aunt and cousins. Fyve frowns. This time, Sevin has actually run off. She's never done that before, no matter how upset she was.

Then again, he's never seen her this upset before.

Determined to find her and somehow make this right, Fyve treks back to the beach. The Trial must be over because people are moving around the village, a few giving him sympathetic glances that set his teeth on edge. He doesn't care about the Trials. But he does care about Sevin, and right now, she's hurting in a way he never wanted his only sister to.

And it's all his fault.

Fyve spends hours looking for Sevin. She's not in the village. Not out at the rat traps—which are empty, as if Terra herself is punishing him. Not down at the beach where the Trials are being held, reliving the moment he let her down. At first, he assumes she's hiding from him. But when the sun passes the midday crest and begins to trek to the west through the low hanging clouds, he begins to worry. Sevin's never been gone this long.

Something is wrong. Very wrong.

A light, steady rain settles in as he does another quick sweep of the village, even asking several people if they've seen her, but no one has. One or two people shrink away from him, as if his bad luck in the Trials is contagious. Casting his net wider, Fyve circles the village, checks the rat traps one more time, and then decides he'll circle the whole island if he has to.

It's late afternoon when he makes his way to the beach and heads east, conscious that the sullen clouds mean dark will come sooner. What's more, he discovers the fine droplets that have rivulets running down every inch of his skin were enough to wipe the beach clean. There's no way to know whether his sister came this way.

Flicking his sodden hair out of his face, Fyve trudges on. Up ahead is the tiny bay where they laid Coal's body to rest. He's not surprised his mom and aunt chose that as the location for their final goodbyes. His mother comes here often. In fact, he noticed as a child she came here more and more in the lead up to her absences. She'd always stand at the water's edge, staring out at the red ocean, her expression anywhere but here. He stopped following her once he realized what she was doing— listening to the call to leave.

"Sevin!" he shouts over and over, uncaring that his voice is becoming hoarse. Each time, all he gets is a scowling gray sky and rainwater sucked into his lungs.

Fyve reaches the small circular bay and stops, staring out at the darkening sea. It's calm, the surface peppered by the rain like a thousand little needles. Coal is beneath it, or what's left of him. The acid works quickly once it dissolves the skin.

"I miss you, Coal," he whispers hoarsely. He didn't realize

how much his cousin balanced him. He was the optimism to Fyve's realism, the faith to his doubt. Now, his world has progressively become more unstable. Is it possible he went too far with throwing the Trial? Sevin's words echo through his mind.

You want what's best for you.

He was doing all this so he didn't lose Sevin, too. Yet, it feels like that's exactly what he's done.

Fyve blinks rapidly, not sure whether it's rain or tears running down his cheeks. "Where are you Sevin?"

He doesn't know how, but he has to make this right.

He blinks again when something out on the ocean catches his attention. Fyve narrows his eyes, squinting through the misty rain. He takes a step forward. The expanse of the ocean that surrounds them is even less interesting than the uneven stretches of Treasure Island. It's always a blank canvas. A vista only broken by storms. Never...a shape.

Fyve half-jogs the few feet to the water, stopping when it swirls around his ankles. He ignores the tingling that's the beginning of a sting as he wipes the water from his eyes. "It can't be," he gasps.

Is it the ship?

Has Elijah been telling the truth all along?

He quickly realizes it's too small to be the grandeur that Elijah's been promising. It's little more than a squiggle bobbing on the calm, pock-marked sea. One that's strangely familiar.

"Sevin!" Fyve roars.

His sister is out there! On their mother's raft!

She spins around, her movements sharp with alarm, then faces the never-ending expanse of water ahead of her and breaks into frantic paddling.

It's not only his sister, but she's trying to get away from him!

"Sevin!" he shouts, even as he realizes what's happening.

Sevin has decided to go find Tomorrow Land herself, just like their mother has spent most of her life doing.

All because she failed today's Trial. The one he sabotaged.

Not seeing any other option, Fyve runs until the water reaches his knees, his hips, then splashes his face as it hits his chest. Pushing off the sandy floor, he breaks into strong strokes, determined to reach her.

The warm seawater is pleasant for the space of a breath. Then the mild acid finds any cut or scrape he's accumulated throughout the Trials, seeps into his eyes, even fills his mouth as if it's corroding his lips. But Fyve doesn't slow. Sevin can't leave. She'll die out here.

A few minutes later, her voice reaches past the sounds of splashing. "Fyve! What are you doing?"

Thank Terra. His skin is starting to feel like it's peeling. The raft appears through his blurry vision and he beelines for it, clamping a hand on the edge. Fyve hauls himself up as Sevin helps him. He rolls onto his back, slowing the motion when the raft rocks, water flowing over its rough surface and stinging his skin all over again.

Sevin sits back, looking stunned. "You just swam out to me!"

He sits up, panting. His skin is an angry, burning red. "I noticed."

"That was a stupid idea," she half-shrieks.

"And going off to find Tomorrow land isn't?" he demands.

She scowls. "No, it's not."

Fyve glances around, noting it's stopped raining as he waves his arm to encompass the endless miles of nothing in almost every direction. "It's the height of stupid, Sevin!" He realizes he just shouted the words, but he doesn't care. "You'll die out here!"

"I'd prefer that than dying on Treasure Island," she hollers back, her face scrunched with conviction.

He rears back as if he was just slapped. "You don't mean that," he chokes.

"I really, really do," Sevin says, tears pooling in her eyes. "And now that we failed the last Trial, this is the only way I can do that."

To follow in their mother's footsteps. To leave those she loves behind, risking death each time she goes out.

Fyve shuffles forward, taking his sister's hands. "We don't know that we didn't pass," he says, urgency filling him. He has to get Sevin back to the island. To safety.

She looks at him as if the acidic water has addled his brain. "We didn't even finish the Trial. Of course, we failed."

"Terra works in mysterious ways, remember?" he says, finding a grin. "And Mom's sure we've passed."

Sevin arches a brow. "Since when did you agree with Mom?"

"Since my only living sister set off on a raft, paddling out to a certain death," he retorts.

"Exactly," she says, yanking her hands away and crossing her arms. "You're just saying this to get me back to Treasure Island."

Fyve thinks over her words. That's definitely the reason he said that. But he's also realized exactly how important these Trials are to his sister. She's willing to die for them. Just like Coal. Tomorrow Land may or may not exist. The ship may or may not exist. But they both represent hope. And Sevin's not willing to live without it.

Fyve can't be the one to take that away from her. And if he really does love her, he needs to go one step further than that.

"No, I mean it." He leans forward, holding her gaze with his. "If we don't pass this Trial, I'll come with you."

"What?" she asks in a whisper.

"You heard me. If we don't pass, we'll go out on this raft together and find Tomorrow Land."

Sevin leaps with such enthusiasm that the raft rocks danger-ously as she lands in his arms. Fyve spreads out his legs and supports her weight as he chuckles, enjoying her exuberant hug too much to do much else.

"Thank you, Fyve," she says in a choked voice. "I really do love you."

He squeezes her tight. "I love you, too."

She pulls back, joy making her young face beautiful. "You really mean it? We'll go out, just like Mom does?"

Not quite believing this himself, he nods. "That's what I said." If that's what it takes to keep Sevin not just safe, but as close to happy as one can get on Treasure Island, then he'll do it.

She beams. "We'll find Tomorrow Land, just you watch."

Rather than answering, he picks up the paddle. "We'd better get back. Gratitude will be soon."

Sevin nods, adjusting herself in the center of the raft. Fyve jams the paddle in the water, glancing down at the large, thick piece of blue plastic his mother has kept safe all these years just so she can do this—spend endless hours on a futile mission. One Fyve just committed himself to doing, too.

He grits his teeth as he focuses on getting them back to land. For the first time since the Trials began, he's desperately hoping he passes.

If he doesn't, he's just promised to become the one person he's never wanted to be.

His mother.

HALO

"There'll be no room for us in here soon." Halo points to the pile of gifts stacked up against one of the walls in their hut.

Ajax grins proudly at the offerings the people of Treasure Island have been bringing for their father. It's significantly increased since the beginning of the Trials. "And you think that's a problem?"

"I do, actually." Halo throws out her hands. "Why do you keep accepting them? It won't make any difference to the elimination. Our father is literally unable to be bribed."

Ajax goes to the stash and steps around a parcel of soap blocks to pick up some dried rats wrapped in cloth. He holds the precious meat to his nose, then scoops up a wide-brimmed hat and sticks it on his head.

"I accept the gifts for Cloud," he says. "For my child. They can live well while they wait for my return. It's the least I can do."

"The gifts are for Dad," she points out. "Maybe he'll take them on the ship."

"And leave his grandchild to starve?" Ajax takes off the hat and puts it on Halo. "The great Elijah would never do that."

Halo remains quiet. After Coal's death, she's not certain what her father is or isn't capable of.

"Besides," says Ajax. "Maybe Terra will look favorably on anyone giving Dad a gift? It shows how much they really want this."

Halo shrugs, knowing full well that the people giving these gifts can't spare what they're offering. Is that what Terra wants? For the people to have nothing, so that one man can have plenty? That doesn't seem right. If her father really loves his people, shouldn't the gifts be flowing the other way around?

"Oh, Cloud adores these." Ajax picks up a jar of dried crickets and shakes it. "Lots of protein for the baby."

Halo takes off the hat and goes to her brother, putting a hand on his arm. "You know, if you're so sure the ship will return here for everyone left behind, then you could always choose to stay here with Cloud and wait."

Ajax's eyes flare and he shakes his head. "It's not up to me. It's up to Terra. We still have Gratitude tonight. If Terra doesn't want me on that ship, she'll eliminate me."

"But what do *you* want, Ajax?" Halo locks eyes with him, aware she'd asked this same question of Fyve, although their situations are quite different. Fyve wants to stay behind because of the people he loves. Ajax wants to leave regardless.

"I want what Terra wants." He glares at her, clutching the crickets and rats to his chest as he walks toward the door. "I'll see you at Gratitude."

Halo lets out a sigh as he slams it, causing the walls to shake. She's tired of people hiding behind Terra to explain their actions. At what point do people need to take responsibility for themselves? Ajax isn't staying behind because, quite simply, he doesn't want to. He's choosing a better life for himself over providing one for his child.

An overwhelming urge to see Fyve seeps into her every cell. He may not be her blood, but he's the best person she's ever met. He's worth a hundred of her brother. And the way he threw today's Trial, made it clear he has no intention of getting on the ship. Which means that soon they'll be separated.

She walks to the door, accepting she got everything wrong. Rather than putting distance between them, she needs to make the most of the time she has left with Fyve. Surely, it's better to have loved someone for a short time than never to have loved them at all? But is that what this feeling she has is? Is this what love feels like?

She runs down the village road, wanting to reach Fyve before he leaves for Gratitude. Maybe she can see how his breeding rats are getting along while she's here. The gestation is short for rats, so with any luck she'll get to see some babies before she leaves. That's assuming she makes the cut. With twice as many teens still in the Trials as places on the ship, anything could still happen.

Halo taps on the frame of Fyve's door and waits. It's his mother who pulls back the cloth that acts as a door.

"Hi." Halo smiles, warmly. "I'm here to see Fyve."

"He's not here." Dee returns her smile, although hers is laced with concern. "He's out looking for Sevin."

"She ran off?" Halo glances back down the street. "Was she upset about what happened in the Trial?"

Dee shakes her head. "She was upset with me."

"Oh." Halo is curious but doesn't pry.

"I wanted my children to have strength for the next Trial," she says, drawing Halo into their hut.

Halo looks around, feeling uncomfortable with how much she has compared to Fyve's family. Her own hut might be small, but it's a palace next to this tent-like structure with only a few possessions scattered about. There are two sleeping mats, and she can only assume Fyve shares one of them with Sevin. It's no wonder he's so protective of her. She's more like his child than his sister.

"I did what needed to be done." Dee holds up two skinned rats. "Sevin was upset. Fyve was furious. They didn't understand."

Halo lets out a long breath, devastated for everyone involved. "Those two rats could have become eight, then twenty, then fifty, if only you'd waited a few weeks."

"But my children don't have a few weeks," says Dee. "In a few weeks, they'll have sailed away on the ship. I can breed rats after that if I want to. They need the sustenance now."

"How can you be so sure they'll be on the ship?" Halo asks. "Their barrel tipped. There's a good chance they'll both be eliminated tonight."

Dee shakes her head. "My children are the best of the best on this entire island. Terra knows their worth. She won't leave them behind."

Halo frowns, not able to reconcile the loving mother she sees before her with the version Fyve talks about. It's clear she killed the rats thinking she was doing the right thing. And the way she'd cared for Halo after the second Trial showed just how tender she can be.

"I know what you're thinking." Dee sets down the dead rats. "That I'm a terrible mother."

"I was actually thinking the opposite." Halo reaches out to touch her on the arm. "I can see how much you love your children."

"Fyve can't see it." Dee blinks back tears. "He thinks when I go out looking for Tomorrow Land that I'm forgetting about today. He thinks the present is more important than the future, but I disagree."

Halo nods.

"I've lost a lot of children," says Dee, looking years older as she speaks with the weight of her pain. "I can't just sit here, happy in this moment, if it means I might lose the only two I have left. I have to think of tomorrow, even if Fyve hates me for it."

"He doesn't hate you," Halo quickly reassures, even though she can't speak for him on this. "I don't think he understands, that's all. Have you ever told him what you just told me?"

Dee puts her hand on Halo's. "He's not ready to listen."

Halo wonders if perhaps Dee understands her son a whole lot better than he understands her.

"I'm going to go to Gratitude," Halo says. "Maybe Fyve will be there with Sevin."

Dee nods. "I hope so."

Halo leaves and takes the road toward the beach, keen to get Gratitude over and done with. Is Dee's confidence that her children will make it through misplaced? Because she's right that Fyve and Sevin are the best that Treasure Island has to offer. But will that be enough? After all, Fyve had clearly thrown the Trial. Is that the kind of person Terra wants aboard her ship?

There's a stone on the path and Halo kicks it, expelling some of her frustration into the sharp movement. The contact stings her toes, but she chases after the stone and kicks it again. A week ago, her life was simple, mapped out before her with the most exciting thing being finding a new part for her motor or the tree she'd built. And now she's fallen for a guy who wants the exact opposite of everything she does. And he comes with a little sister who wants everything the same...

"Urgh!" She kicks the stone again and it hits the sand.

Walking down onto the beach, she joins the gathering crowd, standing off to one side, disappointed not to see Fyve or Sevin here. She's sure they can still be eliminated even if they don't turn up. In fact, it probably makes it more certain.

"Hey there."

She looks across to see Striker beside her, grinning.

"Hey." She returns his smile. "How are you?"

"Confident." He puffs out his chest.

"So was the team who were eliminated in the first Trial," she points out.

"That was different." He glances toward Zake, who seems to have adjusted to his fate by being even more obnoxious to those around him. "They were a pack of assholes."

Halo lets out a small gasp at his language.

"Sorry." Striker holds up his palms. "But it's accurate, isn't it?"

Halo laughs. "Yeah, I'll give you that."

"We made a good team," says Striker. "We should pair up in the next Trial."

"We don't even know if it will be teams." She shrugs, trying not to commit to anything before she hears who passed.

There's a tap on her back and she turns to see Sevin and Fyve behind her.

"We're here," says Sevin, somehow knowing that's exactly who Halo had been waiting for.

"Hi." Fyve looks at Halo as if daring her to glance away.

She holds his gaze, wishing she'd been able to find him alone like she'd tried to. There's so much that needs to be said, and here they can say nothing.

"Right," says Striker. "Why didn't you tell me?"

"Tell you what?" Halo turns to him.

"That you're already taken." He rolls his eyes. "By him."

Had that one look she'd shared with Fyve really told him all that?

"Women are not property," Sevin points out. "But yes, Halo loves Fyve, so you can rack off."

"Sevin!" Fyve and Halo exclaim in unison.

A flush rises to Halo's cheeks as three words reverberate inside her mind.

Halo loves Fyve.

Is that true? It's certainly starting to feel like it.

189

Striker pats Fyve roughly on his arm. "Lucky guy."

Fyve doesn't seem to know how to respond to this, but he doesn't complain, which Halo takes as a positive.

She opens her mouth to stop Striker as he stalks away but closes it again when she realizes she's quite happy for him to leave.

"My people," Halo's father calls from the beach. "Thank you for gathering on this glorious evening to thank Terra for all she does. The sun is getting low, so let's get straight to our elimination so we can focus on expressing our Gratitude."

There's a low murmur of agreement in the crowd. Everyone is keen to get onto the elimination, but not for the reasons her father's suggesting.

"My instructions are simple tonight," her father says. "If your barrel successfully made it back to the scales with the correct weight, you are safe from elimination."

"That's you, Halo," says Sevin. "You're safe."

Halo lets out half a breath, trying to make herself feel happier. Safe is what she wanted. But now it doesn't feel enough. She needs to hear the rest of the announcement.

"If you didn't make it back to the scales, or you had the wrong weight, you are eliminated," her father says, and a groan echoes across the crowd as several teams realize that includes them.

"What about my sister?" Zake calls out. "What about teams that got to the scales but tipped over before they could get weighed?"

Halo's father looks directly at Fyve as he answers Zake's question. "There were four teams in that situation. Terra is satisfied that three of the teams had the correct weight before they tipped and would like them to continue through to the next round."

"We might still be in," Sevin whispers to Fyve, her face lighting up.

"Shh." He tilts his head as he listens.

Halo's father raises his hands to regain his people's attention. "The final team to be eliminated is Farrah, Triad and Sola."

Fyve reaches down and hugs his sister, genuine joy caressing his face. And men say women are confusing! Halo had been certain he'd thrown the Trial on purpose. So, why is he celebrating having made it through?

Fyve stretches out an arm and pulls Halo into the hug with Sevin who wraps one of her skinny arms around Halo's back.

"Sevin and I reached an understanding," Fyve says, by way of explanation.

Halo smiles into his chest, not sure she actually gets it, but pleased regardless. Maybe she'll get to hold onto Fyve beyond the next few days or weeks. Maybe, just like his mother, she can dare to dream of the future, instead of being forced to make the most of today.

Fyve loosens his grip and Halo steps back.

"I want to be on your team for the next Trial," she says.

"What about your brother?" Sevin asks.

"What about him?" Halo counters. "Not all brothers are built the same. You got lucky with yours."

Fyve flashes her a smile, and she drowns just a little in the dark pools of his eyes.

The sun hits the horizon sending out golden rays of light and the people let out a gasp, still moved by the extraordinary beauty of nature, no matter how many times they see this spectacular sight.

"Praise Terra," says Halo, unsure if this is habit or genuine gratitude for all the wondrous moments of her life.

"Terra is great," a girl nearby replies.

They watch as the sun disappears, and the crowd breaks apart as the people turn to each other to discuss the results of the elimination.

"Oh," says Sevin, reaching into her pocket and holding out a fuse. "I nearly forgot. I found this earlier. Is it useful?"

"It could be." Halo scruffs Sevin's hair. "Why don't we go and check?"

"Can I come?" Fyve asks with an exaggerated pout.

Halo laughs. "As long as you're good."

Sevin skips ahead, knowing the way to the falling-down shed in the back section of the village that Halo uses as her workshop.

As they set off to follow, Halo's hand brushes Fyve's and he immediately entwines his fingers with hers.

"You were distant today," he says.

"So were you." She squeezes his hand gently, enjoying the warmth of his touch. "I was scared."

"Of what?" He looks genuinely concerned.

"You," she says. "I'm scared to get close to you, in case…"

He slows his steps a little to glance across at her and she lets out a long sigh, wondering if Sevin might be right. Does she love this guy?

"In case we're separated?" he asks.

She nods. "It hurts to lose people."

Fyve purses his lips, and she knows he's thinking of Coal. "I know you saw what I did with the barrel in the Trial."

"And I know why you did it," she replies, before he can jump to any conclusions. "You did it for Sevin."

He nods. "I did. But I've now realized I can't hold her back. She's determined to find Tomorrow Land and I owe it to her to help her with that."

"You know you don't owe anybody anything, don't you?" She wishes he could understand that. But just as her own brother is selfish, Fyve is the definition of selfless.

"I do owe it to her," he says, unable to see her point. "Someone has to owe that girl something. So much has been taken from her already."

"No more than has been taken from you," she says. "You love her more than you love yourself. That's admirable."

"Maybe you're right." He lets go of her hand to drape his arm around her shoulder. "At least someone understands me."

"Your mother understands you better than you think she does." Halo bites down on her lip, regretting her words the moment she says them.

"You've been talking to her again?" Fyve's hand falls from her shoulder.

"I was looking for you!" She throws out her hands. "Your house seemed like the logical place to start."

"She's not the saint you think she is," he says, with a bitter note to his tone.

"Nobody is," she points out. "Not even my father."

He laughs at this, his lips finally heading skyward. "Believe me, I don't think your father's a saint."

"What about me then?" Halo asks, hating that she's fishing for confirmation that he feels as strongly about her as she does about him. "What do you think of me?"

"I think you were appropriately named." He pretends to straighten something above her head. "Sorry, Angel, your halo was a bit crooked."

"My mom used to call me that sometimes." She gives him a sad smile.

"Oh, sorry." He looks aghast.

"No!" She loops her hand in the crook of his arm. "I like it. It's nice to hear you say it."

Sevin reaches Halo's ramshackle workshop and enters. Halo follows, smiling at the way Fyve needs to duck his head to get through the door. It's going to be cramped inside with the three of them.

"Where is it?" asks Sevin, looking around. "Did somebody steal it?"

A sick feeling winds its way through Halo's gut as she stares at the empty space on the floor where her motor should be. There are drag marks on the ground heading to the door. She's been working on this project since she was younger than Sevin, collecting parts and painstakingly fitting them together. Years of hard work have just been extinguished!

"Who would do that?" Fyve clenches his fists. "I bet it was Zake. That guy's got it coming to him!"

He turns to leave, but Halo catches him by his shirt and pulls him back.

"It wasn't Zake," she says, the truth settling in her stomach like a stone.

"Then who?" he asks. "Who else would do this to you?"

"The man who's not a saint." She crosses her arms, trying to hold herself together. "My father did this."

FYVE

*H*alo looks as if she's slowly crumbling. Her mouth turns down. Her green eyes fracture. Her belief in her father, the leader of Treasure Island, shatters before Fyve's eyes.

He turns to Sevin. "Go and see if you can track where the motor was taken."

She hesitates, her gaze darting to Halo, and Fyve tenses. Now isn't the time for his sister to assert her independence. He doubts very much that she wants to hear what's about to tumble from Halo's mouth. But then Sevin nods, and with a last glance at Halo, darts out the door.

"Why do you think Elijah did this?" Fyve asks quietly.

Halo's lip trembles. "Because I suggested we use the motor to move the entire island."

Fyve blinks in surprise. "The whole of Treasure Island? To find Tomorrow Land?" She was trying to save everyone, not just a chosen hundred?

"Yeah." She tightens the arms wrapped around her waist. "He said it was heresy. That I'm going against Terra."

Fyve is still struggling to comprehend this. Elijah accused his own daughter of heresy? He thought Halo's brilliance is a threat to Terra?

He takes a step forward and tilts Halo's chin up so she can see his eyes. "Your father's wrong."

She draws in a shuddering breath. "I think it's more than that," she says, her eyes pooling with pain. "I…I'm not sure Terra is even real, some days."

The moment the admission escapes, the rest of Halo's body gives out. Fyve catches her, even though he's reeling from the same words that have echoed in his own heart, but never had the courage to be more than a shadow. He hauls her against him and cradles her, sobs shuddering through her slender frame.

Halo clings to him as hot tears soak his shirt, burying her face in his neck as if she desperately wants to hide from what she just said. He bands one arm around her back while he spears his other hand into her hair, holding her tightly. "I feel the same," he murmurs against her ear. "The Terra I believed in would've wanted to save all of us."

That Terra would've watched Coal's face as his gaze first landed on Tomorrow Land. She would've gloried in the wonder. The joy. She would've witnessed Fyve's family delighting and celebrating alongside every other person on Treasure Island.

His words trigger another round of shuddering sobs from Halo, but these ones are different. They're not sobs of heartbreak. They're ones of relief. She pulls back enough to gaze up at him, green eyes swimming with tears and something else. The same knowledge coursing through Fyve.

They're connected. In ways they'd never realized.

And they're not alone.

This kiss is an inevitability. An affirmation of what they've just discovered. A promise of what it could mean. Their mouths crash together and open, suddenly keen to explore that. Their lips slide breathlessly, their tongues explore hungrily. Fyve dips his head lower as Halo pushes up on tiptoes, both ensuring more pressure. More heat.

More evidence that beauty does indeed exist.

It's a kiss that began bathed in tears. A kiss that ends with two soft smiles. They pull apart, panting a little as their foreheads rest against each other's.

"Your father's wrong," Fyve says again, wanting to make sure the words weren't lost in their moment of passion.

"I know," she says heavily, then sighs. "So, who's right?"

"You always ask the hard questions, don't you?" he asks, grinning.

A rueful smile tips up Halo's just-kissed lips. "It seems so."

It's Fyve's turn to sigh. "We need to get on that ship to get answers, don't we?"

She nods. "According to my father, Terra is sending it."

Fyve's hands slide down Halo's arms and he threads his fingers through hers. "I need to know," he says, realizing it's the truth. His life has been defined by loss, and he needs for that to make sense.

Is Terra real? And if so, whose version? And what does she want for the people of Treasure Island?

Halo's fingers tighten around his. "So do I."

They stare at each other for long seconds, determination cementing the air around them. There are two more Trials, and they need to pass both of them.

The sound of rapid footsteps reaches them and a moment later, Sevin appears in the doorway, not looking in the least surprised to find them close and holding hands. "Halo, I found it." She twists her fingers in her shirt. "I'm so sorry."

A calmness settles over Halo. "Where is it?"

"He threw it in the ocean," Sevin says miserably. Halo gasps, as if she didn't expect Elijah to go that far. Sevin wrings her hands even harder, stretching her shirt until it looks like it's going to tear. "I tried to pull it out, but it's too heavy."

Halo rushes to slip an arm around her shoulder. "You didn't need to do that. You're right, it's far too heavy. And the seawater isn't good for your skin."

"Show us where it is," Fyve says, his voice like flint. "We'll get it out together."

Halo shakes her head. "You don't need to—"

"We need to try," he says resolutely.

Sevin ducks back out of the hut and they follow a line gouged through the sand directly to the beach. Even though the sun has sunk below the horizon, the motor wouldn't have been hard to find. Elijah took the shortest route he could to dispose of it.

Fyve strides straight into the gently breaking waves, ignoring the warm prickly sensation of it against his ankles, then calves, then thighs.

"It's right about there—"

Sevin's words are cut off when Fyve's foot hits something hard, eliciting a low curse. He grips his toe, talking through gritted teeth, "Found it," he calls back.

The sound of sloshing water alerts him that someone's approaching. He can just make out Halo's outline when she speaks. "It's heavy. You'll need two people to carry it."

He squats down, keeping his mouth closed as water sloshes up to his chin, and hauls it up. "I've got it," he grunts, hoping she doesn't notice the slight stagger as he makes his way back to the beach.

"I can help, Fyve," she protests.

But he keeps walking, his legs slicing through the water, glad Halo can't see his face in the dark. She's right. It is heavy, but he's determined to do this himself. He doubts Striker would be able to carry this motor single-handedly, through acid seawater no less.

Fyve drops it the moment they're past the reach of the waves and it lands with a muted thud. His biceps ache, and it feels like something dug into his forearm, but the brush of Halo's hand on his shoulder makes it all worth it.

"Thank you," she says softly.

He clears his throat. "No big deal."

"It is to me."

Halo squats down, not giving him a chance to answer, and he's once again glad for the cover of darkness. His cheeks feel like they've been dipped in seawater.

"It's already corroded," Halo says unhappily, running her hands over the surfaces almost tenderly. "Who knows if it was going to run, but now..."

Sevin squats down, too, squinting hard. "We can fix it."

Halo's shoulders have drooped again. She reaches out and runs a forlorn finger down something that looks like a fan.

"We won't have time," says Fyve. "We'll be on the ship on our way to Tomorrow Land."

"We will?" Sevin gasps.

Halo pushes to her feet slowly. "Yes, we will," she says, her voice once more full of the promise they'd made in the workshop.

Sevin leaps to her feet and wraps her arms around his neck. "Coal would be so proud," she whispers.

His heart swells and constricts simultaneously. "Of you, too," he says gruffly. He pulls away, clearing his throat when he's pretty sure he sees Halo's teeth glint thanks to a smile. These girls are going to make him soft. "Let's get this somewhere safe."

"I don't think so," says a hard voice.

Fyve spins around as he recognizes the owner. "Zake."

"That's me," he says, a sneer making it sound like the words just came out his nose. "And you ain't taking that thing nowhere."

Fyve takes a step forward, anger hardening his muscles, when Halo plants a hand on his chest. "He can take it."

"But—"

"You're working for my father, aren't you, Zake?" Halo asks.

Anger coils even tighter through Fyve as he remembers Zake throwing the ocean water at Halo in the second Trial.

"I'm helping Terra," he snaps back. "And your father is rewarding me for it." There's the sound of a soft footstep as he moves closer. "And he told me Terra said this hunk a metal needs to stay in the sea."

Fyve takes his own step forward but Halo's hand pushes harder against his chest. "Then it's yours," she says, her voice equally as sharp. "I hope you drop it on your toes."

"Or your face," mutters Sevin.

Zake lets out a low growl and the desire to cut it short—possibly by dropping the motor on his head—swells through Fyve.

"Come on," says Halo, now tugging on his arm. "We need our rest for the Trial tomorrow."

The snarl is effectively cut off by Halo's words and Fyve almost finds himself smiling. He drops his arm around her shoulders and grabs Sevin's wrist with his other hand. "Good point."

"Yeah," says Sevin. "And it'll probably be busy on the ship, too."

They walk away, a string of curses staining the night air. They're almost at the edge of the village before Fyve stops. They may have shut up Zake, but there was no win back there. He takes Halo by the shoulders. "Why did you do that? We could've got the motor back."

She shakes her head, her hair brushing the back of his hands. "What for? I doubt I could ever have got it going, anyway."

"You could've," says Sevin on Fyve's right. "You're smart."

"And you've worked so hard on it," adds Fyve. The motor meant something to Halo, and her father knew that by throwing it away he was sending a message to his daughter. Even though she's now determined to be chosen in the Trials for her own reasons, not because she's the daughter of the great Elijah, losing it would hurt.

"What you said is true, Fyve," she says, wrapping her hands over his. "We won't need it. We're going to be on that ship."

Sevin giggles. "All waving to Zake."

"I'll be giving him a different sort of hand signal," Fyve mutters.

Halo giggles, too. "So, we're in agreement, the motor can dissolve at the bottom of the ocean." She steps in and embraces Fyve before he can object. "And we really do need to get some rest for the Trial tomorrow."

Instinctively clasping her back, he feels the tension easing in his body. Halo is fast becoming his new equilibrium. One he's finding it hard to let go of. A loud yawn has them releasing each other with a soft laugh.

Fyve turns to Sevin. "Come on, let's get you back to the hut."

She mumbles an agreement and not giving himself too much time to think, Fyve presses a quick kiss to Halo's cheek. He feels her smile and the sentiment echoes somewhere in his chest.

Halo leaves for her hut while Fyve leads a tired Sevin back to theirs. He's pretty sure she's asleep before her head hits the mat, and he can't blame her. Today was intense. Failing the Trial, then taking the raft out. Gratitude, then discovering the motor gone. He thinks that's what used to be called a roller-coaster.

But despite his own exhaustion dragging at his every cell, Fyve sneaks back out of their hut.

He's not letting that motor disintegrate like every other dream on this island.

As he makes his way back through the village, Fyve hopes he doesn't have to wait too long for Zake to fall asleep, and he guarantees the lazy scumball will do exactly that. Although by the time Fyve reaches the beach, he considers just knocking the guy out. He'd quite enjoy doing it, to be honest. He's just decided that's what he'll do when Zake's soft snores ripple along the beach.

Disappointed, Fyve takes a wide berth of the grating sound and slips back into the water. Walking far more cautiously this time, he finds the motor even closer. Seems Zake couldn't be bothered carrying it very far. Fyve hauls it out of the ocean for the second time and carries it back to shore. The metal feels rougher and more jagged after even longer in the acidic seawater, and he grits his teeth as he trudges back to his hut. Elijah probably has damaged this thing beyond repair.

Yet, Fyve carries it all the way back to their hut. Despite the weight that grows with each step. Despite the tiredness that multiplies with each second. He even goes to the effort of tucking it in the half-barrel they'd dug into the ground for the rat breeding. He's just sliding the lid on when Sevin stirs.

"You brought the motor back, didn't you?" she mumbles sleepily.

Fyve quickly curls around her, not wanting to wake their mother, too. "Yes, I did," he whispers. "Now, sleep."

She relaxes with a sigh. "Good."

As Sevin's breathing evens out again, Fyve feels his own muscles unwind gratefully. He closes his eyes, wondering to himself why he bothered rescuing the motor when he no longer intends on staying. Maybe because it's a symbol of hope in some ways. A smile hovers on his lips. Perhaps one day Bloo will find it, or Jett or Rubee, and be inspired in the same way Halo was.

The smile fades. He'll never know because he won't be here. He meant what he said—he's determined to find the truth.

About Tomorrow Land.

And Terra.

HALO

*H*alo rises early and leaves before her father wakes. Ajax had spent his first night with Cloud in the hut they'd built for themselves, which was a relief as Halo hadn't had to talk to him when she'd returned after finding her dreams submerged in the ocean.

All she'd wanted was to find a way for her people to search for a better Tomorrow, without having to leave the Today they'd built for themselves. It's possible to move the island given they're not pinned down to land. They already move in the ocean currents. At least a motor would've given them control over a destiny that's always been handed down to them instead.

But it looks like Terra remains firmly in charge of their future.

Halo takes the road toward her workshop, not wanting to retrieve her years of hard work, but just to sit in silence for a few moments and accept its loss.

She could hear her father muttering all night through the flimsy wall that separates them. She'd strained her ears, trying to get some clues for today's Trial, but it was no use. It seems Terra likes to speak more than she likes to listen. All Halo had managed to hear was her father agreeing to whatever it was that he was being told.

Which means one of only two things. Either Terra exists, or her father has completely lost his mind.

Reaching the beach in the early morning light, Halo steps onto the prickly sand and sees a dark figure asleep. *Zake.* Her adrenaline spikes as the fear she'd felt when he'd attacked her floods her system.

She walks further down the beach, drawing in deep breaths and hating that someone can provoke such intense feelings. If she's going to board a ship and sail out into the ocean, she needs to learn how to protect herself, not just from the elements, but from humankind itself. Maybe Fyve can teach her how to fight? Although, if she's honest, there are a whole host of other things she'd prefer him to teach her. That kiss they'd shared in her workshop had produced far more sparks than her motor would ever have been capable of.

She focuses on how she felt, and the fear of Zake slowly leaves her body, being replaced by all things Fyve.

"Halo!" a young voice calls.

She turns, expecting to see Sevin following her. But, instead, she sees Justice.

"Hi." Halo smiles, unsure what Zake's little sister could possibly want. Just when she'd managed to push him out of her head, too. "What are you doing out so early?"

"It's my favorite part of the day. Look! It's here." Justice points toward the ocean, pulling Halo to a stop.

Halo quickly spins, squinting to see if Terra's ship has finally arrived. Except, there's nothing but calm ocean and the tip of the golden orb of the sun peeking over the horizon. This is what Justice has come to watch. The sunrise. A timeless symbol of new beginnings and hope.

"I watch it every morning," says Justice wistfully.

"It's beautiful." Halo takes a moment to appreciate just how spectacular this sight is. The light dances off the mirrored surface of the rust-colored water. Giant leatherskin sharks circle in the distance, hunting for breakfast, while a flock of ravens swoop, hoping to collect any leftover scraps. There's not a cloud in the sky, an indicator that it's going to be another scorching hot day.

"Gratitude should be held in the morning." Justice tips back her head as golden rays of light streak across her face. "Isn't it more important to say hello, than to say farewell?"

"Goodbyes are important," says Halo, wondering if they're still talking about the sun. "If we make it through these Trials, we'll be saying goodbye to everyone we know."

"I don't like goodbyes." Justice shrugs. "The only person I cared about is dead. And I never got to say goodbye to her."

"Your mother?" asks Halo, aware that Justice and Zake live with their father.

Justice purses her lips and nods, her pain evident without words to confirm it.

"We actually have quite a bit in common," says Halo. "I lost my mother, too,"

"I know." Justice seems to be resisting rolling her eyes. "Everyone here knows everything about you."

"Not everything," Halo replies, quickly.

"Tell me one thing about you that I don't know," Justice dares.

Halo lets out a long sigh. There are so many things she could tell this girl. But none of them seem any of her business. She's not used to having conversations like this.

"I'm scared of not making it onto the ship," says Halo.

This time Justice does roll her eyes. "Everyone's scared about that."

"I'm also scared of making it onto the ship," she says, truthfully. "You know, facing the unknown and all that."

Justice tears her gaze from the glory of the sunrise to look at Halo. "Then we have nothing in common."

"What do you mean?" Halo is surprised by the harshness in the girl's tone. "We live with our father and brother. We both lost our mother. We're both trying to pass the Tri—"

"Your life is easy!" Justice spits out. "If it wasn't, you wouldn't be afraid to leave it."

"I...all I was saying was..." Halo's words float out to the ocean. Maybe Justice is right. Her life on Treasure Island is easy compared to most. Is it fair then that she takes up a place on the ship when someone like Justice could be given a second chance?

"It doesn't matter, anyway," says Justice. "You'll pass the Trials, no matter what."

Halo groans. "Not this again. I swear it's not like that. My father tells me nothing. I have no advantage at all. I'm desperate to know what today's Trial is about."

"See, we're nothing alike." Justice takes a step away then sighs and looks back at her. "Because I know."

Halo's jaw falls. "How could you possib—"

"Teams of four. We're building something." Justice smirks. "Most likely something that floats."

"Wait!" says Halo when Justice takes another step. "How do you know this?"

"I always know," she says. "Everyone always knows. My father told me when he got home from setting everything up. Seems he wants to get rid of me just as much as I want to go."

Halo's jaw drops as Justice walks away. So, all this time people have thought she's had an advantage in the Trials when it's been the other way around! The people who've been helping her father have also been helping their children.

She continues walking in the same direction Justice had gone, heading toward the section of beach where the Trials are being held. Now that the sun is up, there are a few others doing the same thing, keen to get a glimpse of what they're in for today. Those who don't already know, of course... It won't be long before this whole beach is full.

In the distance are piles of various shaped objects set up along the sand. She does a quick count. For teams of four, the number seems correct. And it most definitely looks like they'll be required to build something. Which means Justice was right. But she'd said they'd have to build something that floats. That bit can't possibly be accurate. The ocean is far too dangerous, even on a calm day like today. If a boat isn't made just right, it will get eaten right up, if not by the acid in the water, then the leatherskins themselves. Perhaps they have to build something to push out into the water and see whose structure takes the longest to break apart?

Halo's mind whirls with options of how to best get an object to float. It's basic science. If something's more dense than water, it will sink. If something is less dense than water, it will float. She thinks of her motor and how it had sat on the ocean floor. That had been as dense as the person her father had asked to dispose of it for him. It's no wonder it had sunk.

She gets a little closer and sees the piles are made up of an assortment of items including steel poles, pieces of wood, tires, sheets of tin, concrete blocks, and sections of fiberglass. Each pile is different, like in the first Trial. This challenge is going to be just as much about which stack you choose as how you use it.

More people are gathering on the beach, their stomachs as empty as their curiosity is primed. Striker is there and Halo decides to approach him. Now that he knows she's with Fyve, hopefully he'll drop some of his bravado and behave more like a regular person. Apart from the arrogance he possesses, he does seem to be a decent guy. If they really are in groups of four, then they could use him on their team.

But before she can get to Striker, Ajax is by her side.

"Which pile should we go for?" he asks. "We don't want to get stuck with the one with the concrete blocks."

Halo hesitates. When she'd pictured her team, it had been with Fyve and Sevin, not her brother. They're getting toward the end of the Trials now and she can't afford to jeopardize her chances just to be nice to a sibling who's made it clear he has little respect for her.

"I'm not teaming up with you," she says plainly.

The hurt on his face is palpable and she winces. Despite her complicated feelings for Ajax, she doesn't want to cause him pain.

"We need to divide up," she explains. "To reduce our chances of both of us being eliminated at once."

He pulls back his shoulders. "I was thinking we should do that."

"How's Cloud?" she asks, changing the subject. "Was it nice to be in your own home?"

Nodding slowly, he takes a step away. "Yeah, it was good." Without saying anything else, he walks off, no doubt to scout for a team.

Pushing down feelings of guilt, Halo makes her way over to Striker.

"Let me guess." He smiles to see her. "You've seen the light and ditched Fyve for a better option."

She smirks. "Not quite."

"Worse luck." He grimaces. "Just as long as he knows how lucky he is. You're quite the catch, being Elijah's daughter and all."

"I'll make sure I tell Fyve that," she says, knowing it had been no contest. Fyve's probably the only person on the island who sees her bloodline as a negative rather than a reason to be with her. Which means, he actually likes her for who she is as a person.

"I've just done the math," says Striker, scanning the piles lining the beach. "Looks like teams of four."

Halo nods, not saying she'd already figured that out. "Ajax is looking for a team."

"No offence to your brother," Striker says. "But he was pretty useless in the last Trial. I'm strong. You're smart. We make a good team. Sadly, your brother is neither of those things."

Halo's eyes widen and she wonders why it feels okay for her to think these things about her family, but it stings when pointed out by someone else.

"I'll have to check with Fyve and Sevin," she says. "I'm teaming with them today."

"They'll want me," Striker says, flexing his biceps. "I mean, who wouldn't? Other than you, of course."

She laughs. He might be arrogant, but he sure takes rejection well.

"What do you think we're going to need to do this time?" she asks.

Striker points out to the ocean, and she sees something she hadn't noticed before. There's a buoy bobbing in the water about two hundred yards out.

"My guess is we're building a raft," he says. "We'll have to row out to that buoy and back."

"But that's impossible." She looks from the piles of trash to the buoy. "Nothing will hold together for that long."

"I'm never wrong." Striker smirks smugly. "You'll see."

A flurry of movement catches Halo's eye, and she turns to see her father walking down the beach, his people surrounding him like a human shield. A few of them are desperately stating their case as to why they shouldn't be eliminated. Others are listening intently, hoping to pick up a clue about how to pass. It's a spectacle that's been growing with each Trial that takes place, just like the gifts that have been appearing on their doorstep.

Fyve and Sevin step onto the beach and Halo lifts a hand to get their attention. Fyve breaks into a smile, then sees who she's standing with, and his expression shifts to a frown. If only he knew what little competition Striker poses. Nobody in all of her tomorrows could ever compete with what she has with Fyve at this very moment.

"How are you?" Fyve pulls Halo into a hug, and she rests her head on his chest. "Did you manage to sleep?"

"I'm okay," she says truthfully. "I've just been speculating with Striker about the Trial."

Striker scoffs at this. "Not speculating. I've been telling Halo how it's going to run."

"And how do you know that?" Sevin jams her hands on her hips. "Is Terra talking to you now, too?"

"It's pretty obvious." Striker points at the piles lined up on the beach. "The number of piles means teams of four." Then he points out to the buoy. "We'll be building rafts, going to the buoy and back."

Fyve lets go of Halo and nods slowly as he takes everything in. But Sevin doesn't seem so eager to readily agree with her brother's rival.

"You don't know any of that for sure." Sevin crosses her arms tightly. "We could be in teams of eight with a Trial that has two rounds. We might have to build a weapon that can fire something that hits the buoy. Or we could have to choose which one of us will go out on the raft. There are a lot of variables."

Halo shakes her head, impressed at the way Sevin's young mind works. She could do great things one day if only given the chance.

But Striker seems to find Sevin amusing, and he playfully pats her on the shoulder. "Don't doubt the Striker. I was just telling Halo that I'm never wrong."

"Well, we're about to find out." Sevin juts her chin toward Halo's father, who's now standing alone on the beach with his arms held out wide.

"My people." He pauses, waiting until he has everyone's

undivided attention. Halo notices how tired he looks, which isn't really surprising given the kind of night he had. "Thank you for honoring Terra by gathering for our fourth Trial."

"Praise Terra," calls out one of the competitors, keen to impress the all-seeing-but-never-seen judge of whatever it is they're about to do.

"Terra is good," echo a few others, not wanting to be outdone.

The great Elijah smiles warmly, stirring up a whirlpool of complicated feelings inside Halo. This is the man who raised her. The one who's always cared for her. Yet...he destroyed years of her work last night without any shadow of guilt. And all for what? To ensure that her future is filled with the dreams he has for her, without any regard for what she wants for herself.

"Today, you'll be working in teams of four," he announces.

Striker coughs, nudging Sevin with his elbow while she stares directly ahead, pretending he's not there.

"This is a Trial of trust," her father continues. "Your team will divide in half. Two of you will be required to build a raft while the other two wait at the shoreline. They will be required to row that raft out to the buoy, circle around it, then come back to shore. Any team who successfully completes this is guaranteed to be safe from elimination."

"Told you so," whispers Striker.

"You said all of us would go out to the buoy," Sevin hisses back.

"Shh," hushes Halo. This is the first time they've been given a clue as to how the elimination might work. They need to pay attention.

"What about the teams who don't make it to the buoy?" Justice calls out.

Halo's father increases the wattage of his smile. "There are no guarantees for those who don't complete the task. I wish you all well. You may begin."

The competitors around them blend into teams almost seamlessly.

"Justice!" calls Sevin, waving her hands to get her attention.

Justice glares back at her, shaking her head as she loops arms with a tall girl standing beside her. She's clearly still unimpressed with the stunt Fyve pulled at the last Trial, even if they made it through.

Striker coughs once more. "You do realize that the pick of the bunch is standing right here, don't you? Halo can vouch for me as a teammate."

"It's true," says Halo, putting a steadying hand on Fyve's back. "Striker works hard."

Fyve shrugs, looking down at his little sister then the guy who's made it clear he'd like to fill his shoes if he decides to step aside. "Fine with me. Besides, I don't think we have a lot of choice."

"Fine," huffs Sevin, realizing he's right. There are no available teammates anywhere near them.

"So, who's building and who's rowing?" asks Striker, rubbing his hands together. "I'm probably better at rowing, given my strength. Halo's smart, so she's better off building."

"But that…" Fyve looks at Sevin, realizing that if Halo builds and Striker rows, he'll be separated from his sister.

"We need to think about this carefully," says Halo, trying to buy him some time. "If both Striker and Fyve row, the raft will need to hold more weight. We're increasing our chances of it sinking. If Sevin and I row, we risk running out of strength."

"Then Fyve builds with you," says Striker. "I can handle the raft on my own with only one skinny rat as a passenger."

"Not on your life!" scowls Sevin. "I'm not going out there with him."

"Agreed," says Fyve, putting a protective arm around his

sister. "I don't want Sevin going out on the water. Or Halo. Striker and I will row. Sevin and Halo will build."

"Not on your life!" says Halo, repeating Sevin's words. As much as she respects Fyve's need to protect his sister, that option makes no sense. "We need to divide our weight. Sending you two out there will be a disaster. You're far too heavy. I'll go out with Striker."

"But we need you to build the raft," Sevin protests. "You're the only one smart enough."

Halo laughs at this. "No, Sevin, I'm not. You can do this. You're so much smarter than you realize."

Sevin's eyes widen at this compliment as she dares to believe this might actually be true.

"It's settled then," says Striker. "Sevin and Fyve build. Halo and I row."

"I don't like that plan." Fyve's face is filled with anguish. But Halo knows his need to try to keep everyone safe is outweighing his ability to make the best decision for the team.

So, she makes it for him.

"Build us a good raft." Halo winks at Sevin. "Hurry, before we get stuck with the concrete blocks." She walks off toward the shoreline, Striker trailing behind her.

"Halo!" calls Fyve. But Halo doesn't turn. This is the only way any of them have a chance at this Trial, unless Fyve's prepared to take Sevin out on the raft. But that's not an option Halo's prepared to entertain, either.

"I like a girl who knows what she wants," says Striker, chuckling. "Although, I'd like it better if *I* were what you wanted."

Looking down the line of competitors on the shore, Halo's not surprised that Ajax isn't here. Of course, he'd insist on building the raft rather than risking his life on one. If this is a Trial of trust, then it's clear her brother trusts nobody but himself.

Justice is on the shoreline though, pacing as she keeps a keen eye on her team, the tall girl still beside her. It seems her team had decided to send out their lightest members. Halo just hopes they also have enough strength.

"We need a plan," says Striker, his eyes fixed on the ocean.

Halo nods, impressed with his focus. "What are you thinking?"

"I'm going to assume that kid's as smart as you say she is," he says. "And that we're given a raft that actually holds the two of us."

"It will," says Halo confidently.

"Which leaves us a few challenges." Striker rubs his chin. "First, the distance, but I think I've got that covered. I can row, if you can help steer. Do you know how to do that?"

Halo hesitates. "I know the theory…"

"Drag the oar in the water on the left to swing right." He mimics putting an oar in the water. "Drag it in the right to swing left."

"Got it." Halo nods. "What else?"

"The water's calm right now, but that might change." He points his face to the sky. "I can feel a bit of a breeze picking up. That might impact the currents. It also means we're going to get splashed. Your skin didn't cope well in the water during the last Trial."

"I'll be okay," she reassures him. "Just as long as I don't fall in."

"And if you do fall in?" Striker turns to look at her, his face more serious than she's seen before. It's only now that she realizes he wants this just as much as she does. "Because there's a good chance our raft won't hold. What will you do then?"

"I'll swim to shore," she says.

"And you know how to swim?"

"Well, no." She crosses her arms. "But again, I know the theory."

"You can't fall in," says Striker. "No matter what happens, you can't fall in. Swimming is harder than it looks."

Halo nods. "Is that it?"

He shakes his head. "There's the leatherskins to think of."

"But they're too far out," Halo says, squinting to see a giant fin in the distance.

"Not once the water starts churning they won't be," says Striker. "We need to hit them with our oars. Aim for the eyes. That's their weak point."

"Won't they just tip us in?" she asks.

Striker lowers his voice. "Not if they're focused on another team. We need to get in, move swiftly, and get out."

"This is suicide!" she breathes, wondering if she chose the wrong role. But having Fyve or Sevin stand here in her place seems even worse. At least this way she has some control over her destiny. And this time, there's not a damn thing her father can do about it.

"We just have to know our dangers," says Striker. "Then we can beat them."

"Acid water, hungry leatherskins, unpredictable weather," she lists. "Add to that the risk of drowning when our raft breaks apart...anything else?"

He seems to be thinking this over, rather than being amused. "I think they're our main risks."

"So, what do we do now?" she asks.

"Conserve our energy," he says, sitting on the sand, then lying back and covering his eyes with his arm.

Halo looks back up the beach to where Fyve and Sevin have selected a pile of colorful objects and are busy getting them sorted out. She wishes they'd spent more time discussing which pile to choose instead of who was doing what task. But there had simply been no time.

Deciding Striker may be right, she lies down next to him and looks up at the sky.

"Why do you want to pass?" she asks, wanting to know more about this guy who she only just realized is far more complicated than she'd thought.

"I'm too good for this place," he says, simply. "I was meant for something better. I just know it."

"You're so..." She bites her lip as she tries to find the word.

"Arrogant," he finishes for her. "It's okay, you can say it. Won't be the first time I've been told."

"Confident," she says instead. "You really believe in yourself. That's admirable."

He removes his arm from his eyes and turns his face to her. "Maybe that's because nobody else has ever believed in me. I gotta do it for myself."

"I believe in you," she says, glad she has him as a teammate.

Striker hoists himself up on an elbow and leans toward her, closing his eyes as his lips pucker.

"Striker! No!" Halo recoils. "I said I believe in you, not that I want to kiss you!"

"Oh." He lies back down, seeming unaffected by the rebuff. "Your loss."

"Let's just rest." She folds her arm over her face and focuses on the sounds around her. The waves are crashing on the shore, Striker is snoring, having somehow fallen asleep instantly, people are arguing, others are encouraging each other, and then there's the sound of banging as rafts are being built. Her father wasn't wrong—this is a Trial of trust. Or perhaps, stupidity.

Minutes pass. Then hours. Eventually, Halo stands up and stretches. There's one team with their raft at the water's edge and it sets her nerves on edge. The raft is flimsy at best, the hungry water lapping at it, ready to devour it whole. There's no way she'd risk her life going out on that.

"Striker," she says, nudging him with her toe. "It's starting. The first raft's going in."

He sits up, instantly alert.

Two competitors take the raft from their teammates and push it out into the water and climb aboard. Halo holds her breath as she watches.

"What have they made it with?" asks Striker. "That's not a metal pole, is it?"

"The poles are their oars," she says, grimacing.

"They're too heavy." Striker looks aghast.

Halo nods. "That's the least of their problems. They've made it out of timber, which should work, but it's being held together by thin wire. The water will break that apart in no time."

"We should tell them." Striker stands.

"Do you think they'll listen to us?" she asks. "We're their compet—"

The raft tears apart without warning, first one timber plank slipping out then the rest spreading out on the waves like a fan. The two competitors are plunged into the water, forced to wade back to dry land, their limbs thrashing as the water nips at them.

"They're lucky they only got that far out," says Striker, as three more teams make their way down the beach with their rafts.

Fyve and Sevin are still working frantically and Halo's glad they're taking their time. If she can be sure of one thing, it's that Fyve and Sevin will do their best to make sure they build something that will keep her safe.

A piercing scream shatters the air, and Halo spins around.

Another team is balanced on their raft several yards out from shore, and Halo sees one of them is Justice. Her taller teammate has shuffled to the back of the raft as she holds out a shaking hand, her finger extended. The raft tips precariously as the tall girl screams again. It seems the thrashing in the water from the other team has attracted some very unwanted attention.

A leatherskin is heading straight for them, its giant black fin slicing through the water with ease.

There's another team on their raft and they start paddling madly, but rather than helping Justice and her teammate, they head for the buoy while the leatherskin is distracted. This is exactly the strategy Striker had suggested earlier, but somehow, seeing it played out in reality feels so much more cruel.

"Watch out!" cries Halo, as the giant leatherskin flips Justice's raft, sending the two girls flying.

Justice hits the surface and scrambles to her feet in the neck deep water, clutching her oar. Her teammate is flailing beside her, unable to find her balance in her panic. The leatherskin launches forward, opening its massive jaws in a giant yawn of death.

Justice swings her oar, hitting the shark on the nose, but this seems to only make the beast more agitated, and it snaps its jaws closed on the screaming girl beside her, cloaking the beach in instant silence.

"Swim!" Halo cries out again. Justice can still get away if she's fast.

There's a quick blur of movement as something takes hold of Justice and hoists her in the air. It takes a few seconds for Halo to realize it's not the leatherskin.

It's Striker. She hadn't even noticed he'd left her side.

Striker flings Justice over his shoulder like she weighs nothing at all and wades back to shore while the leatherskin finishes the breakfast it had waited so patiently for.

"No," sobs Halo, grateful Justice is safe, but devastated another life's been lost.

But just as the water reaches Striker's waist, the leatherskin jackknifes and heads straight for him.

"Striker!" Halo screams, running down to the shallows. "Hurry!"

Striker turns and sees what's coming for him. He flings

Justice forward, catapulting her to safety while he faces what's coming for him.

"Remember the eyes!" Halo calls, even though she's certain he can't hear her. "Go for the eyes!"

Striker leaps through the water at the same time as the leatherskin, landing on its back. He grips onto the enormous fin, reaching forward, trying to gouge the beast's bloodshot eyes. It's both the most heroic and foolish act Halo's ever witnessed. The leatherskin thrashes in the water, trying to flick Striker off its back, but he holds on tight.

Clearly distressed, the leatherskin turns once more and heads to deeper waters, picking up speed before plunging itself and Striker under the surface. Striker must let go as for just one hopeful second, Halo sees his fist punch through the water. But it quickly disappears, replaced by a growing circle of deep red liquid that spills into the ocean.

There's no way he could have survived that. The guy who was certain he was meant for better things has just had his dreams dashed. Tears run down Halo's cheeks as she holds out a hand, wishing Striker peace.

"You were one of the good guys," she tells him. "I believed in you."

"He saved my life," says Justice, emerging from the water and panting heavily by Halo's side.

Halo nods. She has nothing else left to say.

These Trials aren't worth it. They can't be. The one hundred teens to step aboard the ship won't be the hundred most worthy. They'll be the hundred who somehow managed to stay alive.

FYVE

*T*he breathless second of silence after the realization that a leatherskin has not only killed the girl, but also taken Striker, seems to last forever. No one moves. Fyve's breath is tangled in his too-tight throat. His heart is strangled by his ribs.

But then terror explodes across the beach. Screams erupt. The water becomes a thrashing cauldron as teens run in a frenzied panic for the safety of sand. Those already there scramble backward, as if they expect the leatherskin to reach them even on land.

Fyve's the only one running toward the sea. He reaches Halo and grips her arm. She instantly turns around and throws herself into his arms. "Poor Striker."

Fyve holds her tightly, trying not to look at the bloom of red that's slowly being stretched by the tide. The leatherskin just devoured two teens, leaving little behind.

Halo pulls back, her green eyes swimming with pain as she looks up at him. "We were wrong, Fyve. How can these Trials be worth it?"

His heart stutters, the sensation triggering a shudder down his spine. "I…"

"Of course, it's worth it," Sevin cries from beside them.

Justice gasps. "I knew you were crazy." Looking horrified, or perhaps disgusted, she stalks away.

Fyve turns to watch her. They're the only ones still standing on wet sand. Everyone else is further inland, all pale and wide-eyed, some sitting as if their knees gave out, a few holding each other. The same thought echoes across their faces.

It's not worth it.

Sevin rushes around to face both of them. "It's worth it," she says, conviction lowering her voice and making her sound much older than she is. "Terra promised it would be."

Fyve and Halo glance at each other, their conversation from her workshop hanging between them.

Halo confessing, *"I'm not sure Terra is even real, some days."*

His relieved response. *"I feel the same."*

Fyve looks out to the ocean, the words he said next wrapping around his gut and yanking tight. *"The Terra I believed in would've wanted to save all of us."*

But she didn't save the girl. Or Striker, despite the fact he saved Justice. There's no guarantee she'll save Fyve, Halo, or Sevin either. Well, maybe Halo because she's Elijah's daughter, but there's nothing special about Fyve or Sevin. Once again, he has to make a decision that could mean life or death for his sister.

"Look!" Sevin says, pointing past the location of the carnage.

The team that paddled away from Justice and her teammate has reached the buoy safely. In fact, they're making their way back, no doubt excited to celebrate their win.

They're going to pass the Trial.

They're one step closer to seeing Tomorrow Land.

They're one step closer to knowing if this was all worth it.

Halo chews her lip, watching them paddle with renewed

vigor. The victory lighting their face is apparent even from here.

The other words that were uttered in the workshop quickly follow.

I need to know.

Then Halo's unwavering answer. *So do I.*

Sevin hoists her hands on her hips. "The danger is gone. It's safer to go now than it was before."

The ocean is calm, the only sign that two fewer people are alive is a piece of timber bobbing close to the water's edge and the fast-dissipating pool of blood. In an hour or so, that will be gone. As if Striker and the girl never existed.

As if the leatherskin was never here.

"I doubt it will be coming back," Halo says, sounding as if she's a little surprised to be agreeing with this.

But she's right. The leatherskin's belly is full. Plus, it didn't look happy to have Striker on its back, trying to gouge its eyes out.

Fyve looks down at her. "If we do this, we can learn the truth."

Staying on Treasure Island will mean death anyway. An ignorant one.

Halo looks out at their raft a few feet away, blinks, then frowns. "You made the raft out of wood and tires?" she asks incredulously.

Sevin walks over to it and squats down. "Staying afloat is a simple matter of weight distribution."

Halo nods and Fyve waits, having already heard this. It's the reason he followed each of Sevin's instructions without question.

"Of course, surface tension is exerting its own force, which I also considered. A tire standing vertically would sink." She grins. "A tire lying horizontal and filled with plastic bottles, one that Fyve removed the steel wire from to make it lighter, will most definitely float."

Halo's eyes widen. "Yes, it most definitely would."

"We tied them tightly together with twine." Sevin raps her knuckles on the staggered planks of timber on top. "And it should float high enough that the seawater only splashes the wood. It'll last more than long enough to get to the buoy and back."

Halo looks at Fyve, blinking. "We're doing this, aren't we?"

He swallows, realizing that's exactly what they're going to do. "Yeah, we are."

Sevin leaps to her feet. "Yes!"

"But you're staying here," Fyve says before she can get too excited.

Sevin's smile flatlines and quickly becomes a scowl. "But—"

"No, Sevin. Elijah said only two can go on the raft. We'll row faster. And the whole reason we're considering something as crazy as this is so we pass the Trial."

She crosses her arms but doesn't say anything, a deep groove settling between her brows. Drawing in a steadying breath, Fyve turns back to Halo. "We paddle hard, get there fast, get back even faster."

She nods. "Agreed."

They bend down to drag the raft to the water's edge, surprised to find Sevin helping them. "Just because I don't like it, doesn't mean I can't help," she says grudgingly.

Fyve throws her a look of thanks, finally allowing himself to acknowledge he respects his sister's commitment to these Trials. Even the threat of death hasn't stopped her. She wants this, that's for sure, although possibly for the wrong reasons.

"Come on," he says to Halo. "The sooner we get there, the sooner we're back."

"They're going in!" says an incredulous voice somewhere behind them as they make their way down.

"Fools."

"Don't they realize that some of us will pass anyway? Only one raft's made it to the buoy."

"They don't want to leave it up to chance."

The last voice is Justice, and Fyve's not sure, but he thinks he hears the hard edge of respect in her tone. He wonders if she still had a raft, whether she'd be as crazy as they are, and go out, too.

The raft reaches the water and just as Sevin predicted, it floats, and high enough that the wood tied to the tires isn't touching the water. Fyve grabs the two oars Sevin fashioned out of the lightest steel bars she could find and flattened pieces of plastic and climbs on. She even wrapped twine around the top half for better grip. The raft wobbles but he quickly finds his center of gravity. He holds his hand out to Halo. "Ready?"

She takes it and steps on. "Ready."

The raft dips again but they sit down side by side, shuffling until they're centered, and it balances once more. Fyve passes her the second oar, and they dig into the shallow water, preparing to push off.

It's Sevin who gives them a big shove and propels them into the water. "Be quick," she says, the tension around her eyes the first sign she realizes what heading out means.

Fyve flashes her a smile. "I'll be back faster than Mom killed those rats."

She shakes her head. "That's because you'll be using the energy those rats gave you," she retorts.

Turning back, he focuses on gaining momentum considering the waves are trying to push them back to shore. Halo does the same, and with their combined efforts, they make it past the low cresting white caps. The moment they're on flatter water, Fyve glances over his shoulder. Sevin is standing on the shore, hands clasped in front of her, looking as if she's squinting. He goes to wave but stops himself. He needs to focus on getting to the buoy, and he's not sure Sevin would be able to see his hand, anyway.

"I say we row steady there, then sprint it back," he says to Halo.

She nods once. "Good idea. Reserve our energy, then get out of here as quickly as possible."

They quickly develop a rhythm, digging their oars into the water, then hauling them through, over and over. They pass the single piece of wood that's left of Justice's raft in silence. Then the smeared pool of blood that is all that's left of Striker.

Looking away, Fyve gauges the distance to the buoy. It should only take them several minutes to get there. But then something catches his attention.

"Halo," he says in a low voice.

She follows his line of sight and draws in a sharp breath as she registers the triangular fin.

The leatherskin is still in the distance. It's not close, but it hasn't left.

"Smooth, easy strokes," she says quietly.

They learned that thrashing will only draw the predator's attention. They draw their paddles in deeper and harder, determination mirrored on their faces as they keep their motions fluid and steady.

Sweat beads on Fyve's forehead as long minutes pass, and he's not sure if it's the strain or the tension. Probably both. He and Halo alternate between glancing at each other, the buoy, and the deadly carnivore that seems to be happy circling. Although it's far enough for the outline of its fin to be hazy— Fyve doubts Sevin would be able to see it—it still feels too close. The leatherskin could cover the distance between them far quicker than they could row back to shore. He wonders if the same words are echoing through Halo's mind.

Please let this be worth it.

Reaching the buoy doesn't feel like the victory that it is. They still have to get back to Treasure Island. Alive.

They slow the raft and focus on navigating the bulky thing around the buoy. The thick tires bounce against it a few times, but they make their way around. Once they're facing toward land, Fyve glances at Halo. "We paddle hard, and we paddle fast."

She nods resolutely, then glances over her shoulder. She freezes. "Fyve!"

The shock in Halo's voice has each of his muscles coiled, ready to paddle with every shred of energy he has. He turns to look, filling with terror as he expects to see the leatherskin slicing through the water toward them with sickening speed. But even as he imagines the monstrous predator leaping, rust water slicking over its glistening skin, its mouth a cavern lined with razor-sharp teeth, one thought thunders alongside Fyve's heartbeat.

It was worth it.

He'll die seeking. Proving. Honoring Coal and Sevin and even his mother.

But the leatherskin is gone.

Fyve blinks, ensuring he's not dreaming or imagining or hallucinating.

He sees what had Halo gasping.

The outline of a giant, hulking ship is sitting proudly on the peaceful sea, its name emblazoned across its hull.

The Oasis.

The ship that Elijah promised has arrived.

HALO

The hulking sight of The Oasis makes a spectacular backdrop for Gratitude. Unable to get too close to shore due to its sheer size, the ship sits in the water quietly as it waits for Terra to decide who will have the chance to climb aboard.

When Halo's father had promised them a ship, she could never have imagined something this large. It's like an entire city as it stretches toward the sky with multiple levels and more windows than Halo can count. It could easily house the entire population of Treasure Island, bringing into question why they can only take one hundred from the Trials.

"Who do you think is on there?" Sevin asks for approximately the hundredth time since the ship appeared.

Fyve shrugs, tired of saying that he doesn't know. From what they've seen, there doesn't seem to be anyone on board at all.

"It can't have sailed itself," says Halo, wishing her father would hurry up and give them some answers. If he even has them himself...

"Maybe Terra's onboard," says Sevin. "Maybe she's a real person just like us."

"If that were true, don't you think she'd have shown herself by now?" Fyve points out.

"And how has she been talking to my father all these years?" Halo adds.

Sevin holds up her palms. "It was just a theory, okay."

Halo's father walks down the beach. There's no need for him to stretch out his arms, as he already has the undivided attention of his people. They've never been more keen for him to speak.

"What Terra promises, Terra delivers," he says with pride. "The Oasis has arrived, ready to take one hundred of our fittest and smartest to a land of new beginnings. And isn't she beautiful?"

The people nod, their eyes filling with tears to see such hard evidence of Terra's love for them.

"Praise Terra!" a man calls.

"Terra is great!" the crowd echoes.

"And when we find Tomorrow Land," her father continues, "this same ship will return to bring the rest of you to join us. There'll be a new tomorrow for everyone."

The crowd cheers. Halo finds herself clapping, desperately hoping what he says is true. Treasure Island has kept her people alive but hasn't provided them with much of a life. She yearns to see a real forest, listen to the sounds of birds calling to each other from the canopy, and pick fruit from the trees.

"When can we go on the ship?" someone asks.

"When the Trials are complete," Halo's father says. "Terra is pleased with your performance at the Trial today. And we will now take a moment to pay our respects to Striker and Regal, who made the ultimate sacrifice."

Halo bows her head. Striker deserved to make it through the Trials. He deserved the better life he believed he was destined to enjoy. If he'd stayed on the beach beside Halo, instead of going to Justice's aid, he'd be alive. But, instead, he'd given his life to save another. She can't think of a more heroic act. Maybe he'd had a right to be so full of confidence in himself because he really had been a very awesome human.

"Striker and Regal," Fyve murmurs beside her.

Halo spares a thought for Regal, Justice's terrified teammate who'd become nothing more than an appetizer for that primitive beast of a shark. It was an end that she wouldn't wish on anyone. Except maybe Zake.

Her father raises his arms and the crowd settles. "Before the Trial, I told you that any team that made it around the buoy on their raft would be safe from elimination. Ten teams managed to do just that, and Terra welcomes you with open arms to proceed to the final Trial. Please step forward if that includes you."

Sevin slips a hand into Halo's and another into Fyve's and drags them forward. The other competitors who made it around the buoy join them. There are thirty-nine of them in total and Halo's heart aches once more at the space beside her where Striker should be standing.

She looks up and down at the faces of people who will potentially become part of her future, wondering which of them will make the final cut. Ajax isn't amongst them. Nor is Justice.

"Terra is pleased with every one of you who completed this Trial," Halo's father says. "So pleased that she would like each of you to choose two people to make it through to the next round. She's putting the future directly in your hands."

There's a gasp as the ramifications of this decision echo across the crowd.

"Please make your selection," her father says. "You have five minutes."

Chaos erupts around them as people do the math.

"Forty times two is eighty," says Fyve. "That's less than a hundred."

Sevin rolls her eyes. "It's forty times three. You have to count those who made it through. That's one hundred and twenty. But without Striker, it makes only one hundred and seventeen."

"Okay, genius." Fyve rolls his eyes.

"I'm going to choose Justice," says Sevin. "So that Striker didn't save her for nothing. Plus, I like her. She deserves to make it through."

Halo smiles. She was going to do the same thing. "Good choice."

"Let's get this over with," says Fyve. "Try not to get crushed in the stampede."

He's not actually joking. The remaining competitors are grabbing the arms of those who've made it through and begging to be chosen. The air is swirling with desperation.

Halo walks into the crowd looking for Ajax, wondering if he really deserves his place on the ship more than anyone else. And is choosing him fair to Cloud? Perhaps he'd be better to be forced to stay so he can care for the child he sired. Maybe he'd even thank her one day.

Someone takes hold of her arm, and she spins around, expecting to see her brother. Except it's Cloud, appearing almost like Halo had conjured her.

"Choose Ajax," she says, her belly looking even more full of Ajax's child than it had the day before. "You must."

Halo stares at Cloud, her head frozen between a shake and a nod. She wrenches herself free and walks away, wanting to make the impossible decision for herself.

More people put their hands on her as she moves.

"Please, choose me," one girl says. "I've worked so hard for this. I deserve my place."

"My raft was strong," says a guy. "It almost floated. Terra would want me on her ship."

"I'm a friend of your brother's," says another guy. "Please, pick me."

"I've already chosen my two," Halo lies, desperately needing clear space to make her choice.

They peel away from her like she just developed an infectious disease, launching themselves at another target to state their case.

Halo sees Ajax standing off to the side. He looks calm. Confident. Like a man who's certain he's safe. Which perhaps he is. There's no way Halo can deny him this opportunity no matter how much her conscience is screaming at her to choose someone else.

"Sister," he says, as she approaches.

"Brother." She gives him a smile, even though she feels sick. "You were waiting for me."

"No," he says. "I'm all good."

Her brow furrows. "You don't want me to choose you?"

He shrugs. "You don't have to. Your boyfriend already did."

Fyve appears beside her with another guy she's fairly certain lives in the hut next to his. It seems he's made his choice. And in typical Fyve style, he's considered her feelings in the process. He knew she'd be torn over what to do about Ajax, so he spared her by making the choice for her. It's what she would have ended up doing, yet now she doesn't have to live with the guilt.

"That's settled then." She turns to look at the desperate faces around her, with no idea who she might choose.

There are two sisters with long manes of red hair who catch her attention and Halo walks toward them. They're not begging anyone to choose them. They're holding hands and keeping their spines straight, waiting for their fate to be decided.

That's who Halo wants on the ship with her. Not a bunch of pushy people, desperate to put themselves forward. These sisters look kind. The sort of people who will balance out some of the testosterone that's been fueling these Trials.

"Have you been chosen?" asks Halo.

The sisters shake their heads.

"Then I choose you," says Halo proudly. "You're my two picks."

"No," the older one says forcefully, then seems to catch herself as she gives Halo a sweet smile. "Would you take my two sisters instead?"

A younger, skinnier girl with the same red hair steps out from behind her. Halo hadn't even noticed her in the frenzy around her.

"Oh." Halo had thought this was an easy choice. But how can she separate these sisters? That would be like tearing Fyve away from Sevin.

"Halo!" cries Sevin, dragging Justice along by the hand. "I need one more. Who should I choose? Is your brother safe?"

Halo nods. "I've chosen two of these sisters." She doesn't ask Sevin to choose the third, not wanting to make that decision for her.

Sevin takes the youngest of the sisters by the hand without delay. "Come on! I choose you."

Halo breathes a sigh of relief.

With their selections made, they return to the beach. Halo avoids all eye contact, her heart breaking for every one of these teens not chosen. This entire process seems so arbitrary. But then again, so have the Trials. Does Terra even really care who makes it through to the end? Maybe the ship's going to sink, and Halo's just sent these three sisters to their death. She shudders at the thought.

Fyve is standing with Sevin, and Halo notices Ajax has chosen to remain off to the side, which is fast becoming a pattern with him.

"Time is up," Halo's father calls over the crowd, to bring them to order. "The selection has been made. Tomorrow you will take part in the final Trial, after which our one hundred will be chosen. With only seventeen further eliminations, your odds of making it through have never been better."

The teens around Halo are beaming, but she knows better than to celebrate too soon. There are no guarantees for any of them.

"You will require your raft for tomorrow's Trial," Halo's father says. "You will be working in the same teams as today's Trial. If you are the only team member remaining, then you will work alone. If you no longer have a raft, then you will need to build a new one tonight. Further rules of the Trial will be issued in the morning."

Justice groans as she scans the crowd. "Rake and Bolster didn't get chosen. I'm on my own *and* no raft."

"I'll help you build one," says Sevin proudly.

Halo's heart swells. Just like the three sisters, Sevin is exactly who Terra should be choosing for her ship. Smart, strong *and* kind.

Fyve drapes an arm around Halo's shoulders as her father leads them through the rest of Gratitude. When the sun dips below the giant hulk of The Oasis, it lights up the gleaming white steel, making it look like an apparition more than a vessel that's going to take them to their very real future.

"Let's go and check on our raft," Fyve says, as the crowd of people start to break away. "Make sure it's in good shape."

"But we already know it is." Halo tilts her head.

"We have to be sure," he says, taking her by the hand. "Sevin, I'll see you later. You go and help Justice, okay?"

Sevin nods. "Sure."

"Are you trying to get me alone?" Halo asks when Sevin has walked away. "It's not like you to try to shake your sister."

"Something like that." Fyve leads Halo down the end of the beach to where they'd left their raft after they'd hauled it out of the water after the Trial.

"Do you think it got damaged?" Halo kicks the raft gently with her toe.

"Sit down," says Fyve, looking up at the sky. "Let's wait for it to get dark."

"But aren't we better to repair it while it's still light?" She plants her hands on her hips. "Fyve, you're behaving quite strangely."

He steps closer and slides his hands around her. "We're not repairing the raft," he whispers. "We're going to row it."

"What?" She looks up at him, wondering if he's lost his mind. "Why would we do that?"

"I want to check out the ship," he says. "There's no way it traveled here by itself. I want to see what it's like up close and I'm not waiting to pass the next Trial to find out."

"Fyve!" Halo tugs at the front of his shirt. "We could get claimed for doing something like that!"

"Only if we get caught," he says, his face alive with excitement. "Come on, Angel, we said we wanted answers. This is our chance. Nobody will expect it. Let's find out what's going on here."

Halo groans, already knowing she's going to agree to this crazy idea despite her every cell screaming at her to say no. He's right. They said they were going to find out what was happening here and this is a prime opportunity. Nobody will expect them to disobey Terra and go out to the ship.

"Okay," she says.

"You're the best." Fyve leans down and kisses her. His lips are a contrast of soft yet firm, just as his breath is cool yet laced with heat. She'd follow him to the ends of the Earth. Which is exactly what they're trying to do. Head to Tomorrow Land and start a new life. There's nothing she wants more.

She closes her eyes to the dwindling rays of light of the day and pushes up on her toes, wanting to be as close to Fyve as possible. If Terra catches them, this could be their last kiss.

Although in the world they live in, with no promise of a future, every kiss could be their last.

He pulls back slowly, covers her face in gentle kisses and encourages her to sit on the sand beside him while they wait for darkness to cloak them. She rests her head on his shoulder, watching the water lap at the shore, the pale pink foam appearing white under the light of the rising crescent moon.

"What if they see us?" Halo points to the other competitors scattered along the beach, working on their rafts.

"We'll launch a bit further down," says Fyve. "Besides, they're too distracted right now to pay us much attention."

Halo nods, still unable to believe what she's agreed to. And when the night finally turns to black, she's no closer to accepting what they're about to do. Yet, her feet still move, her hands still carry the raft, and her heart still thuds like it's trying to jump free from her ribs.

They set the raft down in the water and Halo climbs on, careful not to get her feet wet. Fyve pushes it out, climbs on beside her, and they each pick up an oar.

"Did anyone see us?" she asks, quietly, impressed with how well the raft is holding up. Sevin's design was far better than anything Halo could have come up with.

"We'd know if they did," he replies, dragging his oar through the water.

"This reminds me of my tree," says Halo. "It's the same feeling of doing something important that most people wouldn't understand. Especially my father."

"Maybe he understands more than anyone," says Fyve.

"Or maybe less," she adds.

"That's why we're doing this." Fyve seems to pick up his pace and Halo works to keep up. It's better to get this craziness over with as quickly as possible.

"How are we going to get on the ship?" she asks.

"What?" Fyve seems surprised. "You want to go *on* it? I thought we were just going to check it out from the water."

"Oh." She smiles in the darkness, somewhat relieved that the crazy factor in their plan just got dialed back several notches. "That's fine with me."

They row closer and with each stroke its outline looks larger until it's looming above them like nothing Halo's ever seen before. The tallest structure on Treasure Island is the hut she lives in. Or maybe the hump of land where she built her tree, but that's hardly a structure. This ship is like looking up at a wall of never-ending blackness.

Fyve lets out an impressed sigh. "It should be called The Ominous, not The Oasis."

They navigate the raft around the ship, listening and watching for any signs of life. But the ship is as quiet as it is large.

"Look," says Fyve, pointing with his oar. "Is that a ladder made from rope?"

Halo squints. "Why would they drop down a ladder?"

"Maybe they're expecting us," he says.

The world falls out of the bottom of Halo's stomach.

"It feels like good luck to me," says Fyve, paddling forward. "Seems we can get on the ship after all."

"No," Halo protests. "This feels like a trap."

"Don't blame me," he says with a good dose of amusement in his voice. "It was your idea."

Fyve maneuvers them to the edge of the ship and sets down his oar so he can grab hold of the bottom of the ladder, which is dangling just above the hungry surface of the acidic water.

"I need a way to tie the raft to the ladder," he says. "Any ideas?"

Once again, Halo feels like she's at a crossroads. This is pure madness. But the way her heart is thumping, the adrenaline coursing through her body, she's never felt more alive. This might be a trap, but it might also be the most exciting thing to ever happen to her. And she's doing it with Fyve.

She reaches in her pocket for her lucky cord and passes it to him. "Don't you dare lose this."

"This is perfect!" He takes the cord and loops it through the rope ladder then one of the thick pieces of twine Sevin had used to secure the raft. They lay their oars flat in one of the deep grooves between two planks of timber and Fyve slowly gets to his feet.

"We don't have to go if you don't want to," he says, his body language in direct contrast to his words.

Even though she can see he's never wanted to do anything more in his life than to climb that ladder, Halo believes him. If she didn't want to go through with this, there's no way he'd make her. Nor would he leave her alone out here.

"I'll be right behind you," she says.

Fyve hauls himself onto the ladder, moving quickly and quietly upwards. Halo follows, finding it far more difficult than she expected. The ladder is swinging, making it hard to get a good grip, but she pushes through, determined to make it to the top. All the answers to all her questions are on this ship, she just knows it.

About halfway up, Fyve pauses and points to his left. She climbs up a few more rungs to get closer to him and stops.

"It's a light," he hisses. "Look."

Halo's eyes widen to see he's right. There's a light burning in one of the rooms. She can see an unmade bed with a pillow. Sleeping in that would be just like lying down to rest on top of a cloud. But there's no person in the bed, or in any other part of the room that she can see.

Fyve starts climbing again, and Halo follows, her arms burning with the strain of the climb. She pushes more with her legs, trying to get them to do most of the work. Looking down into the darkness, she's glad she can't see how high up they are.

Just when she thinks she can climb no more, Fyve is lifting a leg over the top edge of the ship, then turns and reaches to help Halo up.

"That was a hard climb," he whispers. "I can't believe you made me do it."

Halo smiles in the dim light of the stars. They're on a deck that has what looks like a large pond of water in the middle of it. She's heard of the existence of pools, where their ancient ancestors would swim simply for the enjoyment of it.

"It's beautiful," she says.

"Let's see what else there is." Fyve tugs on her hand, and they hurry off to a door. The solid timber of the deck under her bare feet feels strange, so different to the dirt floor of her hut or the prickly sand on the beach. She's never stood on anything so smooth before.

They slip through the door and down a staircase, which is another strange experience, like moving down a hill but in tiny stages, one step at a time. She holds onto the railing, feeling like she might fall. There are small lights at intervals, casting the stairwell in a dim glow and the smell makes Halo's nose crinkle. The air is stale, steeped in the scent of memories and decay.

Fyve stops at one of the doors and looks at Halo. "Are you okay to continue?"

She nods. "Never better."

"I think this is the floor that had the light on," he says, keeping his voice low as he turns the handle. It hadn't even occurred to her to count the floors. She really needs to get better at this whole secret reconnaissance thing.

Noticing a map on the back of the door, she takes a photo of it with her mind. Knowing where they're going will be important in a foreign place like this.

Fyve opens the door, and they step into a long hallway lined with more doors. They walk in silence, keeping their footsteps light and their eyes wide. At the end of the hallway is a set of double doors that are open.

Halo slips her hand into Fyve's and they walk into the expansive room.

"What is this place?" asks Fyve in awe.

Halo looks up at the chandeliers hanging from the ceiling that light up the cavernous space, her feet padding forward on the frayed emerald and burgundy carpet. "According to the map on the back of the door, it's called a ballroom."

"Coal and I played with a ball when we were young," he says.

"Not that kind of ball. The dancing type." She loops her arms around Fyve's waist and sways from side to side.

Fyve laughs, although being so close to him, she can feel his heart beating just as hard as hers. And it's not because of how close they are. What they're doing is dangerous.

There's a loud clunk from another section of the ship and it has them freezing.

"Come on. We're too exposed here." Fyve takes her hand and leads her out of the ballroom to a door at the rear of the ship. There's another staircase and they walk down, Halo letting go of Fyve to grip the handrail.

"I don't like stairs," she says, still feeling the need to keep her voice low despite not having seen another soul since they stepped aboard. But someone—or something—had to make that clunk.

The staircase takes them to a well-lit room and Halo blinks as her eyes adjust.

"Oh, sweet Terra," she exclaims. "This is the engine room. Look, Fyve!"

They're surrounded by the kind of machinery that Halo has only dreamed of. It makes her little half-built motor that's sitting on the ocean floor look like child's play. Which is perhaps exactly what it is. It's no wonder her father threw it away if he had any inkling that something like this was going to come into Halo's life. There are desks with glowing screens, computers and control panels, and walls lined with tools. And then there's the engine itself with fuel pumps, cylinder heads, and exhaust manifolds like she's only seen diagrams of in books. There are piston rods twice her height, and a row of generators, air pumps and boilers that dwarf her with their sheer volume. It's so hard to take it all in.

"What is all this stuff?" Fyve asks.

"Magic," she breathes, her hungry eyes trying to take every last detail in. "It's like magic."

She's never seen anything so incredible. It makes risking her life in the Trials seem so worthwhile. She has to pass the final test. This ship is her future. She can feel it in her bones.

"Halo," a voice booms from a mezzanine balcony above them.

She jumps, looking up to see her father gazing down on them.

"What are you doing here?" he asks, leaning forward.

Halo's legs begin to shake as her voice fails her.

"What are *you* doing here?" Fyve counters.

"Terra requested my presence," he says, keeping his voice calm. "Did she also request yours?"

Halo and Fyve both shake their heads, knowing there's no point in lying.

Her father walks to a staircase, then down to their level. He goes directly to Halo and puts his hands on her shoulders. "Halo, you're as foolish as you are stubborn."

"I'm s-sorry," she stammers. She knew this was a bad idea. "I just wanted—"

"We wanted answers," Fyve interrupts, taking his portion of the blame.

"And you'll get your answers." Her father looks directly at Halo, ignoring Fyve. "Pass tomorrow's Trial and this engine room will be yours."

"You mean…" Halo blinks. "We're not going to be claimed for disobeying Terra?"

"Move quickly," her father warns. "Keep your gaze ahead. Get off this ship as fast as you can. Use the ladder you scaled to get up here and leave immediately. It's not safe."

Halo nods, hardly daring to believe he's going to let them get away with this.

"Go!" her father says, more urgently. "You don't have much time."

Halo looks to Fyve and he nods.

She's not sure why her father has chosen not to punish them, but she knows they must listen to his warning. Because as much as he's the leader of Treasure Island, he's also her father and his need to protect her had been brimming in his eyes.

She links hands with Fyve and together they run. They have as many answers to their questions as they're going to get for now.

The only problem is that they also have a thousand more.

FYVE

*T*he final Trial. Fyve can't quite believe he's here, standing on the beach, nervous energy churning in his gut. He was so adamant he didn't want this. That leaving wasn't the answer.

And now, five days later, he's realized leaving is the only way to get answers. He's never seen Sevin so full of energy, despite the physical demands of the Trials. He can practically feel Coal smiling. The ship that Terra promised sits patiently out at sea, looking proudly glorious in the dawn light. The Oasis. A promise of life in a world of death. A beacon of hope in a land where hope is scarce.

Fyve glances down at the amazing person holding his hand. Halo is right beside him. She looks up, her eyes green pools of everything he's feeling. Determination. Uncertainty. Excitement about what their tomorrows could look like.

Because their future is here, waiting to be carried away on the ship Terra promised.

"The odds are good," Sevin murmurs. "Really good." She glances over her shoulder toward where their mom is standing several feet away, flashing her a smile.

His sister is right. Less than a hundred and twenty teens will be taking part in the final Trial. A hundred will be climbing aboard The Oasis. But now isn't the time to get cocky, so Fyve keeps his face serious. "Let's find out what the final Trial is."

As if Elijah heard him, he appears, striding down the beach with his shoulders back and his chest out, carrying the knowledge that his foretelling of a ship came true. He truly is Terra's messenger.

He turns to the people of Treasure Island and a rousing round of applause explodes. Elijah raises his arms, beaming. "Terra has provided," he booms. "Just like she promised."

The crowd's response is lifted to the sky with jubilation. "Praise Terra! Terra is great!"

Elijah drops his hands. "The final Trial is here," he continues. "By the end of today, the final hundred will be chosen for the quest to find Tomorrow Land. They will come aboard The Oasis."

Halo shuffles a little beside Fyve, no doubt thinking of last night. They've already been aboard the ship. It was far more fantastical than he'd ever imagined. Rooms with walls and ceilings intact, beds that weren't made of dirt, corridors and more corridors full of shade and protection. Or maybe Halo's thinking of the fact they were caught by Elijah. Although it had been a shock, and he'd looked frustrated, it's also the first time Fyve's seen the man look like a father, not a leader. He'd been exasperated, but almost...understanding. Maybe Elijah knows his daughter and her irrepressible curiosity. Although maybe he understands how much The Oasis means to the people of Treasure Island, period.

"Why can't we all go?" shouts a woman on Fyve's left. A few people tuck their heads in and shift away from her, not wanting to be associated with the challenge in her tone. But a few more push up on tiptoes or shuffle to look around the person in front of them so they can get a better view of Elijah. They want to know the answer to the question.

Fyve eyes the monstrous ship, understanding why. Several floors high, it's taller than anything on Treasure Island. There's more than enough space to house everyone.

Elijah's smile falls. "Are you questioning Terra?"

Two people trying to disappear move away from the woman, clearly uneasy, but she raises her chin. "I have been faithful to Terra. I've gifted her with food when I was hungry." Something flashes across her face. "I lost my daughter, Regal, to the Trials. Why would she stop me from going on that ship?"

"It is not about space." Elijah opens his arms expansively. "Treasure Island has more than enough of that and look at how we must scrape through to survive. It's about surviving out on the ocean. There are only so many bodies Terra can care for on The Oasis. Only the chosen can seek Tomorrow Land." He stares at the woman, waiting to see what she'll do.

Challenge him.

Or accept his words as the truth he says they are.

Fyve holds his breath, noting the way everyone else is watching with close attention. He sees his mother look away, and for some reason, the gesture feels ominous. The woman drops her head and steps back, retreating, and Fyve finds himself releasing a breath.

Until a skinny man in threadbare clothes steps in close to her. "We talked about this. Don't let it stop you," he hisses. "We'll die anyway if we get left behind."

Halo stiffens. The man is encouraging the woman. And this is something they've discussed...

"I'm just going to sneak on," the woman mutters under her breath. "Nothing's gonna stop me from getting aboard that ship."

Fyve pulls Halo a little closer, surprised at the barely concealed dissent. Then again, he kind of isn't. He's thought this all himself. He's taking part in the Trials so he can uncover the truth about Terra and what she really wants. Because he wants more for his sister and himself and the people of Treasure Island. And now these people have a beacon of hope that can take them all away from this. They won't give that up easily.

"People were talking last night," Sevin whispers. "About swimming out if they have to. Mom tried to tell them to stop but they chased her away."

Ice trickles down Fyve's spine. The Oasis is proof Terra exists, that the quest for Tomorrow Land is possible. It's brought the promise of something better. But it's also raised the question of her selectivity. Of why some people should be left behind.

Elijah must pick up on it, too, because his hard stare combs through the people of Treasure Island. "No one is to board The Oasis unless they are chosen."

Fyve waits, his breath once again locked in his lungs. Elijah hasn't given many direct commands, but then again, he hasn't needed to.

Although no one speaks up, a ripple of murmurs carries through the crowd. And they aren't murmurs of assent. Mutiny is trying to be born.

Suddenly, the woman who spoke cries out and Fyve winces, already knowing why. She drops to the ground, her hands clamped against the sides of her head. Her back arches, the sinews of her neck looking as if they're about to snap. Less than a heartbeat later, she crumples onto the sand, blood gushing from her eyes and ears.

It's the next cry that takes Fyve by surprise. The scrawny man who encouraged her to speak up also collapses with a garbled scream. He writhes on the sand, fighting this longer than the woman did. Although the result is the same. He stills, sightless eyes staring up at the sky, bright red blood pooling beneath his head as it pours from his eyes, ears, nose, even his mouth.

The third cry has Halo gasping. "Not another one."

A young man on the other side of the crowd drops from sight. Far younger than the other two, he looks like he just missed the age cutoff for the Trials. Which is probably why he resented Terra's decision... The people around him look away, their faces pale.

Sevin scrunches up her face. "Mom tried to tell them."

Fyve pulls Halo in even closer, unsure if he's offering or asking for comfort, possibly a little of both. Three people are dead. Claimed. He's starting to realize what a privilege it is to have the chance to be on The Oasis.

Elijah scans the people, his face dark and thunderous. "Terra spoke to me last night. She has heard your murmurs. The discontent. Your greediness and lack of gratitude."

The people shuffle, a few hanging their heads.

"Terra sends you this," he calls, his arm waving toward The Oasis. "And this is how you thank her?"

"Terra is good," Fyve's mother calls out. "Terra is great. We do not question her wisdom."

"She cares for those who believe," adds Cloud, her face alight with faith even though three dead bodies are now littered amongst the crowd.

But the anger on Elijah's face doesn't lessen. "She's no longer sure a hundred should be chosen. It might be fifty. Or twenty."

"Twenty?" Sevin gasps in a whisper. "But..."

That reduces their odds of getting on that ship significantly.

"It is fitting that this Trial is about what you can give to Terra, rather than what she can give you," continues Elijah. "Today, you will take your rafts out onto the ocean and find her a gift. A symbol of your gratitude. Terra has provided for you, now you provide for her."

Silence is his answer, and Fyve tries to think of what they

could possibly find in the ocean that would be a suitable gift for Terra. One that's better than anyone else's. Even Sevin looks at a loss. The ocean is more of a wasteland than the island.

"All those who are eligible and wish to take part, step forward," Elijah orders.

Fyve and Halo move simultaneously, Sevin with them. He isn't surprised to see every teen who passed the last Trial step forward from the crowd, their backs straight and heads held high. They've all learned exactly how precious this opportunity is. An opportunity others have died for.

Elijah regards them, his gaze flickering over Halo without stopping. "The more pleased Terra is, the higher the number of people to be chosen. You have until Gratitude to bring her your gift."

He walks away, and Fyve's not sure, but he doesn't look like he's holding himself as tall as when he entered. He's disappointed? Angry? Disgusted?

"Let's get to the raft," says Sevin, already turning and walking away.

His lips pressed in a tight line, Fyve follows her with Halo. Their raft is where they left it, the others lined up along the beach. A smaller version is to their right, and Justice stands beside it, looking exhausted and overwhelmed. She would've been working all night after Sevin gave her instructions on how to build it.

And now they have to find something that possibly doesn't exist.

And if they don't, there's a high chance they won't be chosen.

Sevin picks up one of the oars. "We need to get out on the water."

Fyve isn't going to do that without a plan, but Halo speaks first, her eyes scanning the hazy purple line where the ocean meets the sky. "Maybe we need a net. Or something with clear plastic that we can use to look into the water." She looks at Fyve. "Otherwise, we'll have to take turns swimming."

He doesn't answer, unsure which is the best option. Lose time fashioning a tool to drag or scan the bottom of the ocean, or spend time diving into acidic water, hoping to find something of value before they dissolve. Something that will be better than anyone else finds. The sound of feet splashing in the water tells him another group is already on their way out. They need to make a decision.

Sevin huffs. "We're not doing either of those. I know exactly what we're going to gift Terra."

Fyve glances at Halo, but she doesn't seem to know what Sevin's talking about, either. "What are we going to pluck from the ocean, off the comfort of our raft?"

His sister grins. "A leatherskin."

Fyve's jaw goes slack, and it feels like it takes long seconds for him to be able to yank it back up. "Are you crazy?"

"Think about it," his sister says, not bothered by his incredulity. "It's the ultimate gift we can give Terra. Food for everyone on the island. We'll definitely be chosen."

Fyve's at a loss for words. This is too far.

Halo shakes her head. "What are we going to kill it with?"

Sevin's grin only grows. She unwinds the twine that covers the end of the oar she's holding, revealing a pointed tip. "With our harpoons."

"You said the twine was for grip!" Fyve gasps, still full of disbelief. She used weapons for oars?

"These were the thinnest, lightest lengths of metal I could find, and they already had this." Sevin taps the sharpened end. "So, of course I had to cover it over. Now, it's worked in our favor."

Fyve turns to the sea, his stomach dropping when he registers the faint outline of a fin where they saw it yesterday. The leatherskin hasn't left. Flashes of its jaw opening as it took Striker yesterday are like a punch to his hollow gut.

A hand presses on his upper arm and he looks back to find Halo there. "She could be right, Fyve. We went out there in the last Trial, knowing the leatherskin had just killed."

"Not intending to fight it," he says. "Look what happened to Striker when he got overconfident."

"But we were willing to risk it." Her hand tightens. "No matter what."

Fyve's gaze falls on his sister. She wasn't there for that, though, and this time she has to be. That's the rules. He was willing to put his life on the line, for Halo to make the decision about hers, but Sevin's? Trying to kill a leatherskin is the most dangerous task they've faced.

She twists her hands in her shirt. "Please, Fyve. It'll guarantee us a place on the ship."

A life of hope and dreams and Tomorrow Land.

But to do that, they have to risk death.

Justice steps in closer. "It's a good idea. And I'll help, if you'll let me."

Fyve takes in the three sets of eyes regarding him. All knowing the price of choosing this and facing it unflinchingly. Coal would've done the same.

"Okay," he says, his chest tight. "We kill the leatherskin and bring it as a gift for Terra."

There are no whoops of excitement or anticipation, just four somber faces as they push the rafts toward the water. They're about to take part in the final Trial.

And the stakes have never been higher.

HALO

Fyve and Halo push the oars through the water with Sevin crouched at the front of the raft as she keeps her gaze focused ahead. This is hands down the craziest thing Halo's ever done. Even crazier than sneaking onto The Oasis last night. Or going on the water after the leatherskin killed Striker and Regal. But she'd lived to tell the tale of both those adventures, so surely, this is possible as well.

Justice is following in their wake. If only Terra had allowed the teams to divide, then Sevin could have gone with her. She'd done an excellent job of helping Justice with her raft last night. Built using the same technique of tires filled with plastic bottles, it's smaller than theirs, but just as sturdy. Justice is doing an impressive job of keeping up, her determination to live a better future fueling her depleted muscles.

"Are you still sure this is a good idea?" Fyve asks as they get closer to their target.

Sevin spins around and glares at him. "Don't you dare change your mind now. It's the only plan we have."

Halo smiles. "Your sister's kinda cute when she's grumpy."

Sevin pulls a face at Halo and turns back around to resume

her lookout position. She has a smaller oar clutched in her hands. Well, not so much an oar, as a spear. She'd been insistent that each of them be in possession of a weapon, including Justice.

"So, if we're going to do this..." says Fyve. "Why don't we make some splashes here to attract the leatherskin? Instead of rowing all the way out there."

Sevin turns again. "That's the worst idea I've ever heard. We want to catch it by surprise. We're the hunters, not the prey."

Halo pokes Fyve in the ribs with the tip of her finger. "Seems like you're here for looks, not brains."

Fyve bares his teeth playfully at Halo then focuses back on Sevin as he continues to row. "Then what's our plan exactly, my genius sister?"

"Careful," says Halo when the tip of his oar gets a little too close to her for comfort. "Those spikes are lethal."

"Exactly," says Sevin. "They are lethal. We're going to get as close as we can to the leatherskin without alerting it to our presence. Then we throw the spears."

"Striker said their eyes are their weak spot." Halo still feels pain at the mention of his name. But he'd want to help them if he could. Even if he's no longer here to do that.

"Three spears. Two eyes," says Fyve. "But even with those odds, there's no way our aim can be accurate enough when we throw our spears. We're better off to wait until it notices us. We hold our nerve and when it gets close, we go for it."

Halo weighs the oar in her hands. "And how do we get it back to shore? Actually, how do we even get back without our oars?"

"Maybe Justice can tow us," says Sevin. "Anyway, we're not that far out. We'll wash back up on shore eventually. The leatherskin will, too."

"I don't know about this." A sick feeling winds its way through Halo's gut. "This is madness."

"Oh," says Fyve, rolling his eyes. "Welcome."

Sevin lets out a sigh. "Come up with another plan then! How else are we going to get on that ship? You heard Elijah. He might only take twenty of us now. It's time to do something bold. Something sure to get Terra's attention. This is all we've got."

Halo scans the ocean for the other teens. They're mostly paddling aimlessly. A couple of people are in the water and there are the sounds of moaning floating as they beg to be pulled back up to their rafts. She wonders what would have happened if they'd all refused to take part in this Trial of Madness. Would The Oasis have sailed away without a single person on board? Would Terra have claimed them all, just like those three unfortunate souls on the beach this morning? Whatever the case, it's too late now.

"Sevin's right," she says. "This is our only idea. And if it works, we'll all be on that ship. Justice included."

Fyve nods, falling into silence as he rows them closer. Halo does her best to keep up with him, stroke by stroke, but at times it's impossible and she sends their raft veering to the east, and he has to pause to wait for her to get them back on course.

She glances back at Justice who's paddling valiantly behind them. Halo doesn't think she's met anyone as determined as her. Except perhaps Sevin.

"It's circling," says Sevin, sounding surprised. "Why is it circling?"

"They have to keep moving," says Fyve. "To keep the water moving through their gills."

"You're more than just a pretty face, after all," says Halo, trying to lighten the mood.

"I know why they keep moving," says Sevin. "I'm asking why this one's circling. They only circle when they're interested in something. It helps them understand what they're looking at. Their eyesight isn't so great."

Halo decides that's something Sevin has in common with

these giant beasts. If she'd only just noticed the circling motion, her vision is even worse than she suspected.

"How do you even know all this?" Fyve asks.

"Coal told me about it once." Sevin shrugs. "But what has this leatherskin so interested? Why's it circling that one spot?"

"No idea," says Halo. "But I'm grateful. Your plan of a surprise attack might just work if it remains distracted."

They row a bit further, then Fyve stops and rests his oar across his thighs. "Everybody ready? This is our last chance to back out."

"Let's do it!" Sevin holds her spear above her head and growls.

Hoping this is the same beast that killed Striker and Regal, Halo nods at Fyve. "I'm ready."

Fyve looks back at Justice who waves her sharp-tipped oar at him to show she's ready, too. Halo just hopes the three of them can succeed without Justice having to get too close. Although, it will be harder for her to claim the kill as her own gift for Terra if she doesn't at least participate.

Halo pushes her oar in the water, her frenzied strokes outdone only by the rapid beating of her heart. Sweat beads on her forehead as the sun beats down and she focuses on steadying her breath and channeling her inner-Striker as she steels herself for what's about to come. Confidence is exactly what they need.

"We can do this," she mutters more to herself than Sevin or Fyve. "We can do this."

"We can totally do this," says Fyve.

One leatherskin is all that stands between their future together.

The water swells from the movement of the shark and the raft tips up. Fyve jams his oar in the water, both steadying them and turning them, putting him in the direct line of danger.

"Fyve!" Halo calls out in protest. Trust him to position them like this. Forever the protector, she just fell in love with this guy a teeny bit more.

The leatherskin makes an abrupt turn as it takes in their presence and its giant nose catapults toward them. With water beading down the slick leather of its skin, its fin stands tall in the water as its muscled body catches the sun and it heaves forward.

Fyve raises his weapon while Halo and Sevin try to steady their raft.

The shark launches at them with impossible speed and Fyve slams the sharp tip of his oar directly at the leatherskin's eye. But his aim is off just by an inch and the spear slides down its head and lodges in the gills.

Writhing in pain, the shark flips backward, sending the raft airborne. Halo reaches out and grabs Fyve's shirt, stopping him from being thrown into the water, while Sevin shifts her weight, bringing the raft back to horizontal just before they slam to the surface like it's made from cement. The violence of the motion jars Halo's spine but she has no time to dwell on that right now. With all three of them still on the raft and two spears still in play, every second counts.

The leatherskin turns back to them, pure evil blazing in the dark blue of its corpse-like eyes. It charges and this time Halo is ready with her spear.

She lets out a scream as she slams it into the shark's head. But her aim is even worse than Fyve's and it bounces off the tough skin, flies into the water and sinks.

Thankfully the blow had been enough to send the shark reeling and it swims away with Fyve's spear still pointing out of its bloodied gills, turning the water deep red.

Justice paddles closer, her face frozen in determined terror as she clutches her sharpened oar.

"It's not done with us!" calls Halo, warning her back.

"I'm not done with it!" Sevin shouts in reply. "I still have my spear."

"Give it to me." Fyve makes a grab for it, but Sevin hauls it out of his reach.

"So you can miss again?" she asks.

"It's coming!" screams Justice.

All eyes turn to the injured beast as it slices through the water, just as powerful as ever. But this time it's trying a different approach. It dives into the ocean, the tip of its tail the last thing to disappear as it heads for the depths of the playground it's ruled its whole life.

"Be ready!" calls Halo as Sevin gets to her knees, her spear held above her head.

Chaos erupts as the leatherskin emerges from underneath their raft and Halo's world spins upside down when they're thrown off and into the air. Before she lands, she sees the sharp movement of Sevin's oar sailing past. Their only hope is that it manages to find its mark.

Halo is plunged into the warm water, and she squeezes her eyes closed to protect them from the inevitable sting. She's never been fully immersed in water before, and the sensation is so foreign that for a moment she's not sure which way is up. Somehow her body seems to know, and she flaps her arms like the ravens she sees swooping through the sky and her head breaks through the surface.

Blinking rapidly, her eyes feel like they're on fire as she tries to take in the scene around her. But before she can figure out what the flurry of movement is about, she sinks again. The water feels like it's filled with something squirming and squishy, but that could just be her senses going to mush. It's difficult to identify any of her feelings right now other than pure terror and pain.

She flaps her arms again but this time the action doesn't work, and she remains immersed. Unable to stop her lungs from screaming for air, she gasps, and the sharp sting of acid bites at her throat. Clawing at the water, she tries again, half expecting the leatherskin to come along and finish the struggle for her.

But, instead, she feels a sharp tug on her hair as she's dragged upwards. The pressure shifts to her shirt as a strong hand hauls her to the safety of a world of sweet, fresh, air. She coughs up water as she grips onto Fyve, who's holding onto the edge of the raft with his other hand.

"You're okay," he says, directing her to hold the raft herself while he dives underwater again.

With shaking hands, she clings on, drawing in deep breaths as she steadies herself.

Moments later, Fyve appears again with Sevin. She's lighter than Halo and he manages to lift her high enough that she can scramble onto the raft.

"Halo," calls Fyve. "Get up there."

She doesn't need to be asked twice. She tries to climb up, but finding herself too weak, she has to rely on both Fyve and Sevin to help her. Once up, she lies on her back and looks up at the clouds, every muscle in her body aching, her skin feeling like it's covered in molten lava. She expresses more gratitude than she ever has for simply being alive.

She turns to her stomach to reach out to help Fyve, only to find him already beside her, panting heavily.

"That wasn't fun," he says between breaths.

"It wasn't meant to be." Halo props herself up on her elbows. "Did we at least hit our mark? I saw the spear—"

A loud sobbing cuts off Halo's words. It's Sevin, pointing with one hand and tearing at her wet hair with the other.

"I made a terrible mistake," she says.

Halo sits up to see what she's pointing at. Justice is sitting on her small raft, bobbing a few yards away. She's deathly pale with a short spear sticking straight up out of her leg.

"Justice!" Halo cries. "What happened?"

But as soon as she's asked the question, she knows the answer. That's unmistakably Sevin's spear. Justice's oar had been far longer. Sevin had found her mark, except it was the completely wrong one. In the frenzy and with her limited vision, it seems Sevin had managed to catch Terra a gift—Justice.

Fyve dips his hands into the harsh water and paddles them closer.

Justice looks unsteady as she sits there in silence, like she's about to faint.

"Stay with us, Justice," calls Fyve. "We've almost reached you."

Halo scrambles up beside him and dips her hands in the water to help.

"What happened to the leatherskin?" she asks, scanning the water. If it comes back for them now, they have no defense. Not only will the Trials be over, but so will their lives.

Justice turns to look at Halo. "I got it," she says. "Right in the eye, just like Striker said. Except all it did was make it swim away."

And that leaves them with a whole lot of problems way beyond Justice's horrific injury. A dead shark is a gift to Terra, but a gift is not a gift if you can't give it to someone yourself. She highly doubts Terra subscribes to the theory of it being the thought that counts. Which means all of this has been for absolutely nothing.

They're now stuck out in the ocean and the only oar they have is lodged in Justice's leg. This Trial could not have gone any worse. They've completely ruined their chances of getting on that ship. And Justice's life is in danger. In fact, all their lives are on the line if that leatherskin chooses to return. It seems it's time to let go of any of the remaining hope that Halo had been clinging to. It's over. This time, the Trials really have slipped from their grasp.

"I'm so sorry," sobs Sevin as their raft bumps into Justice's.

Fyve removes his shirt and uses it to quickly tie the two rafts together, then scrambles over to check on Justice's injury. Sevin is far too distressed to do anything of much use.

As Halo checks his knot is secure, something in the water catches her eye.

"What is that?" she says pointing down. "What are those things in the water?"

This must be what she'd felt brushing against her legs when she'd been thrown off the raft.

"You're going to be okay," Fyve tells Justice as he glances over at Halo. "I'll be back in just a moment. You sit very still and whatever you do, don't pull the oar out of your leg."

"But we need it," says Justice. "We'll never get back to shore without it."

"We need you not to bleed out even more," Fyve replies. "Sevin, can you get over here and sit with Justice while I check out what Halo's seen?"

Sevin looks aghast but does as she's told. She waits for Fyve to climb off Justice's raft before she takes his place.

"I'm so sorry," she says again.

"You didn't mean it," Justice replies. "But it really was a very bad shot."

"I know," Sevin wails.

Fyve is beside Halo now and she points again into the water. Dozens of translucent creatures with tiny wings outstretched are moving about each other in an intricate dance.

"Those things," she says. "What are they? I've never seen them before."

Fyve gasps. "Those are the squishy things, like the one that Coal found on the beach after the first Trial. He ate it and said it was like an energy shot."

"Do you think…" Halo looks up at Fyve and he breaks into a grin.

"I do think!" He leans forward and kisses her quickly on the lips. "We've found our gift for Terra."

She touches her lips with her fingertips, wishing the kiss had lasted longer. Although, the way her skin is stinging from her swim, it's probably best it hadn't.

"Do you think that's what the leatherskin was circling?" Sevin asks from the other raft. "Was it trying to catch some of those for its lunch?"

Halo nods. "That makes sense."

Fyve reaches into a tire on their raft and takes out one of the tightly packed plastic bottles. Lying down on his stomach, he leans forward and dips the bottle into the middle of the school of tiny creatures.

"I got three!" he exclaims, handing the bottle to Halo, and removing another one.

"We can't take out all the bottles," Sevin warns.

"I know." Fyve nods. "Halo, empty some of the water out from your bottle. Be careful not to lose any squishy things. I'll get some more to add to them."

He leans over the raft again, this time catching a whole lot more.

"Are you sure you can eat these things?" Halo asks, as he transfers them to her bottle.

Fyve tips four of them into his hand, passing them out so they each have one.

"Let's eat one now," he says. "For energy. We're going to need it for our trip back. Especially Justice."

Sevin pulls a face. "But it's so squishy!"

Halo doesn't hesitate. If it was good enough for Coal, then it's good enough for her. She puts it straight in her mouth and bites down hard. It's bitter but far better than the acid that had been stinging her throat, and she swallows the two halves.

"Not bad." She nods encouragingly at Justice and Sevin.

Fyve eats his ball of squish and Justice and Sevin glance at each other before following suit.

"Gross!" Sevin complains.

"It's food," says Fyve. "Be grateful."

"It's way better than having an oar stuck in your leg," says Justice, her face still worryingly pale.

Sevin's eyes flare in horror. "Actually, it wasn't that bad," she quickly adds. "I feel more energized already. Don't you, Justice?"

Halo focuses back on the task at hand, working with Fyve to collect four bottles full of squirming little squishy things with wings.

"That's enough," says Fyve. "I don't think we can afford to lose more bottles from the tires. And this way we have one bottle for each of us to present to Terra."

Everyone nods in agreement.

"Now to get back," groans Halo. They still haven't worked out what they're going to use for oars.

There's an almighty howl from behind them and Halo spins around, certain the leatherskin must be back. She gasps when she sees what it is.

Justice has pulled the oar from her leg and blood is flowing out at a rapid rate.

"What did you do?" squeals Sevin, taking hold of the oar. "Fyve told you not to do that."

"You'll never get back without the oar," Justice says, her voice laced with pain. She lies down on her back and covers her face with her hands. "I had to do it."

"Sevin!" says Halo urgently. "Swap places with me. Quickly. And give the oar to Fyve. We need to get Justice back to shore."

Sevin scrambles off the smaller raft back onto the larger one and Halo carefully climbs aboard. There's blood ballooning into the water. If the injured leatherskin doesn't pick up its scent, another one is sure to. They don't have much time to get to safety for so many reasons.

She balances herself next to Justice and takes her lucky cord from her pocket. It's been used for many purposes over the years, but this is going to be its most important one yet. She needs it to save Justice's life. Perhaps all of their lives.

Wobbling slightly as Fyve begins rowing, Halo threads her cord underneath Justice's leg. She scrambles with the rough timber of the raft and breaks off a loose piece about the size of her finger, wincing as it splinters into her palm. She quickly ties the cord around Justice's leg a couple of inches above the wound, placing the stick in the knot. Then she turns the stick until Justice is yelping and the blood circulation is cut off to her leg. The bleeding immediately slows down.

"We're going to get you back," she tells Justice. "Fyve is strong. You're going to be okay. I know it's hard, but just try to relax. Focus on your breathing. And don't move."

Justice's whimpers. "Does it have to be so tight?"

"I'm sorry, but it does." She hates that she's causing her so much pain. "I had to stop the bleeding. What you did was really stupid. But also one of the bravest things I've ever seen."

"Striker saved me," Justice says in a low voice. "It was my turn to do the same."

Halo's eyes brim with tears.

Life on Treasure Island is cruel.

Unfair.

Unkind.

But despite that, it still managed to produce people like Justice and Striker. She looks across at Fyve and Sevin, and adds them to her list, along with Coal.

What will life in Tomorrow Land be like? Because surely the four of them have done more than enough to make it on that ship.

She looks at the sun getting lower in the sky. Soon, the final Gratitude will be held. Soon, they're going to find out.

FYVE

The sun setting over the ocean is usually spectacular, but today, it's as if Terra knows this Gratitude is special. Significant. The sun is a glowing, orange orb hovering just above a calm, crimson ocean. It frames The Oasis as if it's saving the last of the light just for it. Fyve glances down at the four bottles of slowly moving creatures sitting on the multi-colored sand, marveling at the way their luminous bodies seem to absorb the rays of sun, as if they're trying to capture this moment and hold on. He can't blame them.

The people of Treasure Island are about to learn who will be leaving on the giant ship that's patiently waiting. And Fyve, Halo, Sevin and Justice will be among them. They have to be.

They're the only ones who found anything of worth to present to Terra.

Their four bottles are lined up with the other *gifts*. A single shoe, brown and partially dissolved. A length of rope, tangled and frayed. A few jagged shards of stained plastic, with no way to identify what they once belonged to. And then four bottles holding something everyone on Treasure Island never stops praying for, something those on The Oasis will need for their journey—food.

Fyve can still feel the jolt of energy the little being infused him with. It has him feeling alert in a way he hasn't experienced in a long time. Possibly ever. Each of those ocean butterflies is a nutrition injection. He can see it's had the same effect on Halo, Sevin and Justice. Halo's taller, her face brighter, making her impossibly more beautiful. Justice made it to Gratitude, despite her injury. Admittedly, carried here by her brother Zake, who's fussed over her like he's discovered he has a heart. Fyve would even swear Sevin is squinting less.

Those four bottles are their ticket to Tomorrow Land. And hopefully, for ninety-six other teens, too.

Elijah turns from where he was facing the setting sun and The Oasis, smiling broadly. No, beaming. Terra's messenger is about to deliver the final verdict, and he's looking forward to it. Fyve's first instinct is a flash of revulsion. Of course, Elijah's only focusing on the promise of The Oasis. His place was always guaranteed. There will be little or no acknowledgement of those who died today or in the other Trials, including Coal, or those left behind. But Fyve quickly pushes the thought away. He's here, alive, being provided an opportunity others have made the ultimate sacrifice for. And that's something to be grateful for.

Tomorrow Land is the future. And he'll be forging it.

For Coal.

For Won, Too, Threy, Fore, Syx, and Ate.

He glances over his shoulder, spotting the wild hair of his mother. Even for her endless, fruitless searching. He's going to find Tomorrow Land for her, too. So that missing out on a mom for so much of his life wasn't for nothing.

"My people," Elijah intones, his voice low but still creating a ripple through the crowd. "Terra is truly great."

Echoes of his words rise into a sky now the same color as the ocean.

"She has cared for us. Graced us with her love and protection. And now she has sent us The Oasis. She will guide us to Tomorrow Land. We praise her."

"Praise Terra! Glory to Terra!"

Elijah nods, obviously pleased with the fervent response. There's no sign of the discontent from this morning. "Would those who took part in the generous opportunity she presented us please step forward."

His heart a hammer against his ribs, Fyve does just that. Halo's on his right, Sevin on his left. Zake helps Justice, seeming to wince at every one of his sister's grimaces of pain. He makes sure she's stable as she leans her weight on her good leg, the other wrapped in a stained bandage, then steps back. Fyve feels Halo tense beside him as Zake passes them and he can't blame her. He doesn't trust the guy's new attitude, either.

Elijah nods at the motley crowd of teens. A few are leaning against each other, others look as if standing is taking a whole lot of concentration. "The final Trial is complete. Terra has chosen. Line up and you will learn if you have proven your worth."

Fyve squeezes Halo's hand and releases it as the teens spread out along the beach, forming a long line facing the setting sun. A strange sensation fills his gut, his chest, his heart. A warm one. An excited one. He draws in a sharp breath as he realizes what the alien emotion is.

Hope.

Sevin bounces on her toes beside him, and he knows the same feeling is fueling her. It almost makes him smile. Did he gift it to her? Or did she gift it to him? Or was it Halo, with her beautiful, clever, determined mind who was the essential ingredient for the emotion to thrive? He has no idea, but he's looking forward to nurturing it with them.

Elijah moves to the north end of the line, meaning Fyve and the others are about twenty people down. Only a few minutes away from being chosen.

Or not.

Fyve straightens his shoulders. Their gelatinous butterflies of the sea are still moving in their plastic bottles. They couldn't have failed this final Trial, just like they hadn't all the ones before.

Elijah glances at the first person in the line, a tall, too-skinny kid who's trembling, and walks straight past. No one's sure if that means what they think it does until Elijah touches the second person, a girl who looks little older than Sevin, on the shoulder. "You are chosen."

The girl lets out a half-gasp, half-sob. "Terra is great," she chokes out through tears of happiness.

The young man who was first in line drops to his knees, burying his face in his hands. "No." Although the word is whispered, it's heard down the line long past Fyve. Maybe because they can all relate to the devastation that has the power to carry it for miles. It's the same emotion they'll all experience if they're not chosen.

Elijah moves to the next teen. "You are chosen." Then the next. "You are chosen." Then the next. "You are chosen."

Sevin bounces even higher. "One hundred must've passed!" she whispers excitedly.

Fyve can't help but think she's right. More people are being chosen than skipped.

"You are chosen."

"You are chosen."

The next is already puffing out her chest, but Elijah glances at her then continues on. She deflates, a low keening sound pouring out of her tightly clenched lips, her disappointment compounded because she'd allowed herself to become confident. Fyve frowns, realizing that's exactly what he's been doing.

"You are chosen."

Fyve registers the next one is Halo's brother, Ajax. He nods, the movement short and curt, almost as if he's been given a task rather than an honor. Behind him, a strangled sob has him stiffening, one that Fyve isn't sure whether it's a happy or an anguished sound.

"Cloud," Halo murmurs, sounding pained.

Ajax's partner. The one carrying his child.

The one who will be left behind.

"You are chosen," Elijah says to the next teen, and they whoop and punch the air.

The words muffle as Fyve's pulse fills his ears. Elijah is only a few teens away. Halo will learn whether she's chosen. Then he will. Then Sevin. His breath saws in and out of his chest. The moment feels like it's coming too fast. Like he's not ready.

Elijah stops at his daughter, and something shifts in his gray eyes. "You are chosen."

A blinding smile explodes across Halo's face, but she quickly snuffs it out. The same happiness burns Fyve with the same intensity. Halo's been chosen. She'll be able to spend as much time as she likes in the engine room as she seeks Tomorrow Land.

Elijah reaches Fyve, and everything stops. His roaring pulse. His turbulent breathing. His ability to think.

"You are chosen."

It takes a second or two for the words to infiltrate, but when they do, Fyve still struggles to believe them. He's been chosen?

He's been chosen!

Joy is a song in his veins. A dawn in his mind. A dance in his heart. Impulsively, he reaches out and grabs Halo's hand, the feeling only growing when she clamps his as tightly as he has hers. They've both been chosen.

They're going to Tomorrow Land.

A place of plenty. A place of hope. And most importantly, a place where lies can't hide.

Elijah moves onto Sevin and Fyve grips her hand, too, waiting to feel her own burst of happiness. His sister is practically vibrating beside him.

Elijah glances at her, his lashes flicker, and he moves onto Justice. "You are chosen."

For the second time, Fyve's world stops, but this time, it's frozen by denial. Sevin wasn't chosen. She won't be coming on The Oasis with him.

"No!"

But it's not Fyve's throat the word is wrenched from. He spins around to find their mother running toward them. "No!" she screams again.

A whimper fractures through Sevin. A second later, she streaks away, past their mother, past the crowd, and disappears into the village.

Their mother hesitates for a second, then continues her trajectory toward the beach and the line of teens. Toward Elijah. "They promised!"

Elijah sucks in a sharp breath. "Dee—"

"No! After everything I've sacrificed, my daughter is supposed to be chosen!"

"Terra has spoken," he says sharply.

"Well, Terra isn't—"

She drops to the ground, her hands clamping over her ears, and Fyve instantly realizes what's happening.

"No," he gasps, rushing toward her. "Mom!"

She pitches forward, another scream ripping through the air, but this one is full of a different kind of pain. It's not grief. It's agony. Fyve catches her before she plows into the sand, dropping to his knees beside her.

His mother writhes in his arms, her eyes rolling back to reveal what should be white but is already blooming with blood.

"Mom," he says frantically, even though he has no idea what he's asking for. "Please."

She goes rigid, her back bowed at an unnatural angle, her breath scraping out in fractured pants. Fyve can feel warm blood pooling in his palms as he cradles her head. Her mouth works stiffly. "Don't...trust..."

"No, I need to tell you—"

"Terra."

"Mom, please, listen," Fyve chokes. The blood is now running from her eyes like a waterfall of tears. "I love you."

But it's too late. She's gone.

Claimed.

A gentle hand lands on his arm, but it still makes him flinch. He turns to find Halo looking up at him, eyes swimming with compassion. "Fyve, please, don't—"

He yanks his arm away. "I have to check on Sevin," he whispers. Moisture glimmers along Halo's eyelashes and he turns away before it can pool into tears. He can't stop them any more than he could stop the losses that just tore his heart to pieces.

Terra hasn't given him anything. She's taken everything. His mother is dead. Sevin will die here.

And he and Halo no longer have a future.

He walks away, back in the direction of the village, heading toward the tomorrows he was destined for all along.

He won't be leaving Treasure Island.

HALO

*H*alo leaves Gratitude with no idea where she's going. The place that's been her home all her life suddenly feels foreign. She belongs and she doesn't. Everything she sees now is the story of her past, no longer her future. Her father had said the ship will sail in the morning. Tomorrow Land awaits her.

Yet...

Is it a tomorrow she still wants? Is a land of plenty worth it if there's no Fyve? No Sevin. No Coal. No Striker. Because it was clear from Fyve's face just now that he won't be joining her on The Oasis. And how can she blame him?

Her only friend will be Justice, who's really more like a little sister. Perhaps when she grows up, the age gap between them will shrink and a different kind of closeness will develop.

She lets out a sigh as she leaves the beach. As much as Halo likes Justice, she's not who she wants with her on that ship. Then she remembers with a wave of shame that there are two other people she'd completely forgotten about—Ajax and her father.

She's spent her entire life until now with these two males,

but no matter how much she tries to imagine her future, she just can't see them in it. Or is that just because she doesn't want to? During the Trials, she'd questioned if blood is thicker than water, and she now has her answer.

It isn't.

Bonds are forged from trust. And she struggles to think of two people she trusts less than her father or her brother. She'd thought she was entering these Trials so that Terra could decide if she was worthy, and instead she'd discovered her worth all for herself. She *is* worthy of a better future. But no more worthy than Sevin, which makes the entire process the biggest deception Treasure Island has seen yet.

She takes the road in the direction of Fyve's house, plagued by thoughts she can't quite slot into place. There's something going on here. Something big. *No.* Bigger than big. The entire population of Treasure Island has been fooled into believing something that simply can't be real.

And that's Terra herself.

There are so many things her father isn't telling them. And Fyve's mom's words as she was being claimed had been undeniable. She'd said that after everything she'd sacrificed that Sevin was supposed to be chosen. That it was, in fact, *promised.* Who exactly had promised her that?

Halo reaches Fyve's hut and bows her head, aware of the pain that will be contained within the flimsy walls.

"Hello?" she calls out. "Fyve? Sevin?"

There's no answer so she dares to lift back the fabric that acts as a door.

Sevin is curled on her sleeping mat with her face in her hands. Fyve is nowhere to be seen, which is odd. She'd thought he'd gone to look for his sister.

"Sevin," she says gently. "You're here."

Sevin pulls back her hands to reveal her tear-stained face. "And it's where I'll always be. Forever."

"That's not true," Halo soothes. "The ship will return for anyone left behind once we've found Tomorrow Land."

Sevin sits up and glares at Halo. "And if you believe that then you're not as smart as I thought you were."

Her words punch Halo in the chest, partly because of their force, but mostly because of their truth. There have been so many lies already. Why should anyone believe the ship will come back? If Terra wanted all of them in Tomorrow Land, she'd have found a way to take them all on her ship.

"Have you seen Fyve yet?" Halo glances at Dee's empty sleeping mat and realizes if Sevin hasn't seen Fyve, she won't have heard what happened. But is that Halo's place to tell her such news? Surely, those words would be better to come from Fyve.

Sevin shakes her head. "I knew he'd come looking for me, so I hid until after he'd checked our hut. Then I knew it would be safe to go inside."

"You're avoiding him?" Halo squats down on the mat beside Sevin.

Sevin nods. "I don't want to hear what he's going to say. He'll tell me he's staying behind. That he can't leave without me. But he has to go! It's not his fault I wasn't good enough."

Halo puts a tentative hand on Sevin's back. "You *are* good enough, Sevin. I don't know how these choices were made but it has nothing to do with that. You're better than everyone else on this island. You've more than proven that this past week."

"It's because I can't see very well," says Sevin. "Terra thinks it's a weakness. It's why she took Coal, too. She doesn't want our defective genes in her precious Tomorrow Land."

"Coal was the two hundredth competitor to..." Halo's words fade as she realizes nobody actually has any idea what number person Coal was to step on that trap. Sevin could be completely right.

"My mom will be so disappointed," says Sevin on a groan.

Halo winces. Sevin needs to know what happened. It's not fair to keep information from her like this.

"I'm going to find Fyve," she says, standing up. "You two have a lot to talk about. Can you promise me you'll wait here?"

Sevin doesn't seem impressed. "I already told you I'm avoiding him."

"But he needs to talk to you." She takes a step toward the door.

"What he needs is to go on that ship," says Sevin, defiantly. "Otherwise, all of this was for nothing. The whole stinking lot of it. Please, you have to convince him. If anyone can, it's you."

Halo groans and sinks back down beside Sevin. "Nobody can convince him to leave you. You know that. As close as Fyve and I have become, there's nobody he loves more than you. He'll never leave you. And...maybe I shouldn't either."

Sevin gasps. "Not you, too! You have to go. You *want* to go. I can't be responsible for both of you losing your chance at this."

"You're not responsible. You need to remember that. Always." Halo places her hand on Sevin's, hating how broken this already broken girl is going to be when she hears what Fyve has to tell her. "None of this is your fault."

"Fyve needs to stop treating me like a baby." Sevin crosses her arms. "I can look after myself. I know what I'm doing. I have plans of my own, you know."

There's something strange in the way Sevin says this last bit that has Halo's hackles rising. She's up to something. But, what? She remains silent, hoping Sevin will choose to fill the air with words.

Sevin shakes her head quickly as if trying to get herself back on track. "I'm going to finish building your forest for a start. Just like you asked me to when you thought I was too young for the Trials. And I'm going to fix this..." She crawls across the small hut to something covered in a piece of cloth and pulls it back.

"My motor!" Halo gasps, even though she's not totally surprised. Of course, Fyve had retrieved it. That's exactly something he'd do.

"I'm going to get it running," says Sevin. "And I'm going to use it to turn the island to face the sun so that it sets in the same place every night. I'm going to build a giant star out of glass, and the sun will reflect the light and make pretty patterns across the water. And I'm going to build the waterfall I told you about, and a giant compass, and—"

"Sevin!" Halo stops her, aware that she's deflecting. "You're just trying to convince me that you're going to be fine so that I get on that ship."

"I *am* going to be fine." She crosses her arms once more. "So, don't you stay behind just because of me. And you can tell Fyve if he stays, I'll never talk to him again."

"And how do you think that will go?" she asks with the hint of a smile.

"I don't need him," Sevin insists. "I have Mom. She won't go out on her raft again if she knows Fyve is going to Tomorrow Land. She'll have no reason to. We'll be fine."

This wipes any kind of smile from Halo's face. It doesn't feel right not to tell her what happened. What if she leaves the hut and Sevin finds out from someone else before Fyve gets the chance to tell her?

"Sevin," she says, reaching for her hand. "After you left Gratitude, your mom was claimed."

Sevin pulls her hand away like Halo had scorched it. "That's not true."

"I'm so sorry." Halo goes to reach for her again but stops herself. "It is true. She was upset about you not being chosen. She spoke up. It was all very quick. But Fyve was there. He was holding her when she died. I really am very sorry."

"No," Sevin whimpers, scurrying over to her mother's

sleeping mat and picking up the soft bundle of cloth she uses as a pillow and holding it to her face. "No."

"Fyve will never leave you," says Halo. "Especially not now. And nor should he. It's time you accepted that."

"Go and find him," Sevin begs. "Please, Halo. I'll wait right here."

Halo stands, glad to be able to do something useful to help this girl. She knows how it feels to lose a mother, and it's the worst thing in the whole entire world. Sevin is going to need Fyve more than ever now.

Although, the question remains, does Halo need Fyve? Because just like him, she's no longer sure she's going to set foot on that ship.

FYVE

*F*yve rakes his fingers through his hair, desperately trying to keep the panic under control. It keeps cinching around his chest, crawling up his throat, coiling through his thoughts. Some moments he can't breathe. Others, his head swims and his eyes blur with tears.

Sevin's missing.

Because Sevin wasn't chosen.

After stopping by their hut, Fyve ran frantically through the village, but there was no sign of her. He'd checked the rat trap, but it was empty, which hadn't surprised him. Today wasn't a day of gifts. He'd even run to where his mother's raft is buried, the same one his sister dug up so she could try to find Tomorrow Land herself. He fully expected Sevin to do the same again. But the ground was undisturbed, and a quick scraping away of the sand had revealed it's still there.

Now, he's running toward where the raft they'd built in the Trials should be, berating himself. Of course, that's the raft Sevin would take. Except its black outline sits on the sand, just beyond the reach of the waves. His sister hasn't left the island.

Fyve curses under his breath as he looks one way then the

other, as if he can make Sevin appear just by sheer force of will. At least she hasn't gone out to sea again, determined to leave alone. Once he finds her, he'll explain they're going to figure this out. Their tomorrows may be here on Treasure Island, but at least they'll see them together. It's a promise Fyve makes deep in his heart. Sevin isn't doing this alone.

Turning around, he trudges back to their hut, resigned to wait until she returns. Then, he'll hold her and reassure her. They'll find solace in each other. In the one constant they've always been able to depend on—family.

Despite the determined vows, the walk takes longer than it usually would. Fyve's feet feel like they've multiplied in weight and each step requires conscious thought. His body is exhausted. A heavy numbness is slowly blanketing his mind.

His mother's dead. Every angry word he's ever thrown at her arrows through his heart. He'd been so busy pushing her away so her leaving wouldn't hurt that he never allowed himself to admit the truth—it hurt. Because he missed her. Whether she was here or gone, she was his mother. And he loved her. Yet, when he finally realized that, when he finally said the words, it was too late.

Could Terra take anything else from him?

He slows even more as he hesitates. His mother's body would've been taken to the small inlet ready for her final good-bye. Dead bodies court decay and disease, meaning they can't be left in the village. When Sevin's back, he'll have to take her there, but that can wait till dawn. He doubts either of them can face doing that right now. Fyve grits his teeth as the next thought impales him. They'll do it after The Oasis has left.

He doesn't care what Terra has promised, or what Tomorrow Land could bring. Family comes first. It always has and always will.

Their hut crouches in the near dark, leaning slightly as if even it's lost the strength to hold itself straight. Fyve slips past the material hanging over the entrance, frowning when he registers Halo's motor has been removed from the half barrel. Why would Sevin take it out, today of all days?

The frown dissolves when he realizes there's something else in the hut. No, someone.

Sevin is lying on her mat, staring up at the ceiling, one arm thrown out wide, the other lying on her chest.

"Sevin," he says, his voice fracturing.

She doesn't answer.

"Sevin," he says again, clearing his throat. She needs to hear what he has to say next. "I'm not leaving. I'm staying with you."

Still no answer.

He steps closer, intending on lying beside her and comforting her. They've shared a mat all their lives. He was the one who held her each time their mother left. Each time a sibling died. Each time they went to sleep, their stomachs painfully empty. Just knowing the other was there meant they could wake up the next morning, willing to go on.

But he stops, Sevin's stillness seeming to freeze every molecule in the hut. Not only has she not spoken, she hasn't moved.

Nor has he ever seen her lie like that. Sevin is a side-sleeper. Someone who's always curled up, no matter how old she grew.

"Sevin?" Fyve asks, his whisper feeling loud in the stillness.

Silence.

One step closer and he sees it, stark against his sister's pale skin. Blood.

It runs in jagged lines from her eyes to her temples. From her nose and down her cheeks. Even from her ears and into her hair.

Fyve falls to his knees. A choked sound claws at his throat.

No.

Not Sevin.

She can't be claimed.

Fyve glances at the motor. Was that why she was taken from him, like everyone else? Because she was dreaming of forging her future even though she wasn't chosen? Is Terra that vindictive?

Pushing to his feet, he staggers backward. He can't say good-bye. It's too much.

First Coal. Then his mother. Now his only sister.

Spinning on his heel, Fyve blindly runs through the village. He has no idea where he's going. Or what the point is. He can't run from this.

They're all dead. His whole family.

He's alone.

He only stops when he reaches the edge of the island. There's nowhere else to go. His legs give out and he crumples to the sand. He falls forward, his hands digging into the sand, his shoulders heaving. Tears fall, darkening the already night-colored sand. Grief wrenches at his insides, shredding them. A howl of agony is trying to escape, only to be twisted and tortured by the violent emotion.

His whole world is collapsing. It will never be the same again.

He'll never be the same again.

"Fyve?"

Halo's voice filters through the pain, the warm, light sound feeling out of place in this black moment.

She kneels beside him. "I'm so sorry, Fyve. Your mother didn't deserve to be taken like that."

He sags back so he's sitting on his haunches. "It's Sevin," he says hoarsely. "She's also been claimed."

Halo's gasp is one of shock. Horror. An echo of the agony eating away at him. Her arms slip around him, and he sinks into the comfort she's offering. The tears start, hot and scalding. Yet cold and drenching.

"I'm so sorry," she whispers as she holds him tightly, as if she knows he's falling apart. And the tighter she holds, the harder he cries, his whole body shuddering and heaving. "How could this have happened? I was just with her."

Fyve doesn't answer, but he's quickly learning that each wracking sob doesn't reduce the pain. Somehow, they seem to amplify it. Each one punctuates the passing of time. The future he now has to face. Without Sevin. Yet, Halo doesn't relax her hold, like she intends on being here as long as this takes.

Eventually, the sobs recede, his exhausted body no longer able to expel the grief. He sags in Halo's arms, his eyes gritty and throat aching.

Halo pulls back, pushing away the strands of hair stuck to his face. "Sevin was special."

He can barely make her out in the dark, but the compassion is almost palpable. "She really was." His sister was meant for great things. She was smart. A dreamer. "But it didn't matter. She's gone."

Halo's hands twitch where they're holding his arms. "Which means there's no longer a reason for you to stay."

Although the words are said softly, gently, Fyve rears back. "What?"

"You know I'm talking about leaving on The Oasis." Halo shuffles closer. "I know Sevin was your world, but I also know she'd want you to do this."

"You want me to do this." He knows the words are harsh, probably unfair, but he can't stop them. Everything is too raw.

Halo flinches. "I do," she admits. "But not just for me. I want this for you. Because I care about you, Fyve. You've crept into my heart."

A flicker of warmth ghosts over his own heart, but Fyve is tired of feeling. He presses the heels of his hands into his temples. "I...I can't think about this right now."

"You have to," she says, sounding like she wishes it were otherwise. "The Oasis leaves at dawn."

"I don't care about any of that," he snaps. "About Terra. Or Tomorrow Land. Or whatever the truth is."

None of it matters anymore.

He hates Terra.

Tomorrow Land no longer promises hope.

And the truth is, he's alone.

Halo takes a step back, and the distance suddenly feels too far. Wrong. Yet Fyve doesn't move. "Hopefully you'll find something you do care about then," she whispers.

She walks away, quickly being swallowed by the night. Fyve listens to her footsteps for as long as he can, even as he remains where he is, staring out at the black sea. It doesn't feel like his heart will ever care again.

Halo's right. He has nothing to stay for.

But that doesn't mean he can bring himself to leave.

HALO

$\mathcal{H}$alo stands on the deck of The Oasis, looking out at Treasure Island. It's strange to see it at a distance. And from this height, too. The island looks smaller, like the lives on it are somehow diminished, even though she knows that's not true. Is that how Terra feels when she looks down on them from her mysterious cloud in the sky?

She pushes away her cynical thoughts and scans the water for a sign of Fyve, hoping he's changed his mind and decided to come aboard. She hates that she'd had to try to talk him into it so soon after Sevin's death, but there had been no time to lose. It makes zero sense for him to stay behind. Not after losing the three people he was closest to. And she can guarantee that his mom, Sevin and Coal would all want him to leave. His hardcore stubborn streak is literally the only thing stopping him.

Which is why she had to make the impossible decision to leave without him. She can't let his stubbornness ruin both their lives.

The raft Sevin made with Fyve is being used to ferry the chosen teens to the ship. It was the only one sturdy enough to have survived that final Trial. Her father's helpers are taking turns to row three people out at a time with another two on Justice's raft being towed behind. The process is excruciatingly slow, but Halo's glad as it buys more time for Fyve to change his mind. She won't let go of hope until the last trip has been made and the rope ladder has been pulled up.

She blinks in the morning light, her eyes stinging from all the tears she shed overnight. Crying isn't normally something she allows herself to succumb to, but Sevin's death had tipped her over the edge. She'd loved that girl. It's so hard to believe she's actually gone. And it seems that Halo may have been the very last person who'd talked to her. Now, not only will Sevin not be getting on this ship, but she'll never be able to fulfill all the big plans she had for Treasure Island either.

Why would Terra claim an innocent young girl? Had she not liked the idea of Sevin's plans? Or had Sevin been in on whatever it was that her mother had clearly been up to?

Halo sighs, trying to accept she'll never know.

She reaches in her pocket for her lucky cord, then remembers it had been used to save Justice's life. It hadn't felt right to ask for it back. And somehow, it doesn't feel lucky anymore. Its purpose was served. She'll need to find a lucky something else aboard this ship. Pain winds its way through her chest. It's not a lucky-something she wants. It's a lucky-someone.

There's a grunting sound from the rope ladder and Halo leans over the railing of the deck to see what's going on. Zake is climbing up and complaining loudly. Halo looks around to see if anyone's going to stop him. He wasn't chosen! But then she looks closer and sees Justice pinned between Zake and the rungs of the ladder.

With her brother's help, Justice hauls herself up another rung using both hands and her good leg. That girl is nothing if not determined. If Sevin were here, she'd be shouting out encouragement as she jumped up and down with excitement.

When Justice reaches the top of the ladder, Zake climbs aboard and lifts her over the railing.

"Don't worry," he says to Halo, noticing her watching him. "I'm not staying. Just helping my sister, that's all."

Halo takes a few steps back, having no desire to talk to Zake. She'll ask how Justice is once Zake has gotten her settled and is well and truly off this ship and out of her life forever. That is one decision Terra got right, and one person Halo definitely won't miss.

Zake picks up Justice, cradling her as he walks across the deck toward the heavy door that leads to the stairwell.

Halo looks down at the raft bobbing on the ocean to check if Fyve is on the next trip across, and when he isn't, she goes to the swimming pool in the middle of the deck. Ajax is standing by the edge with one of the three red-headed sisters who Halo had selected to continue the final Trial. They're looking a lot more friendly with each other than she would expect, given Ajax has only just said his final goodbye to Cloud.

"Hey!" the girl says when she sees Halo. "Isn't it exciting?"

Halo gives her a wan smile, finding it too hard to summon the enthusiasm she knows she should. This is the day they've all been dreaming of. Somehow, it's turned out to feel like a day filled with dread.

"My sisters were both chosen as well," the girl beams. "We're all here together. Just like you and your brother."

"Great to keep the siblings together." Ajax winks at Halo. "Where's your boyfriend? Oh, that's right. His sister didn't make it through."

"She was claimed last night," says Halo, trying to keep the pain out of her voice. "And Fyve decided not to come."

"Oh." That wipes the smile off Ajax's face. He actually seems genuinely upset for her. "That's not good."

"No, it's not." Halo pulls back her shoulders, determined not to let more tears fall. Especially in front of Ajax.

"Well, this might cheer you up," says Ajax pointing at the pool. "Look what Viney just noticed."

It takes Halo a few beats to figure out that Viney is the name of the girl. She supposes that it won't take long and she'll know the names of every one of the hundred chosen to step aboard the ship.

She looks down into the pool, her eyes widening to see what Ajax is pointing at. The squishy winged creatures they'd collected in the final Trial are swimming about in the water. There's a green blob floating on the surface that seems to be providing shelter, or perhaps food.

"They're called pteropods," says Viney. "Or pods for short. Your father said we're going to breed them. That way, we'll have plenty of them to keep us going for the entire trip, rather than just a one-off meal."

"What an original idea," says Halo, thinking of Fyve and Sevin attempting to breed rats. She has visions of people sneaking into the pool for a midnight snack. Perhaps Terra should have tested for integrity as well as strength and smarts.

"I thought you'd be more excited," says Ajax. "It's because of you that these pods are here."

"It's because of Coal." She glances up to the sky. "He was the one who tested if they were safe to eat. And then Fyve was the one who collected them on the raft that Sevin designed. I didn't do much."

Ajax seems to find this funny. He turns to Viney. "My sister hasn't learned yet that if you're the only one left, you may as well take the credit."

Viney grins back at him in the kind of adoring way that makes Halo's stomach roll. She may have made a mistake selecting her to go through to the final Trials.

"I'll catch you both later," Halo says, deciding she'd almost rather risk running into Zake on his way off the ship than talk to these two any longer.

She returns to the rope ladder to find her father hauling it up. Glancing around the deck, she does a quick count, deciding there's close to one hundred teens. Everyone who was chosen is here. Except the one person she most wants.

Going to the railings, she looks out at Treasure Island and sees the entire population has gathered on the beach with their hands in the air, waving their goodbyes. Fyve's aunt and cousins are standing right at the end of the beach where they release departed loved ones into the sea. They must be there to say goodbye to Sevin and Dee. Halo squints, trying to make out Fyve's familiar form. But he's not there.

A wave of disappointment washes over her. She would've liked to see him one last time. Why did he have to be so stubborn? They could have had such a beautiful future together. Life doesn't hand out too many opportunities in a place like Treasure Island. This was their only shot. And now it's gone.

The ship lurches into motion and Halo wonders who's behind the controls, given her father is up here on the deck. That's going to be one of the first of many secrets she uncovers. Except instead of uncovering them with Fyve, she's going to have to investigate by herself.

"Congratulations," her father says in a loud voice, raising his arms. "Terra has chosen you to step aboard her ship to seek Tomorrow Land. You are the strongest and smartest that Treasure Island has to offer, and you should all be very proud of yourselves. Take a moment to say goodbye to your families. It may be a while until you see them again."

The crowd gathers at the railings to wave, and Halo looks for Cloud. Unable to find her in the blur of faces, she looks for Fyve's family at the end of the beach. They're the only people she feels any connection to. The ones who will spend their lives rolling their eyes at his bad jokes and basking in the glory of his smile.

They're waving energetically at the ship and Halo waves

back, wondering how they're summoning such enthusiasm given they just released Sevin and her mother into the ocean. They continue their waving and Halo gasps to realize they're not waving goodbye, they're trying to get the ship's attention.

Because halfway between the shore and the ship is the familiar blue plastic raft that Fyve's mom used to take on her trips out to the ocean. And it's being rowed by the only person who's ever made Halo's heart sing and pulse race all at the same time.

"Fyve!" she calls, as her hand flies to her mouth.

But the ship is already pulling away, so she runs to her father and tugs on his sleeve.

"Fyve's here!" she tells him, hardly able to get her words out in her excitement. "We have to wait for him."

"It's too late," her father says, scanning the ocean until he spots him. "We can't stop now."

"Who can't stop?" she asks. "Someone has to be controlling this thing."

"Terra is," he says. "I'm telling you, Halo. We can't stop."

Her entire body churning with anguish, Halo leans out over the rails. Fyve is moving fast. But is it going to be fast enough?

"Hurry!" she calls out, untying the rope ladder and flinging it over the side of the ship. Her heart is pounding faster than Fyve's arms are pumping as he closes in on the ship. They're moving very slowly as the engines are roaring to life, but that could change at any moment.

Unwilling to take any chances, Halo launches herself over the side of the ship and climbs down the ladder. If Fyve doesn't catch up, she'll throw herself into the ocean. Because she knows now that she made a mistake getting on board without him. She was determined not to let Fyve's stubbornness ruin both their lives but really it was her stubbornness that was responsible. She'd been so fixated on getting on the ship that she hadn't really stopped to consider she could find happiness any other way. Being together is the only thing that matters. She has to be with Fyve!

She reaches the bottom of the ladder and looks out. Fyve is still a few yards away. He powers forward, his strong arms hauling his oar through the water. The ladder swings as the ship begins to move a little faster and Halo leans out with her arm extended.

Fyve gives his raft one last push and surges forward. He stands, leaps, and flies into the air, gripping onto Halo's hand, then swinging himself forward so the ladder takes his weight. She holds on tight, somehow managing to keep herself from slipping off.

He made it! They made it! Tears sting at her eyes but this time from the sheer joy of the moment.

There's cheering above and Halo glances up to see a line of faces peering over the railing. These people she doesn't even know just yet are all happy for them. Perhaps Terra had somehow tested for integrity or kindness after all.

"Are you okay, Angel?" Fyve asks, positioning himself on the ladder so his face is level with hers.

"I am now." She smiles but it's an expression that's quickly smothered as he presses his lips to hers. And there's that feeling that makes her pulse race and her heart sing all at the same time. Because when she's with Fyve, nothing and no one else matters. And now she gets to do this every day for the rest of her life because Fyve chose a life with the love he found over one mourning those he lost.

The ship picks up speed and Fyve and Halo break apart. They climb up the ladder as quickly as they can, and two guys who look familiar from the Trials help them on board. There's more cheering and Fyve takes a bow.

"I like to make a dramatic entrance," he says with a smile.

As the crowd returns to waving at the disappearing faces of their families standing on the shore, Halo's eyes are drawn to the sole tree on Treasure Island, and she watches the wind caress its plastic leaves.

Fyve wraps his arms around her from behind as they look out at the island that's been their home all their lives. His eyes are glued to his family gathered on the beach and he waves, drinking in his final view of them.

"Did you give Sevin and your mom a good farewell?" Halo asks.

"No," he says. "We were about to, but then I realized I'd never make it onboard this ship in time. Aunt Cee will take care of it. She was the one who convinced me to go. It's what Mom and Sevin would have wanted. And Coal."

Halo nods, not pointing out she'd already told him that. Clearly, he hadn't been ready to hear it. Sometimes it's not what you say, but when you say it.

She returns her gaze to her tree, knowing that soon it will get smaller as the ship moves away, then she'll never see it, or anything else on Treasure Island, again.

There's a scrap of movement and Halo narrows her gaze. She has to hold back a gasp when she realizes what it is.

Or rather, who it is.

Sevin has climbed up the tree and is waving at them.

She's alive! But...how is that even possible?

A flood of memories rush back to Halo of that last conversation she'd had with Sevin. She'd been up to something, that had been clear. But Halo hadn't been able to figure out what. And she'd been determined not to be responsible for either Halo or Fyve staying behind just because she hadn't been chosen. She'd wanted Fyve to live the life she was being denied. The same one their mother had died for when she'd spoken up about Sevin not making the cut.

And what's the one thing that could make Fyve leave Treasure Island without his sister?

Thinking she was dead, that's what.

Halo knows it just as clearly as she knows her heart is beating in her chest. Sevin faked her death to make sure Fyve got on the ship. And she knew Halo would look at her tree as they sailed away, just as she knew Fyve wouldn't. Which means she's waving to her. She's telling her a thousand things in that one small movement.

She's telling Halo she's alive.

And she wants Fyve to know.

But not yet.

Not while there's still a chance he'll jump off this ship and try to make it back to her. Which he most certainly would. And at this distance he'd also most certainly die. For real, not like his selfless, ingenious, spectacular sister.

Which means that instead of pointing to the tree and making Fyve's dreams and nightmares come to life all at the same time, Halo turns in his arms and kisses him. As his lips part against hers, she desperately hopes that one day he'll forgive her, in the same way he's going to need to learn to forgive Sevin.

Tomorrow Land awaits. And with it come all the answers to all their questions.

"My people," Halo's father shouts over the wind.

Halo and Fyve break away from each other and turn to see Halo's father stepping away from the railings as he turns to face the chosen hundred.

"We are on our way to Tomorrow Land," he says. "And it's time I introduced you to someone who's been waiting a very long time to meet you all."

"Who?" Fyve mouths to Halo, as a wave of people ask exactly the same thing.

Halo shrugs, having absolutely no idea what's happening.

She looks back to her father and sees him grin broadly as he indicates the door to the stairwell. "Everyone, I'd like you to meet Terra. Please, make her feel welcome."

The door opens and Halo's jaw drops. It seems she doesn't have to wait for Tomorrow Land for all her questions to be answered. Because the biggest mystery of them all has just stepped onto the deck.

The Oasis may have only just departed.

But Terra has arrived.

THE END
Ready for the next installment?
Check out The Oasis Deception, now!
http://mybook.to/OasisDeception

BOOK 12 - THE OASIS DECEPTION

THE THAW CHRONICLES

A hundred teens. A thousand broken promises. A future built on lies.

Fyve and Halo passed The Oasis Trials and boarded the promised ship, alongside a hundred teens carefully chosen by the mythical force known as Terra. They expect to sail to Tomorrow Land—a place where food is plentiful and opportunities abound. What they don't expect is to meet Terra herself…

As danger winds its way through the decaying ship, Fyve and Halo must try to put together the pieces of the most complex puzzle they've encountered yet. How is Terra managing to control things that can't possibly be controlled? Why are people disappearing, and where are they being taken? And what's in the secret section of the ship that Fyve and Halo were never meant to discover?

As the search for tomorrow becomes a quest to make sense of today, Fyve and Halo will need to draw on their strengths to get one step ahead of a power who's been manipulating them all along.

You will be blown away by this epic dystopian adventure brought to you by Tamar Sloan and Heidi Catherine, authors of the smash hit series, The Thaw Chronicles.

Grab your copy now!
http://mybook.to/OasisDeception

WANT TO STAY IN TOUCH?

If you'd like to be the first for to hear all the news from Tamar and Heidi, be sure to sign up to our newsletter. Subscribers receive bonus content, early cover reveals and sneaky snippets of upcoming books. We'd love you to join us!

SIGN UP HERE:

https://sendfox.com/tamarandheidi

ABOUT THE AUTHORS

Tamar Sloan hasn't decided whether she's a psychologist who loves writing, or a writer with a lifelong fascination with psychology. She must have been someone pretty awesome in a previous life (past life regression indicated a Care Bear), because she gets to do both. When not reading, writing or working with teens, Tamar can be found with her husband and two children enjoying country life in their small slice of the Australian bush.

Heidi Catherine loves the way her books give her the opportunity to escape into worlds vastly different to her own life in the burbs. While she quite enjoys killing her characters (especially the awful ones), she promises she's far better behaved in real life. Other than writing and reading, Heidi's current obsessions include watching far too much reality TV with the excuse that it's research for her books.

MORE SERIES TO FALL IN LOVE WITH...

ALSO BY TAMAR SLOAN AND HEIDI CATHERINE

The Sovereign Code

Elemental Games

ALSO BY TAMAR SLOAN

Keepers of the Grail

Keepers of the Light

Keepers of the Chalice

Keepers of Excalibur

Zodiac Guardians

Descendants of the Gods

Prime Prophecy

ALSO BY HEIDI CATHERINE

The Kingdoms of Evernow

The Soulweaver

www.ingramcontent.com/pod-product-compliance
Lightning Source LLC
Chambersburg PA
CBHW052023240626
47153CB00006B/1930